"YOU ARE SAFE," HE WHISPERED AGAINST HER BROW

The warmth of her skin pulsed against his lips.

Gray eyes clouded with doubt lifted to his. "Am I?"

As she looked up at him with fragile hope, a possessiveness toward her overcame him. "No one will harm you while you are under my protection. That I swear with my life."

Belief flickered in her eyes. Drawn by her budding trust, finding he wanted so much more, Alexander lowered his gaze to her tempting mouth. At the first gentle brush of his lips against hers, sultry heat plunged through him, her taste filling his every thought. At her quiet acceptance, he covered her mouth, sinking into the soft sweetness.

BOOK YOUR PLACE ON OUR WEBSITE AND MAKE THE READING CONNECTION!

We've created a customized website just for our very special readers, where you can get the inside scoop on everything that's going on with Zebra, Pinnacle and Kensington books.

When you come online, you'll have the exciting opportunity to:

- View covers of upcoming books
- Read sample chapters
- Learn about our future publishing schedule (listed by publication month *and author*)
- Find out when your favorite authors will be visiting a city near you
- Search for and order backlist books from our online catalog
- Check out author bios and background information
- Send e-mail to your favorite authors
- Meet the Kensington staff online
- Join us in weekly chats with authors, readers and other guests
- Get writing guidelines
- AND MUCH MORE!

Visit our website at
http://www.kensingtonbooks.com

HIS CAPTIVE

DIANA COSBY

ZEBRA BOOKS
Kensington Publishing Corp.
www.kensingtonbooks.com

ZEBRA BOOKS are published by

Kensington Publishing Corp.
850 Third Avenue
New York, NY 10022

All Kensington titles, imprints, and distributed lines are available at special quantity discounts for bulk purchases for sales promotion, premiums, fund-raising, educational, or institutional use.

Special book excerpts or customized printings can also be created to fit specific needs. For details, write or phone the office of the Kensington Special Sales Manager: Attn. Special Sales Department. Kensington Publishing Corp., 850 Third Avenue, New York, NY 10022. Phone: 1-800-221-2647.

Zebra and the Z logo Reg. U.S. Pat. & TM Off.

ISBN-13: 978-4201-0108-9
ISBN-10: 1-4201-0108-0

First Printing: November 2007
10 9 8 7 6 5 4 3 2 1

Printed in the United States of America

Chapter One

"Where are you going?" Lady Nichola Westcott asked, her voice not as steady as she would have liked.

Her older brother, Griffin, Baron of Monceaux jerked on his mantle without looking at her. "I will be gone for several days."

At his curt dismissal, a chill ran through her. "You came in but moments ago." Long enough to change out of his fouled garb from another day of drinking, whoring, and God knew what else. Unkempt brown hair made him appear more rogue than King Edward's advisor to Scottish affairs.

"There are household issues we must discuss, merchants who are demanding to be paid."

His hazel eyes, blurred by ale, turned on her and narrowed. "I will address them on my return."

She banked her frustration as she stepped toward her brother. To lose her temper now would make an already desperate situation worse. Ever since the seamstress had whispered that Lord James had been murdered at dawn, a man to whom Griffin owed a huge amount of money, she'd thought of little else.

Had Griffin killed him?

She wanted to believe the gossip, that her brother and Lord James had brawled mere hours before his death, was a lie. A rumor surely started by one of Griffin's many enemies to further discredit her brother.

As if he needed any assistance in that regard. Over the past year, with the amount he drank and questionable men he kept company with, Griffin had seemed intent on self-destruction. During her brother's many unexplained absences, she'd reviewed their household ledgers and knew their financial state.

Or lack of.

Confront him now.

Her breath caught in her throat. What if he'd finally crossed a boundary she couldn't repair? What if her greatest fear had come true, that he'd slipped from drunkard to criminal?

"Griffin . . ."

Across the room Griffin watched her in silence. For a moment, the hard angles of his face softened, a tender look that brought back the warmth of their past.

An ache built in her chest. She almost ran to him then, desperately needing the sibling who'd comforted her after their parents' death, the brother who'd always kept her world from going awry.

Then his mouth hardened into a thin line. And the cold, callous man, who now drowned his grief in drink, returned.

Her brother adjusted his mantle. "While I am away, stay within the castle walls."

"I will not do your bidding."

But he was already turning away. In a deft move that surprised her, he opened the secret door that led from the solar. He slipped into the beckoning darkness. Before she could react, the stone-coated panel shut behind him. The stale rushes scattered onto the floor, spiraled into stillness in his wake.

Why had her brother used the secret passage? They both knew of its existence, but until now, they'd never used it.

Or needed to.

Nichola raced to the door. She slid her fingers along the near invisible indentation. It didn't budge. "Griffin!"

Silence.

"I need to speak to you!" She tugged, but the panel held. He'd secured the door.

Fear crept through her with destructive precision, wrapping into a tight ball in her gut. Had their dismal finances made her brother desperate? Desperate enough to murder?

Why else would he use the secret passage to escape the castle unseen?

"Stop it!" Even as her voice echoed throughout the solar, doubts of her brother's innocence remained.

Crossing her arms over her chest, Nichola turned and paced the chamber. With a heavy heart, she halted before the colored panes of glass. Dust particles shimmering with reds and golds sifted through the fractured evening light.

She pressed her fingers against a cool panel, remembering the pride on her mother's face as she'd overseen the installation of each crafted pane. The windows were one of the last of the many treasures her family had brought with them when they'd moved to this northern stronghold twelve summers ago.

Now, the beautifully designed panes were but a solemn reminder of how much she'd lost.

She withdrew her hand and curled it into a fist. With their bleak financial situation, how could she have hesitated in demanding answers from Griffin? Hadn't the past few months tested her fortitude many times over?

Upon learning of Rothfield Castle's monetary distress, she'd made her decision. Without her brother's knowledge or consent, she'd discreetly sold several expensive rugs, gems, and pieces of furniture that had belonged to their family.

Her brother would be furious when he found out, but he would have to reconcile with her decisions. If he didn't run with braggarts, spending the last of their money without thought, they wouldn't be in this quandary.

Until now she'd upheld the facade. The Baron of Monceaux's wealth knew no bounds, and their family tie was strong. But with family heirlooms dwindling and creditors demanding payment, a month—two at best—was the most she could hope for before their shattered lives became fodder for gossip.

She shuddered. Unless Griffin was officially charged with Lord James' murder. Then the time remaining before their peers learned the truth might be hours. King Edward would sever his ties with Griffin, their home and any remaining possessions would be sold and they would be left in disgrace.

What would happen to her then?

A discreet cough behind Nichola interrupted her thoughts. She turned and forced herself not to panic.

A stranger stood near the far wall, his feet braced shoulder width apart, his muscled body drawn to its full height. His hair, black as midnight, disappeared behind broad, well-muscled shoulders. A scar slashed down his left cheek; an aged line adding to his daunting presence.

Cobalt eyes, half shielded by long, thick black lashes studied her with unapologetic interest. Eyes of a man who'd seen too much devastation.

Unease slid through her. 'Twas easy to envision him locked in battle, wielding his sword with sheer brute force, sweat clinging to his skin.

As she continued to stare at him, a scowl carved the man's strong-boned face, an expression as unwelcoming as it was dangerous.

Instinct urged her to take a step back, but Nichola held firm. Why was he here? She'd left explicit instructions with her servants to turn away anyone seeking her or Lord Monceaux. Fear scraped her throat like dried rushes against stone. Please let him not be here to bring formal charges against Griffin.

"You startled me," she said.

"My regrets," the stranger replied, but little in his tone supported the sentiment.

She struggled for calm. Mayhap he was an acquaintance of Griffin's? No, the sharp intelligence in his eyes boasted naught of drink. Only determination. A man who savored war as he would a woman's flesh.

Mary's name, what was she thinking? Never would she allow a man into her life again. "What is your purpose here?"

"Lord Monceaux. We have business."

Business. She released a slow breath. He wasn't here to arrest Griffin. "My brother is away."

The intruder's eyes darkened.

Nichola tried to ignore the predatory quality about him. He was a man who wouldn't tolerate being crossed. Was that why he'd come? Somewhere along Griffin's ill-gotten path, her brother had deceived this man?

"If you will tell me the reason you are here, I will inform my brother. Upon his return, he will be in contact with you." Or once alone, she would sell another heirloom to resolve whatever financial matter existed with this man. Even if she told her brother of the stranger's visit, she doubted Griffin would search this unnerving man out or any other he owed money to, whatever the threat.

His jaw tightened. "I was told he was in residence. In the solar to be exact."

Whatever servant had ignored her request for privacy would regret their actions. "I am sorry, you have been misinformed."

The stranger drummed his fingers over the hilt of his dagger sheathed at his waist. A fury lurking beneath his calm facade flickered into his eyes, clear and intense.

"Sir, I do not recall your name."

"As I have not given it, you would not."

His rich velvet voice swept through her like a silken rain, warm and smooth upon her skin. Irritated she'd noticed, Nichola stiffened. She'd learned to be wary of men, more so of those who wielded their words with soft precision.

"Why are you here?" she demanded.

"When will Lord Monceaux return?"

She angled her chin and shot him a withering look, raising her voice deliberately. "Now I understand, it is a problem hearing that caused your rudeness in answering my query."

His eyes narrowed.

Enough of this foolery. "If you have nothing more to say, you will leave."

He didn't move.

A fresh wave of anxiety swept over her. What if her brother owed this dangerous stranger nothing, and he was touched in the head? Whatever reason brought him here, for her own safety, she must convince him to go.

Nichola gestured toward the door. "Sir, I have entertained your poor manners long enough."

"Lass." The faintest burr caressed his voice.

A Scot?

Every nerve in her body went on alert, aware of exactly how much separated England and Scotland. Though King John had abdicated the Scottish throne to King Edward, bands of Scottish rebels continued to attack English troops. She doubted the rebels loyal to William Wallace would ever cease in their quest for freedom and give way to England's dictates.

Nichola studied the stranger. Relief poured through her as she noted the Stanford weave of his tunic. The cut and fabric of his clothes marked him unmistakably English. She was worrying for naught.

Her confrontation with Griffin along with news of the murder of Lord James had left her overwrought. This man's brazen manner put her further on edge. All she needed was time to sort things out.

Alone.

He took a step toward her. Slow. Precise. With intent.

This was her home. She refused to allow him to intimidate her. Nichola held up her hand. "You will leave and—"

"It is no time for debate." He lunged forward. His arm caught her around her waist.

She tried to scream, but he clasped a hand over her mouth and muffled her cry. She bit. Hard.

"By my sword!" the intruder cursed, this time his burr rich and thick.

He was a Scot! Nichola dug her elbow into his chest only to come up against honed muscle. "Release me!"

He caught her arms, then again covered her mouth, this time keeping his hand cupped. "Be still."

While he raped or murdered her? She twisted hard in his grasp.

With ease he backed her up and pinned her body against the wall, his hard frame trapping hers. "Do not fight me," he warned.

Beyond the cold determination, she caught a flash of desire. Hysteria welled up in her. God, no! She struggled harder.

"Cease!"

Unable to break free, she stilled, conscious of every muscle pressed against her, and the power within his honed frame. What was she going to do? She couldn't overpower him. Neither could she allow him to go unchallenged.

"Do not bite me again. And if you try to scream, I will be forced to resort to drastic measures. Do you understand?"

She understood completely. He had the upper hand, and she despised the threat he represented. Nichola glared at him.

A brow quirked in surprise at her defiance. He watched her a moment. As if satisfied she'd obey him, he lowered his hand from her mouth.

"You are a Scot!"

A grudging smile tugged at his lips. "I am that."

"What do you want from me?"

"I am taking you hostage. Rest easy, lass."

"You cannot—"

The warrior smothered her cry again with his hand. "Be quiet!"

Nichola shook her head in an attempt to remove his hand and failed. His body felt like hewn stone against hers. She glanced toward the door, willing a servant to arrive. No, they wouldn't come. She'd informed them she wanted to be left alone.

"Give me your word you will not call out, then I will release you. You will come to no harm, that I promise you."

She narrowed her brows, her breaths coming hard. As if she believed him.

"Give it."

Furious she had no other choice, she nodded.

He withdrew his hand.

"You err in choosing to abduct me. My brother is a powerful man, a Scottish advisor to King Edward. Release me and I will say nothing."

The scar down his left cheek tightened. "I know well of Lord Monceaux's ties. But my decision is made. Once your brother has paid the ransom, I will see you are returned."

A wild sob built in her throat as he called her bluff. As if payment would ever be sent. Griffin was on the run and their coffers barren. "You cannot take me, I—"

He put his finger over her lips, forestalling further protest. "I can. Not a word," he warned. "If you care about your brother's life, you will not scream."

Her heart slammed against her chest. He'd kill Griffin? She had to do something. But what? If she screamed, he'd tie a gag around her mouth and end any chance to cry for help.

At her silence, he lifted her against his chest and strode toward the door.

Nichola fought to pry free. The blackguard would soon learn his outlandish abduction would fail. Before he could make it outside the castle, her guards would seize him and toss him into the dungeon where he belonged.

Except her abductor didn't head toward the main entry. He strode toward the secret door.

Saint's breath! How did he know about this passage-way? It mattered not. Griffin had secured the exit when he'd left.

With arrogant confidence, her abductor pressed his fingers against the almost invisible indentation and pulled.

With smug satisfaction, Nichola awaited his frus-trated curse.

The door swung open.

And she understood. Her servants hadn't escorted the Scot to the solar. When she'd stood by the panels of glass, lost in thought, he must have slipped into the chamber through the secret door.

Griffin!

No, her brother was safe. Why else would the Scot have asked his whereabouts? By some miracle, as her brother had made his hasty departure, in the labyrinth of tunnels woven within Rothfield Castle, he must have missed the Scot.

Her abductor stepped toward the entry.

She couldn't let him enter. If he made it inside the tunnel with her and closed the door, little hope ex-isted for her escape. Nichola planted her foot against the wall and shoved hard.

The Scot caught her legs and pried them free.

Nichola screamed.

He clamped a hand over her mouth as he glared at her with a scowl as fierce as the devil's own. "Cease! I gave my word you will not be harmed."

Images of the violence a man of such build could bestow upon her terrorized her mind.

"I do not lie," he said. "Do not scream again."

She shot him a furious glare. Most men lie. 'Twas their reasons for doing so that varied.

With her caught in his grasp, he stepped through the opening and secured the panel behind them.

Stale air enveloped Nichola and a sense of doom settled over her. Her captor removed his hand from her mouth. Why wouldn't he? His unorthodox arrival into the solar proved him familiar with the maze of tunnels woven throughout Rothfield Castle. He would know the interconnected passageways had been built to ensure a safe and quiet escape.

If she screamed, no one would hear her.

The Scot removed a torch from a nearby sconce and held it before them. Wavering light illuminated the dismal, but sturdily built tunnel. Cobwebs cluttered the shadows, dust coated the hewn stones and aged-oak beams lay overhead. Somewhere in the distance the steady drip of water echoed with a somber plop.

Nichola remained still against her captor's solid chest, but beneath her lashes, she searched for anything to use as a weapon. Not even a loose stone was within reach. She drew in a slow breath, at odds with her pounding heart. To panic now would only make the situation worse.

As the Scot strode down the torch-lit tunnel, she peered through half-open lashes at his face; the hard slash of his cheekbones as unforgiving as his mouth. The cleft in his chin as if carved by an angry god. The scar running down the left side of his face giving his appearance a dangerous edge. She wouldn't call it a cruel face, but that of a man seasoned by war. A man who, when he gave an order, would expect to be obeyed.

How long would her captor allow her to live when he discovered the truth—that they were impoverished? She shuddered. The answer was simple.

He wouldn't.

The irony of the situation wasn't lost on her. Because of her efforts to keep the myth of a happy and prosperous home alive, her abductor believed he would be well paid.

The deception she had so desperately nurtured would seal her own fate.

Shards of torchlight punctured the blackness. The firm slap of his steps echoed around her.

Nichola glanced back as the secret door faded into darkness. She couldn't give up. Maybe she couldn't overpower the Scot, but she'd bide her time, gather her strength, and pray for an opportunity to escape. It would come.

She refused to believe otherwise.

For now, she would pretend to faint in his arms. He would believe she'd succumbed to fear. With a silent prayer that her tactic would work, she closed her eyes and relaxed.

The alluring woman in Alexander's arms went limp, then her breathing slowed. She'd passed out. From a mix of fear and exhaustion, he imagined. He grimaced. He'd not meant to scare the lass, but the matter could not be helped.

In the soft flickers of light, her ivory face framed by her auburn tresses radiated innocence. Her full lips, the color of sun-ripened berries drenched in dew, caused him to linger on them. He wondered at their softness. And taste.

Irritated by his attraction to the woman in his arms, Alexander returned his attention to the tunnel.

By the saints, what was he doing? However tempting her slender frame, her auburn hair that flowed down to spill across full breasts, and a voice that slid through him like warmed honey, he could never forget she was English—a people he despised.

On his father's grave he'd pledged his life to war. To serve his people. To protect their freedom. A vow no woman would make him break.

Pleasures of the flesh were brief, unattached, and at his choosing.

He'd tolerate her presence and no more. Alexander turned his thoughts to her brother. Where was the baron? He, his brothers, and their informant had mapped out the baron's abduction in detail. Nothing should have gone wrong.

But it had.

Used to making quick decisions, however much it vexed him to involve a woman, Alexander had abducted the baron's sister instead. With the rebels urgent need for coin to buy arms, and Alexander's awareness of the siblings' tight bond, her brother would pay a hearty ransom for her return.

Far from appeased at the change in plans, Alexander retraced his path through the intricately woven passageways. He followed each turn and twist that would take him to a field on the outer edge of the castle, a route explained by the laird who'd resided here before the English had seized the stronghold.

As he moved with confidence, the scent of woman, mixed with the fragrance of lavender, teased at his senses. Irritated he'd noticed, he pushed himself harder.

Fresh air, rich with the scent of water, alerted him that they neared the exit. He lengthened his stride. The steady churn of the current grew into a low rumble as he turned a corner. Moonlight carved through the blackness up ahead.

Alexander extinguished the torch, threw it aside and stepped out of the small rock opening onto the moor.

Cool night air greeted him as he studied their surroundings. Beneath the moon's glow, the water flowed down the burn like a silken ribbon. Light wind rippled across a nearby field of rye in a slow caress. Beyond that stood a cluster of elm and oak where he'd hidden his steed.

He'd begun his journey with a second mount, but last night it had gone lame and he'd left it behind. He'd planned to steal another horse, but having taken Lord Monceaux's sister instead of the baron, she was light enough to ride with him.

Alexander noted beneath the half-moon of her auburn lashes, the slight movement of her eyelids. She was coming to. He needed to hurry before she fully awoke.

Through the cover of trees, Alexander turned and scanned the castle walls that rose above a stand of low pines less than a league away.

After assuring himself no guard could see them, he began to pick his way across the fragments of rock jutting above the shallow burn.

Halfway, without warning, the unconscious woman in his arms exploded into action, twisting against him.

"Let go of me!" Her voice echoed in the crisp August night.

Blast it. He covered her mouth with his hand and stifled another scream. "Be still!"

Her wriggling increased.

In her surprise bid for freedom, she'd managed to free her lower body from his hold. He grabbed for her legs at the same instant that she kicked out, throwing him off balance. He lost his foothold.

Cold water erupted around them as they landed in the burn, soaking them both.

His captive sputtered in the knee-deep water as she sat there wet, bedraggled, her eyes glittering with defiance.

From the satisfaction on her face, she had planned this sabotage all along. A part of him was irritated she found delight in besting him, another part admired her courage to try.

Maybe her bravado came from the blue blood pouring through her veins. Or from her classic beauty that she doubtlessly wielded like the finest swordsman to bend men to her will.

He narrowed his eyes on her face. She would soon learn any attempt to defy him, however sweetly delivered, would fail.

The current rumbled around them as Alexander hauled her onto her tiptoes before him. "It is a bold one you are," he said with a fierce scowl, "but I will not—" She gasped, and he made the mistake of looking down.

Her chest heaved against his, her sodden-wool gown clung against her slim figure to outline her full breasts. Doused with cold water, her nipples had puckered into hard peaks.

Lust speared straight through him with a brutal aim the stoutest marksman would admire. His body burned with need. He clenched his teeth. Though raping and pillaging was common, he found distaste in overpowering a woman.

Alexander caught her shoulders, nevertheless yanking her against him for effect. "Hear me now, lass. I am not a patient man and you have exhausted what little I had. I have promised not to harm you. What you believe," he said with icy precision, "or not, is your own choosing. Do not cross me again."

As if sensing how close he was to losing control, fear flashed in her eyes, then she lowered her gaze.

Believing he'd quelled the last of her resistance, Alexander stood. Water sluiced down his tunic as he lifted her up with him. He reached down. A loud rip sounded as he tore a strip from the bottom of her gown.

"What are you doing?" she demanded.

Though fear battered her voice, she stood her ground. His respect for her increased. "What I should have done from the first." Before she could balk, he secured a strip over her mouth. As she struggled anew, her eyes skewering him with loathing, he used another to bind her hands before her.

Without further incident, he carried her from the burn. He crossed a field thick with heather, then slipped into the protective cover of trees. Out of view, he thrust her onto his horse, swinging up behind her.

She stiffened, her slender body snug against his muscled frame.

He tried not to notice how well she fit, or her sweep of wet auburn hair inches from his mouth. Beneath the moonlight, he followed a rivulet of water as it slid down the side of her neck to disappear beneath her gown.

Gritting his teeth, he caught the reins. He refused to allow temptation to sway him from his purpose. Holding her for ransom was the rebels only hope.

But with the lass wedged against him, his blood pounding hot, 'twould seem his decision to abduct her would issue its own consequence. With grim resolve, Alexander turned his mount north and kicked him into a gallop.

And for the first time, he wondered if his abduction of the baron's sister would be something he'd come to regret.

Chapter Two

An owl's cry slipped through the fragments of Nichola's dream. She squeezed her eyes tighter. She didn't want to wake up. Not yet. The pounding of horse's hooves was soothing. The solid heat at her back felt so warm and inviting.

She burrowed closer.

A shaft of pain shot through her and she moaned. She tried to lift her arms to work out the hurt. They didn't budge. Why couldn't she move her arms?

The thickness clouding her mind faded. Nichola flicked open her eyes. A strong muscled arm was wrapped around her waist. Another held reins as they rode. Mary's will, the hard, lean warmth she rested against was her captor!

She stiffened, jerking upright. Another bolt of pain struck. Her breath came hard and fast through her gag, but she couldn't move. Her hands were still bound before her.

"You are awake then," the Scot said, so close that his breath stirred the hair against her neck. "We will be riding for several more hours yet. Fighting your bindings will only cause your muscles to ache more."

A few more hours. Then what? Would he turn her over to rebels awaiting their arrival, or, remembering the lust in his eyes when he had stared at her back at the stream, would he pleasure himself at her expense?

Her ties chafed, her mouth was dry, and she wanted to cry out in frustration. Instead, Nichola steadied herself against the pain. She refused to give up. In a slow sweep, she examined her surroundings in hopes of recognizing a landmark.

Sheets of fog as thin as unleavened bread floated in ghostly slivers around them. A forest, darkened with night-blackened trees, embraced the field they rode through. Shimmers of rolling hills peeked above the canopy of leaves.

She recognized nothing. But, from the position of the disappearing moon, they were headed north—to Scotland.

Fear had her closing her eyes, but determination forced them back open. The thickness weighing down the Scot's burr was evidence of his fatigue. And, by daring to abduct her on English soil, his arrogance. After dealing with her brother, his scoundrel friends, and her ex-fiancé, this was a characteristic she understood well. Before long, confident of his success, her abductor would let down his guard.

And she would make good her escape.

Hours later, when the first pale streaks of sun crept into the eastern sky, her abductor finally drew his mount to a halt. Without comment, he dismounted, his fine English garb now wrinkled and in a sad state. The Scot lifted her from the saddle and set her before him without releasing her.

Nichola's legs were so weak she was forced to grip his arm for support. After riding throughout the night, it was little wonder. She looked down.

A dagger glinted in his hand.

Nichola screamed against the gag and tried to wrench herself free.

"Be still!"

She dove to the left, but his hand caught her wrists and yanked her back. A sharp snap sounded as he cut her bindings, swearing all the while. Her hands fell away.

At the freedom, blood rushed through her arms and made them throb like frozen hands exposed to heat.

Rubbing the numbness from her wrists, Nichola stared up at the powerful man with distrust. Exhaustion carved deep lines across the hard angles of his face, but it didn't diminish the intelligence in his eyes or the determination. That of a predator.

His cobalt eyes narrowed on hers.

Awareness shivered through her, a slow pull that stole her breath. Shaken by her reaction, she looked away. No, she felt nothing toward him but fear.

The Scot stowed his dagger.

Relief poured through her.

"You will be sore, but the stiffness will ease soon enough." He rummaged through the roll tied upon the horse's back and withdrew a garment. "Change into this." It wasn't a request. The Scot tugged her gag free, but he left the limp cloth hanging around her neck. His eyes held a warning. "It stays where it is for now. I will not be replacing the gag or the bond upon your hands unless you give me reason."

"Such twisted nobility that allows you to tie and kidnap a helpless woman," she charged, her voice hoarse from misuse.

He grunted. "Aye, helpless enough to douse us both in the burn." Her abductor handed her the clothes and pointed toward a dense clump of brambles. "Change in that thicket. And be quick."

She hesitated. He'd not taken any gown from her home. "Where did you find this?"

Satisfaction glinted in his eyes. "I stole it. Move."

Weak from the lengthy ride, her legs threatened to give as she did his bidding. Once behind a dense cluster of shrubs, she leaned against a tree for support. All she wanted was to be curled in her bed away from this outlaw who would steal her from her home.

More emotion welled up in her throat. And what of Griffin? Had he returned to Rothfield Castle? Did he even know she was missing? Or was he at this moment imprisoned and charged with the murder of Lord James?

"It is too quiet in there, lass." The Scot's harsh warning cut through the night.

She tore off her gown and snapped back, "It is poor manners of me not to know of a drinking song to offer for your entertainment."

A muffled laugh echoed through the brush.

With a grimace, she pulled on the simple linen gown he'd given her, ignoring its fit and cut. What did it matter how she was dressed? Unless she found a way to escape, once he received word that no ransom would be forthcoming, she would be dead.

Nichola stepped out from behind the bushes to find her captor had changed as well. Gone were the trappings of an English gentleman. Now he wore snug trews that emphasized his well-muscled legs, a broadcloth tunic, a claymore secured behind his back in a leather sheath, and his dagger secured to the belt at his waist.

Oddly, the garb suited his rough strength better than English trappings.

The Scot waved her forward. "Come here."

His quiet burr rippled across her skin. Her body tight-

ened in response. Shame filled her that her abductor
could coax such unchaste yearnings for him.

Though he was fair to gaze upon, she understood a
man's promises—and the lies to follow. Her be-
trothed had taught her well the extent of a man's deception. While he beguiled her with his honeyed
words, his intent was to gain access to her dowry. A
fact she'd overheard when he'd not known she was
near. And a fact he'd rued when she'd called off their
engagement.

She drew in a steadying breath as she stared at the
Scot. No, she wasn't tempted by him. 'Twas fatigue
that played tricks upon her mind.

"Lass." When she remained still, he stepped toward
her with a determined gait. He halted a pace away,
close enough to touch her if he chose. His gaze slid
over her with male appreciation, then rose to her chest
where it lingered. "Your garb should do well enough."

She glanced down. In the first rays of morning light,
she took in the simple peasant gown. The neckline
plunged daringly low and exposed the swell of her
breasts almost to her nipples. She looked like a whore!

Nichola lifted her gaze. At the naked longing in his
eyes, she stumbled back.

The Scot caught her hand. "Calm yourself. I gave
you my word you would not be harmed," he said
gruffly as he pulled her toward his steed.

But she'd seen the heat in his eyes, desire that smoldered like kindling ready to flare. How could she trust
him? The answer was simple. She couldn't.

He held out the water pouch. "You will be thirsty."

With reserve, she took a drink, then handed it back
to him.

The Scot mounted his horse and pulled her to sit
before him. His body was rigid against hers; his male

warmth enveloping her. She tried to ignore him, and failed miserably.

He nudged his steed into a canter. They traveled throughout the day, and the easy flow of hill to field slowly transformed into more rugged terrain.

The hard travel sapped her of strength. Her body screamed for mercy, but except for several brief stops to water his mount, and eat cheese and bread washed down with warm wine, they continued on.

As the sun started to sink in the horizon, they topped a tree-lined ridge. Below, the outline of a small village came into view. A smith's anvil collided with the sound of a dog barking at their approach.

Nichola owed his blunder in exposing her to her fellow countrymen to exhaustion. How could he not be tired? Since he'd abducted her over a day past, he'd not slept.

The sad state of the earthen homes didn't diminish her spirits. English subjects lived here. When they realized the Scot held her against her will, they would seize him, truss him up like a goose and cart him to the nearest dungeon.

Her abductor's fingers worked quickly on the gag still dangling around her neck. Once he'd loosened the tie, he shoved it into the saddle pack and out of sight.

A smile brushed her lips. Further proof that tiredness skewed his mind. He'd nearly forgotten to remove the evidence of her abduction.

"Keep quiet," he warned. "I will do any talking that needs to be done."

She remained silent. If the opportunity came, she'd do whatever necessary to gain her freedom.

As they entered narrow, mud-raked village streets, the stench of refuse hit her first. Children, half-clothed, their garments in tatters, ran by. Several women were beating clothes clean in a stream nearby. As they rode past, a few glanced toward them, then quickly averted their gaze.

With the unrest between England and Scotland, especially in light of her abductor's Scottish garb, why didn't anyone halt them or at least send a messenger ahead to warn the others of their arrival? Or had they already done so?

Unimpeded, they passed several homes, their thatch roofs patched over and again; walls sturdy yet unkempt. No men came into view to challenge their approach.

Her unease grew. These people would help her, wouldn't they?

Her captor reined in his mount before a two-story, ramshackle tavern; the walls cracked, the door thick and marred by deep gouges, and a sign so battered she could make out nary a letter.

The Scot dismounted. His devil's black hair slid backward as he reached up and caught her by the waist. He scowled. "Not a word."

"What is inside?" she asked, the fear in her voice betraying her outward calm.

Irritation dredged deep lines across his brow. "A room we will be staying in for the night."

Nichola tried to pry away his hands, but her own were shaking. Her reputation would be in ruins if he shared a room with her overnight. If it wasn't already. And what was his intent toward her once locked within the chamber?

"Please, let me go. I cannot—"

"Silence." He lifted her from his mount and tugged her toward the entry.

Her aching legs balked as the Scot opened the

door and hurried her inside as if familiar with the decrepit building.

Not a good sign.

Her slippers met with the compacted dirt floor as he tugged her forward. The stench of unwashed bodies made her stomach roil. A few tallow candles scattered about offered meager light and added to the foul smell.

Nauseated, she scanned the crowd. To her horror, unkempt men filled the numerous, roughly crafted tables strewn about. Several of the men's gazes were fixed upon her.

Saint's breath. Where had he taken her to, a den of thieves? From the appearance of the scruffy lot, they would most likely rape her, not help her escape.

She tried to step back, but the Scot's grip tightened on her hand.

At his warning glare, several men nearby turned away. "Stay beside me," her captor hissed in her ear.

As if she dared do otherwise? Icy prickles of fear stabbed Nichola as she kept tight behind the Scot while he wove through the dangerous men. For the first time since her abduction, she found herself thankful for his presence.

Once they'd reached the opposite side of the room, he led her toward a table in a darkened corner where a bald-headed man lurked. As they neared, the man's beady eyes skewered her with such carnal intent her skin crawled.

The baron's sister hesitated, and Alexander gave her hand a reassuring squeeze, but he didn't slow.

Her eyes widened with surprise at his reassurance.

Alexander leaned close to her. "It will be fine, lass." He saw the doubts in her eyes and regretted having to bring a lady inside this squalid tavern, but he was exhausted and little choice remained. Out in the wilds, anyone might come upon them while they slept. At least here he could keep an eye on her without worry of her escape.

Smothering a yawn, Alexander stopped before the tavern owner. "We will be needing a room." He disliked Hammet's overt interest in his hostage, but Alexander had dealt with the tavern owner enough times to know that for the right price, he would see nothing.

From her simple gown and low-cut neckline, Hammet would believe Lord Monceaux's sister was Alexander's mistress; the reason he'd chosen to steal the revealing dress. But earlier, when she'd walked from the bushes with her breasts half-exposed, he'd found himself wishing the story was real.

Alexander grimaced. More than three months had passed since he'd bedded a lass, which explained the lust invoked by thoughts of her naked. Once home and free of her, he'd find a woman to ease his need.

Greed danced in Hammet's beady eyes. "I have a room, but it will cost you."

"A fair price," Alexander demanded.

The tavern owner's mouth thinned. His lewd gaze skimmed over the for-once quiet woman at Alexander's side, then named a steep sum.

Alexander withdrew twice the amount and tossed it to the man.

Hammet snatched the coins from the air and dropped them inside a scarred leather pouch. "Last room at the top of the stairs."

"If anyone is asking"—Alexander paused in an unspoken threat—"you have not seen me nor the woman. A man who loses his mistress tends to be ill-willed."

A sly smile slinked across Hammet's face. He licked his lips. "'It is understandable why you took such a risk."

Lord Monceaux's sister inhaled a sharp intake of breath. Humiliation stormed his captive's face. "Why you—"

Blast it, she was going to give him away. Alexander jerked her close and covered her mouth with his own. The fire that ignited between them almost dropped him to his knees. He'd only meant a stifling kiss, but her taste blazed through him; hot, tempting, and searing his every inch. He fisted her hair with his hand and tilted her head back for greater access.

She stiffened against him in outrage.

Alexander took the kiss deeper, needing her compliance. If the men filling the room learned she wasn't his, they would fight to take her.

At last her body shivered, then she relaxed against him. Her tiny moan of acceptance stole his breath, but her response left him breathless. He took his time now; savoring her taste, the softness of her skin, capturing her every gasp. Needing more, he cupped the nape of her neck to draw her closer.

Ribald laughter and lewd cheers filled the chamber.

Stunned that he'd lost himself in the kiss, Alexander lifted his head. His heart pounding and his breath coming fast, he stared down at his captive; far from appeased to find her gray eyes as wide and as startled as his likely were.

"Aye, the lass keeps a man hard and pleases him well," Alexander growled out as he reined in his lust. He was not a green lad who became weak-kneed at the taste of a lass. That he'd succumbed to the charms of an Englishwoman drove his shame deeper.

If he could, he'd rid himself of Lord Monceaux's sister this instant. But the rebels needed the coin her ransom would bring. And he'd given his word to protect her, so that he would.

Alexander pulled her to the stairs. "Stay quiet," he threatened and nipped at her neck in cover to any who observed their departure.

At the bottom of the steps, she rounded on him, and by the stubborn glint in her eyes, ready to argue anew. Before she could rail at him, he heaved her over his shoulder.

Her scream blended with the rowdy cheers of the men below as he hauled her up the rickety steps. They reached the top of the stairs and thankfully out of view of the very drunk and nondiscriminate crowd below.

She clawed at his shoulder. "Do not rape me!"

Exhausted, his head throbbing from fatigue, he set her down inside the hall, but kept a secure grip on her wrist. Of course she was terrified. He'd abducted her from her home, dressed her in a wanton's gown and hauled her into a tavern filled with the basest of men. Most noble women would have fainted as they'd stepped inside. That she'd but trembled at the sight of the dangerous men raised his respect for her another notch.

"Lass," he said softly. "I am going to—"

She tried to rip her hand free, her chest heaving. "Let me go!"

Alexander softened his grip. "I only want sleep."

His quiet words spilled between them as she eyed him with distrust. With the strength of a saint, he kept his gaze focused on her face and away from the tempting swells below.

She wiped her lips with the back of her hand as if she found his lingering taste offensive. "You let them think me your whore!"

He gave a somber nod. "Aye. Had they known differently, they would have taken you. Or tried."

Her hand went to her throat. "But you are their

enemy?" As if realizing the peril of her condemnation, a flush stole up her cheeks.

"The lot below would not be caring," he said, matter-of-fact. "As long as they believe you are with me, they will not harm you."

"Is that supposed to reassure me?"

"That is up to you." He'd given his word to protect her. He'd not spend all night easing her mind when a bed could be found nearby. Besides, best to let her imagine the worst about him, which she probably did. Not that her opinion would deter him from his plan.

Alexander pointed down the corridor. "Move." When she didn't budge, he dragged her down the hall.

As they reached the door, she gave his shoulder another hard, desperate shove. "No!"

"No?" Was the lass daft?

"I cannot go in there."

Through an exhausted haze, he shot her an intimidating glare. "I gave you my word I will not hurt you."

Panic rimmed her eyes. "I—I do not even know your name."

He blinked in surprise. She had just now decided that being with him was improper? Laughter tugged at his mouth.

An angry blush streaked up her pale cheeks. "It is not funny."

"No, lass," he said tiredly, pulling her against him before she could bolt for the stairs. He immediately paid the price as her slender body wedged intimately against him. Her generous chest rose and fell beneath his gaze, her woman's scent wrapped around him and her taste lingered in his mouth. His body hardened to a painful ache.

Too easy he imagined himself pushing down the wisp of hindering material to expose her to him, a view he'd seen too clearly when her original gown had become soaked at the burn. The firm, round breasts, the darkness of her nipples that begged for his taste. The curve of her slender waist that led to her womanly charms.

Alexander gritted his teeth. No, this definitely wasn't a laughing matter.

Shoving the door open, he hauled her inside. The sturdy wooden bed wedged into the corner looked like heaven.

"My name is Alexander." He closed the door with a firm snap and secured it. "And if you have wits about you, you will not try to run. If you have not noticed, the men below are not a bloody selective lot."

The lass's ample endowments and tempting face had already created an unwanted stir of interest. The last thing he needed was further trouble. Until they departed at the break of dawn, he must keep her out of sight.

She remained silent, her gaze wary.

He scrubbed his hand over his face, feeling as lively as wilted heather. All he wanted to do was sleep, but a tug of conscience had him asking, "I know you are the Baron of Monceaux's sister, but not your given name."

She hesitated. "Nichola," she finally replied, her voice as warm as a chunk of ice.

"Now that we have been introduced properly, we can find our bed," he said in a tone that to him sounded like that of unending patience. With his hand still wrapped firmly around her wrist, he started toward the bed only to have her pull back. He rounded on her. "What now?"

"You are not— I will not share a bed with you. Or this room." She looked down her dainty, aristocratic nose at him. "It would not be proper."

"Proper? We are going to sleep." But the thought of her naked in his bed added to his growing frustration. Damnation!

As if she read the lust in his eyes, her eyes widened. "Let me go."

Beneath her quiet demand, he saw a reluctant desire to match his own, and his blood pounded harder. He moved his hands up to her shoulders to set her away.

Nichola lowered her gaze. She drew in several slow breaths, her shoulders rising and falling slightly with each. Then she calmed, her breathing growing even. Slowly she looked up.

The innocent yearning in her eyes caught him off guard. Alexander gritted his teeth. He needed sleep, not to be tempted, but he couldn't help notice how her lower lip trembled, or how her mouth parted; soft, slow in invitation.

On a sultry exhale, her lashes drifted shut. She leaned toward him.

He should leave her alone, they were both tired. But she wanted him. He'd already kissed her once, what harm could another wee kiss bring? Alexander leaned forward and claimed her lips. As before, her taste exploded in his mouth; hot, sweet, and destroying his reserve. Her body relaxed against his. On a groan Alexander released his hold on her and reached to frame her face with his hands.

Gray eyes opened and flashed with defiance a split second before her knee jammed hard into his groin.

Agony seared his every inch, and his legs gave out. He sank to his knees. Bloody hell! On a ragged gasp, he drew in a shallow breath, then another, glaring up at her accusingly.

Panic widened Nichola's eyes as she stepped back, but triumph flickered there as well.

She took another step back, as if he could catch her? He'd be lucky to move. "Do not"—He gasped for another breath as his body screamed in agony—"try and—"

"Damn you!" She ran to the door, shoved back the latch, jerked the door open, and fled.

Alexander gritted his teeth as he stumbled to his feet. The room blurred.

Rowdy cheers broke out from below.

God no! Cursing the mind-numbing pain, Alexander withdrew his sword and bolted toward the hall.

Chapter Three

Breathless from bolting down the stairs, Nichola stood frozen at the base and stared at the swarm of miscreants before her. A tremor shot through her body. She stepped back.

An inebriated cur grabbed her arm.

Nichola screamed, turned, and lunged toward the scarred door only paces away.

A calloused hand snagged her other arm. "Where do ye think you are going?" A nasty grin curved the foul stranger's lips, giving her the full effect of yellowed teeth.

She shot him her iciest glare. "Release me!"

His ribald laughter escalated her fear.

She twisted to break free and failed. She should have known that she could never slip through these dangerous men without notice. But with Alexander's kiss still tingling on her lips, and the shame of her own reaction, all she had been able to think about was escape.

Nichola scanned the sodden crowd for any sign of help. Lust smeared the faces of the rough-looking men. They were going to kill her. No, they'd rape her first, then she would die.

The stranger hauled her against him and tipped precariously with her in his arms. "She is feisty!" he slurred to the crowd.

To his right, a bald man rose. Mugs clattered to the earthen floor as he slapped them from his table. "Put her down here. When you are through, I want a taste of her meself."

"Bugger off with you," her captor snarled while he hauled her through the men toward the door. "She is mine."

Bile surged through Nichola's body. "Please, release me!"

Bawdy laughter met her terrified plea.

"You can at least be showing us the goods," a man with sagging jowls yelled from nearby.

Her captor wove, then steadied himself. "Would not mind a look-see meself."

Before she could evade him, his fingers caught her bodice and ripped it downward, exposing her breasts.

Cheers rose from the men.

"No!" Oh, God! Nichola managed to free her hand. Grasping the neckline, she tugged up her gown.

Her captor clamped one of her hands in a painful grip and leered down at her. "No protector with ye I see. Wear him out did ye?"

Desperate, she raked the nails of her free hand down his cheek.

Blood beaded on his face. "You bitch!" Teeth bared, he lifted his hand to strike.

"Lass!" Alexander's voice boomed throughout the room. Silence swept the seedy tavern as one and all swung toward the commanding source, who stood at the base of the stairs like a demon capable of trouncing hell.

Alexander shoved his way through the cantankerous

men, his gaze never leaving her. "It is a beating you have earned."

Instead of fear, hope built inside her.

Her captor's hand had frozen in midswing. He glared at the Scot with murder in his eyes. As though acknowledging the other man's prior claim on Nichola, the drunkard muttered under his breath and dropped his arm to his side.

Alexander halted before her. The hard angles of his face twisted into a savage mask.

Nichola struggled to preserve her modesty with the torn gown. How had she believed she would be safer with these men?

"I will not be playing games with you tonight, lass," Alexander roared.

"I will beat her for you," a man yelled from the back. Several men shouted their agreement.

"It is punishment she will get," Alexander vowed without taking his eyes off of her, "but it will be by my hands. And in private."

"And after, reaping the rewards," another drunk sneered, which earned agreeing grumbles from the crowd.

Tension built within the room. Nichola caught her breath. Didn't Alexander realize these men wouldn't give her up? That if he tried to take her from them, they'd kill him?

With a slow, covert move, as Alexander glared at the drunk holding her, his hand eased to the hilt of a dagger secured at his belt.

She swallowed hard. Yes, it seemed he understood the danger. By the determination carved on his face, he was not leaving without her.

A thrill ran through her knowing that this man would risk his life to save her. As quickly, her spirits sank. The Scot wanted her not because he cared for her welfare, but because she was a means to gain coin for the rebels.

The man holding Nichola swayed, his grip tightening on her arm as he righted himself. "I caught her right and square. She is mine."

Alexander bared his teeth like a wolf defending its territory. "Release her."

Without ceremony, her burly captor shoved her into the arms of another leather-clad man at his side. "Hold her while I finish with the fool." He sneered at Alexander. "Then I will have a taste of his whore. If he does not know how to keep his woman abed, I do."

"Alexander!" Nichola screamed as the grimy man hauled her farther back into the drunken crowd, his foul stench almost making her wretch.

His hand wrapped around her throat and tightened.

She struggled for air. The crowd of men around her blurred. Their shouts muted. The stench of bodies and sweat faded. In a haze of pain and fear, her mind plunged into darkness.

Alexander watched Nichola go limp in her captor's arms, and he cursed. One wrong move and they both could die. He shot her captor a savage glare as he withdrew his dagger.

"Release her or die," Alexander ordered.

An expectant hush fell over the crowd. Like vultures, the men watched, their eyes gleaming with bloodlust.

Alexander understood the unspoken rule among thieves. They wouldn't interfere, but would watch for a chance during the fray to claim the woman for their own.

His opponent removed his own dagger, and the surrounding men backed up to give them wide berth. "A fight is it?" He answered his own question by lunging.

Alexander sidestepped to the left, and the man's blade met air as it whistled past.

The man angled his dagger and again lashed out.

Alexander dodged his attack.

Laughter chortled around them.

Red mottled his aggressor's face as he whirled. Snarling, the man thrust his weapon at Alexander.

Alexander easily evaded. Sauced to the gills, the man was a poor opponent. But at his next step back, Alexander hit a wall of men. One of the men behind Alexander shoved him forward into his attacker's blade. The tip drove into his left side. Pain tore through him, a potent reminder he needed to rescue Nichola, not waste time eluding a drunk.

"Alexander!"

He heard Nichola's frightened cry. She'd come to. He had to take her out of here now.

Whirling, Alexander caught his burley opponent's wrist and jerked it behind the man's back. The snap of bone sounded.

The drunkard's weapon clattered to the floor as he howled in pain. "You broke me arm."

Alexander slammed him to the floor, pinning his boot against his wounded arm. The man howled in pain. "It is fortunate I do not end your worthless life." With his dagger raised, he turned toward the wall of men surrounding them. He glared around the room. "Who else dares challenge my right to this woman?"

One by one, the men met his gaze. Menace hummed in their eyes, a dark seething skewed by drink.

Alexander stilled, his dagger readied. They'd reached the critical moment. The men would let them go or kill him and Nichola. He glared at the man holding Nichola.

"Release her!" Alexander demanded.

Tension permeated the silence.

At last, the man shoved her away. "Too scrawny for me liking anyway."

On a cry, Nichola stumbled forward.

Alexander caught her arms. At the terrified cry, the men began to chuckle. Before the mood turned more dangerous, he hauled her to within an inch from his face.

"You have earned the punishment you will receive this night," he said loud enough for everyone to hear. Not waiting for the men to change their minds, Alexander tossed her over his shoulder, strode across the room and up the stairs; the cut in his side aching. Grumbles followed in their wake.

Inside their chamber, he shoved the door shut and barred it. He set her down, the anger he'd banked below pouring through him. Gray eyes filled with fear stared back at him; a fragile, haunted look that dredged deep to his soul.

One wrong move and she would have been brutally raped. And once the men were through with her, they would have discarded her.

Uncaring.

Ignoring her pleas for help.

Until she died.

He swallowed hard, tempted to draw her into his arms and ease her fears. To swear he would protect her always. Shaken by his possessive thoughts, he dropped his hand to his side.

By the saints, he'd not be swayed by a comely face, especially that of an English lass. His concern for her arose from duty. Until her ransom arrived, 'twas his responsibility to ensure she remained safe.

"I told you not to run." He kept his voice hard to discourage further defiance.

Her lower lip trembled. "And let you rape me?"

Alexander caught her chin. "Lass, had I meant to take you, we would still be in bed. But," he said, anger cutting through his every word, "after the way you pressed your body against mine, moaned with pleasure as my lips took yours, little doubt exists that any pleasure you derived from me was not forced. Or would be."

A blush stained her cheeks.

"It was your attempt to escape that nearly cost us both our lives," he continued, damning her defiance. "Had you heeded my earlier warning, we both would have been sound asleep by now."

With her hand clenching the torn fabric of her gown, she looked away, a silent acknowledgment.

Alexander went to his saddle pack and retrieved an undershirt. "Here, wear this until I can steal you a new gown."

She took it and backed away.

By God's eyes, he was tired. At this moment, he could sleep upon a flattened boulder. Before he could lay down and rest, he needed to cleanse the injury. If the cut became infected, he might become gravely ill, or die.

He pointed toward the bed.

Fear swept through Nichola's eyes.

Alexander grimaced. "The bed is yours. I will sleep elsewhere."

At his quiet offer, tears flooded the eyes that had stared at him so balefully moments ago. She hugged his tunic to her chest as if a shield, and her slender body began to shake as if never to stop. Understanding dawned in him. Warriors often shook from their confrontations on the battlefield. This day she'd braved more than any woman he'd ever known.

"Th—The men below—"

Instinct had him stepping forward to draw her slender body against his own massive frame. He stroked his fingers through her hair as soft as silk. "*S e sàbhailte a th' agad fhèin a-nis,*" he whispered in Gaelic. "You are safe," he again whispered, in English this time against her brow. The warmth of her skin pulsed against his lips.

Gray eyes clouded with doubt lifted to his. "Am I?"

As she looked up at him with fragile hope, a possessiveness toward her overcame him. "No one will harm you while you are under my protection. That I swear with my life."

Belief flickered in her eyes. Drawn by her budding trust, finding he wanted so much more, Alexander lowered his gaze to her tempting mouth. At the first gentle brush of his lips against hers, sultry heat plunged through him, her taste filling his every thought. At her quiet acceptance, he covered her mouth, sinking into the soft sweetness.

He pulled away, his body hard with unspent desire, his breathing coming in sharp rasps. 'Twould be far too easy to give into his mind's tiredness, his body's raging need, and do something foolish. Like continue to kiss her.

Or seduce her upon the bed.

Nichola may have delusions of resisting him, but he had none about her acceptance of his touch. Though wariness filled her gaze, desire lingered there as well. If he caressed her in places proven to soften a woman, she wouldn't fight him. Her passionate nature would allow him whatever he desired.

Frustrated beyond belief, he pushed the images of her body arching against his as he made love to her away, thoughts he had no right thinking. Ever.

Alexander released her and gestured toward the straw-filled mattress. "Go to sleep. I will rest on a pallet near the door."

Silence filled the room between them. Nichola slid a hesitant look at the worn-wood floor, scuffed and dented through years of neglect, then back to him, his tender kiss still warm upon her lips.

A kiss she hadn't denied.

Guilt pricked her. Tired lines sagged the Scot's face, his muscled frame drooped with exhaustion, and though his words were firm, concern filled them as well. And he'd given her an undershirt to wear to spare her further embarrassment.

What reason prompted his concern toward her? She couldn't matter to him beyond the ransom she would bring. She had enough experience with men to know they thought little of her beyond her wealth.

Or was he indeed honorable?

In fairness, Alexander had risked his life below to save her. But had his actions to save her life arisen from chivalry? Or greed?

Nichola's body trembled as she reached the bed. She desperately wanted to sleep, to find sanctuary from this horrific night. Two nights ago she'd slept within her own bed, her biggest worry being what heirloom to sell to pay another debt. Now, she was being held hostage by a Scottish rebel, who inspired awareness for him as no other man.

She willed Alexander from her mind, but memories of his kiss, his taste, and the thorough mastery of his mouth lingered. Nichola wanted to owe her ready response to her exhaustion. That tiredness weakened her defenses.

However much she wanted to cling to that excuse, she refused to hide behind a lie. When his lips had covered hers, sensations she'd never experienced before had swamped her. Overwhelmed with emotion, she'd forgotten time, place, and the danger surrounding them.

And that the man embracing her was her enemy.

The soft pad of steps echoed behind her.

She tensed. Had Alexander changed his mind and was coming to share her bed? Praying she was wrong, she turned.

In the dim setting she saw Alexander walking toward the bowl set on a sturdy corner table.

She sighed with relief.

When he reached down to pick it up, she noticed the dark red stain on his tunic beneath his left arm.

"You are wounded," she gasped.

"It is nothing."

Her guilt mounted. "An injury gained in my defense."

A swath of black hair slid forward, casting the hard planes of his face in dangerous shadows. "You are under my protection."

"Is that what you term abduction?" she asked, unable to stop the question.

Cobalt eyes locked with hers. "The reason matters not."

It shouldn't. But against all logic it did. She should find her bed and ignore his suffering. "As I caused your wound, I will be tending to it," she said, matter-of-fact.

He straightened to his full height, his look as unwelcoming as dangerous, as though he too recognized they were playing with fire.

Nichola wondered at her sanity in offering assistance to a man who'd proven he could break through her emotional defenses with a single kiss.

"You will need to remove your tunic." Her quiet words echoed between them.

The muted shouts and laughter from below broke the silence as he stared at her. Cool. Decisive.

Her throat grew dry beneath his hard stare, that of a man who didn't ask, but took.

As if in response to a silent dare, Alexander slowly removed his tunic. His arms and chest rippled in an amazing display of sleek control. His gaze leveled on hers in an unspoken challenge as he dropped the garb to the floor with an unceremonious thump.

Beneath his blatant stare, she shuddered, but fear had nothing to do with the warmth that pulsed through her. Drawn to the sinewy muscles carving through his magnificent body, she studied him with appreciation. Scars crisscrossed a massive chest that tapered down to a rippled abdomen. Numerous cuts, healed over time, topped by a ferocious scar extending from the top of his left chest down to his hip.

A line of red along his side caught her attention. Blood seeped from an angry gash.

"If you are to tend me," he drawled, his burr thick, "be on with it."

On an unsteady breath, Nichola stepped closer to examine his wound. Within a pace, she made the mistake of looking up.

His mouth was but a hand away. The softness of his breath feathered against her cheek. The air grew thick, potent with awareness. She longed to reach up and touch the hard curve of his jaw, to run her fingers down the corded muscles of his neck, then lay her palm flat upon his chest. To feel the steady pulse of his heart within.

Her breathing grew ragged as her mind conjured

forbidden images. If he lowered his mouth but a whisper, he could cover hers with his own.

Dragging her gaze downward, she took in the injury. "The wound is not deep." Her words spilled out in a raspy whisper, betraying desires best left hidden. Unnerved by her reaction to a man she would be a fool to trust, Nichola retrieved a cloth that had been provided with the room and dipped it into the basin of water.

"This will hurt."

He gave a curt nod. "So be it."

She remained silent as she worked.

"You have a gentle hand."

Ignoring the heat that swept through her at his unexpected praise, she wiped away the last of the blood from the wound. "The cut should heal quickly." She folded the cloth, intending to step away.

He caught her hand.

"My thanks." For a long moment he studied her, not with the fury of a warrior, but with the needs of a man. Everywhere his gaze touched, her body responded as if his fingers lingered against her skin. As if he'd won an inner battle, he released her. "Go to sleep."

At his curt order, she set the cloth on the table and hurried to the bed, never having felt so at odds in her life. Worse, for the next few hours she would be locked within the same room with a man who made her body feel anything but imprisoned.

All too aware of his presence, she lay down and faced the wall. She dragged the blanket over her as if a shield, but it couldn't protect her from the truth.

She didn't despise him. She wanted to, but his valiant rescue showed her that he had honor and courage. And although he'd abducted her, he'd given his word to keep her safe as well. A promise he'd risked his life to keep.

Not that safety lay within his hands. Once he learned no ransom would be forthcoming, only God could help her then.

Nichola wished this was but a horrid dream. But with the straw poking into her back and the woolen blanket scratching against her flesh, her situation was anything but an illusion.

Chapter Four

At Nichola's cry, Alexander sat up from his pallet on the floor. Flickering candlelight caught her agitated movements in sleep. He frowned. She was having a nightmare.

Aye, her near-rape by the men below would invite terrors in her mind and account for her unrest.

On a whimper, she shifted onto her back, driving his guilt deeper. He rose to his feet, then stopped. What would his comforting her do but heighten her awareness of how alone they were and cause her further distress?

'Twas best if he left her alone.

This night, the feelings she'd aroused when he'd held her had proved to be a personal mistake. Kissing her more so. Intimacy between them had no place in this abduction.

After they'd returned to the chamber, the fact that she'd noticed his wound didn't surprise him.

Her insistence to tend it had.

Alexander's body tightened as he remembered her tender touch. Her genuine concern. And how after, she'd looked up at him with such innocence.

He'd wanted her.

The awareness smoldering in her gaze had assured him that she'd wanted him as well. But he'd not touched her. Not seduced her to release the craving for her that stormed him like a well-organized charge.

Straw crunched as Nichola rolled onto her side to face the wall. The blanket puddled on the floor with a quiet plop.

So he'd stay away from her to prove that he could? And allow her to suffer her nightmares alone? A sad knight he'd be the day he lost his compassion for the innocent.

Disgusted with himself, Alexander walked over and knelt beside the bed.

With her eyes closed in sleep, she began to shake her head. "No!"

He gently stroked her hair. His fingers glided greedily through the smooth, silken strands. "There now. It is but a dream."

Soft gold flickers of candlelight illuminated her face as she winced, then, slowly, the troubled lines on her face smoothed.

"Go to sleep. Let naught but dreams of fairies frolicking fill your thoughts," he whispered, remembering his mother's words, given to ease his night terrors.

Her eyes blinked open. With a gasp, she clutched the tunic he'd given her against herself and scooted back against the wall.

"Steady now."

"Yo—You said you were sleeping by the door," she accused.

"Aye, and that I am."

She hesitated. "I thought . . ."

He clenched his jaw, understanding all too well her misinterpretation to his nearness. "You thought I would break my word and take you." He stood and glared down at her. "Do not worry, you will be sleeping alone. Unlike the men you have known, I keep my word." Alexander strode across the worn planks to his pallet. He lay on his back and stared up at the ceiling.

"Why—"

"Go to sleep," he ordered.

"Why were you at my side?"

He remained silent. He refused to entertain questions of his honor.

"Will you not answer me?"

"So you can again doubt my reply?"

Her soft exhale whispered through the room. "I am sorry."

Appeased, he nodded. "You were having a night terror." Straw rustled. He awaited her next comment, she'd have one no doubt, that he'd learned from their brief association. Unless he gagged her. An appealing thought.

A corner of his mouth lifted in a grim smile.

"I want to apologize."

The regret in her voice tugged at his conscience. "It is done."

The cold plank pressed against his back as he laid there and listened as she settled into the bed. The chirp of crickets from outside rode in with the cool, nocturnal breeze. A boisterous laugh echoed from the rowdy men below.

Nichola's suspicion of a man's word weighed heavily on Alexander's mind. What had instilled her belief that a man's word meant naught? Who had lied to her? Hurt her enough to cause such distrust? Whoever the man was, he was a fool.

With a covert glance, Alexander studied the lass who seemed a contradiction at every turn.

Candlelight caught the sadness lingering in her eyes as she watched him, a quiet desperation within her that beckoned to him to offer her comfort.

As if she'd offer him such a token of her trust?

Against logic, he found himself wishing she would believe in him enough to share her heartache. He had experienced first hand the tragedies of life. Of hurt.

And the loss.

Familiar grief washed over him. He'd stood with his brothers as they'd buried their father—a father who'd sacrificed his life for Alexander's. And as the last stone was placed on his grave, Alexander had sunk to his knees and sworn to avenge his father's death.

"By God's eyes," he muttered. Alexander shifted to face the door, welcoming the cold, hard wood beneath him and the throbbing pain of his wound. His life was dedicated to war, against any who dared threaten Scotland's freedom.

Not a troubled Englishwoman who held no faith in men.

He tried to rest, but the sorrow within her gray eyes, too close to his own turbulent emotions, lingered on his mind. So he focused on the muted voices of the men below, his duty, and the many reasons it would be foolish to care about her.

But as the thick veil of sleep fell over Alexander, the barriers he'd erected to keep thoughts of her from his mind fell away. Steeped in tender thoughts of her, he drifted off into a contented slumber.

The next day, with hours of travel behind them, Alexander guided his mount out of a glen. He took in the new gown he'd stolen after they'd rode from the inn. The new dress, though worn, dipped daringly low on Nichola's chest. The ill fit couldn't be helped. Out in the wilds, the luxury of choice eluded him.

He scanned the sun-ripened grass sweeping across the secluded valley with a scowl; the scant sleep of last night had done little to ease his exhaustion. All because of a gray-eyed, outspoken lass who'd haunted his dreams.

If he'd bedded her in his dreams, that he could have accepted. With her siren's body and her seductive eyes, a man would have to be daft not to want her. Instead, in the realm of his sleep, she'd come to him needing a friend. Someone she could turn to. Trust.

He tightened his hold on the reins as he glanced down at Nichola. She leaned against him, but with her shoulders sagging and her face pale with fatigue; exhaustion, not desire, guided her action.

He reined his steed around a clump of weathered rocks jutting from the soil. What did her opinion of him matter? Within a fortnight, with her ransom paid, she would be reinstalled within her home. He will have rejoined the rebels; his mind steeped in planning their next assault on English troops.

A sudden gust of wind, cool and thick with the scent of rain, blustered past. The field of grass, which was scattered with heather, bowed beneath its force.

Alexander searched the horizon. A dark bank of clouds rolling in from the west promised a storm. With the night approaching, they would have to find cover. He'd have to reconsider his original intent. The only dwelling he dared stay in was another day's travel north.

However disreputable, he'd not risk returning to the tavern or any other village. "A storm is brewing. We will need to be finding shelter soon."

She tensed against his chest. Caution blanketed

her eyes as she tilted her face toward him. "Where will we stay?"

"If the weather holds, a hideout about an hour north."

"In Scotland?" Though whispered, nerves rattled her voice.

"Aye."

"Please, if you release me, I swear I will not tell them your name."

"No." As the land began to smooth out, he urged his mount into a canter, wanting to reach shelter before the rain began. "My decision is long made."

At Alexander's sharp reply, Nichola turned and stared straight ahead; the rugged land before them as untamed as the man who claimed her hostage. Her enemy. A man she should fear with her every breath.

And didn't.

How could she? Last eve he'd saved her from a brutal attack. After, he'd proved true to his word and had left her untouched. Neither could she forget his tenderness when he'd checked on her during her nightmare.

Was he indeed a noble man of honor?

Against the thrum of hoofbeats, the land raced past. Flowers misted the field in a rainbow of colors. But not even the spellbinding scenery eased her worries. What of this night? Or the days ahead?

With her response to his previous kiss, would Alexander keep his word and leave her untouched? Alexander? She caught the horse's withers as the wind whipped at her face. That she thought of him by his first name disturbed her further.

As the ground angled up, the Scot slowed his horse. His hand moved to gently clasp her shoulder. "What is wrong?"

His protective touch melted her resistance further.
"Naught."

"You are trembling."

Nichola leaned away from his touch. "I . . ." How
did she explain her reaction was from needs he inspired, not fear? She couldn't. An ache built in her
heart. Was she so lonely, so desperate that she'd find
comfort with a Scottish rogue?

"Lie against me." It was an order. At her noncom-
pliance, a deep sigh rumbled in his throat. "Leaning
forward will achieve naught but cause your muscles
to ache."

Nichola yielded, stiffening when her back rested
against solid muscle. He wrapped his hand around the
flat of her stomach. She tried to ignore the steady beat
of his heart; the reassurance his nearness gave her.

The assurance was an illusion.

Over the years, since her parents' horrible death,
trying to save her brother from his self-destructive
ways had shattered her beliefs of love and happiness
she'd once held as a child. The betrayal of her fiancé
severed any remaining belief.

Duty had kept her sane. Given her purpose. However much she dreaded returning home, to learn if
her brother had indeed committed murder, or to
face the army of creditors they were unable to pay,
she must.

Neither could she dismiss the thought of Alexander's anger when he learned their coffers were bare.
Somehow, before then, she must escape.

And use caution. As Alexander had shown her when
he'd appeared in the solar dressed as an Englishman,
the man could appear to be anyone he chose. From
the wanton state of her new dress, anyone she met

would believe her a whore, not a lady. As if she could trust anyone this close to the border.

Alexander guided the horse toward what she recognized as battered ruins of a church. A broken cross lay near the entry like a forgotten promise. How ironic. They would seek shelter in a holy place that now lay in shambles. A sanctuary as battered as her heart.

The churning gray clouds overhead erased any hint of sunshine and cast the warm and sunny late afternoon into a dismal mire. A cool breeze rushed past. Fat drops of cold rain began to splatter the earth.

He drew his steed to a halt before the weathered rock and dismounted, keeping the reins tight in his hand. "Come now," he said, wrapping his free arm around her waist.

She tried to push his hand away, but it didn't budge. "I can dismount by myself."

"Aye, I am sure you can." As if pushing aside an empty trencher, he removed her hand, then lifted her from the saddle and set her before him.

Nichola fought against her awareness of him as a man, ashamed his mere proximity made her shiver. "Must you find every excuse to touch me?"

He stared at her a long moment, then his gaze flicked to her mouth.

She held her breath, unsure if it was because he would kiss her, or that he wouldn't.

Alexander lifted her chin with his forefinger, the chilled air encircling them in a dizzying rush. The fresh taste of rain tingling on her lips. He slid his thumb over her lower lip; sensations strummed through her to her very core.

Saint's breath. The last thing she needed was his attraction to her. Or for him to see she was drawn to him as well. He was a knight. A man driven to war. His decisions quick. Unforgiving.

A muscle worked in his jaw, then he released her. "Stay here." He removed a taper and several other items and strode toward the tumble of timber and rock. At the weathered, but partially standing entry, he turned back as though unable to help himself. His cobalt eyes darkened with a dangerous edge, that of a predator.

Her heart stilled. Had he felt her pulse race? Sensed her body tighten at his touch? Or did his ire arise from his touching her in a manner far outside that of his captive?

In the way a man caresses a woman he desires?

Gripping the hilt of his dagger, he turned, ducked under the timber, and disappeared inside the darkened cavity.

Nichola sagged back. To allow him to believe that a bond could grow between them was a mistake.

But when he'd touched her face, the rough pads of his fingertips gentle against her skin; however wrong, she'd been unable to stop herself from wishing for more.

Alexander emerged from the darkened ruins. He gave a sharp nod toward the decaying structure. "It will do for the night."

Raindrops splattered against her face as she stared at him. Her breath wavered as she turned toward the ruins. "It is unstable."

"And has stood so for more than a decade." He held out his hand. "Come."

She hesitated, wanting to refuse, but the warning in his eyes assured her—he would make her comply, willing or not. She dismissed telling him that since her parents' death she feared the dark, more so during a storm. He already held too much power over her.

Catching the length of her dress with her fingers at each side, she lifted the hem above the fallen rock and walked forward. As she passed him, he tensed. Gathering her courage, Nichola hurried inside the murky opening.

Age mixed with the cool taste of rain greeted her, but the faintest scent of myrrh lingered as well. Her heart pounded as her eyes slowly adjusted to the candlelit interior. One wall was ready to collapse, but the remainder of the small enclosure remained sturdy and proud.

Near the farthest wall stood the decaying remnants of an altar, but she could envision the adornments that would have decorated the humble church: woven tapestries edged with gold thread, finely crafted goblets, carved figures of saints proudly displayed, and other, simpler offerings.

Thunder rumbled in the heavens above.

Nerves had her glancing up. In the wilting light, the gnarled beams shifted into ominous shadows. A shiver stole through her, and she crossed her arms against her chest.

Images of the accident with her parents flashed in her mind. The screams. The pain. The unbearable grief.

Please. Not now. She fought to quell the panic that a thunderstorm evoked.

On her next breath, she focused on the three large cracks near the battered entry; crevices where the rain would be able to slip inside.

Alexander's footsteps halted behind her. His breath, warm and steady, whispered against her neck. "Nichola?"

The strength of his presence lured her to lean

against him, to allow him to shelter her from her fears. By sheer will, she resisted his invisible pull. To allow him knowledge of her weakness would be a grave error.

She gathered her composure and turned to face him.

He studied her a moment with a shrewd eye. "The horse is bedded down in another part of the ruins. With the storm upon us, we will remain here for the night."

Until dawn she would be confined within the aged stone walls with Alexander. A thought that did little to ease her nerves. "It is too early to sleep." But however tired, sleep would evade her this night.

"Aye, it is." He walked past her with the bedroll in his hands, his muscled frame at odds with the decay surrounding him. Near the sidewall, he knelt and brushed away any loose pebbles, then spread out a woolen blanket.

She didn't want to sleep within inches of him, but she had little choice if she wanted to stay warm on this dreary night.

Another blast of thunder sounded, and she jumped. The steady beat of rain increased.

Sweat beaded her brow. Fighting for calm, Nichola walked to the entry. In the waning light, water streamed down the pile of rocks to spill onto a fallen pillar covered by moss. Hard, steady pounding sheets that saturated the earth. Wind ripped at the leaves, tossing saplings to and fro as if shaken by God himself.

Lightning severed the sky in a jagged streak. Thunder rumbled, this time closer. It took every shred of willpower not to curl up into a ball and cry.

Nichola hated the gnawing fear, but she couldn't prevent another shudder, or the all too vivid images of another time during such a thunderstorm; the rain had battered the ground and smeared pools of blood. The raw cries of terror had mingled with those of death.

"Lass?"

She whirled to find Alexander behind her. "You startled me," she said, barely quelling the urge to scream.

Alexander studied her. Startled mayhap, but as she'd stared at the rain pouring down, her face had grown deathly pale. Whatever memories she struggled against, they were far more than those that left one merely startled.

"You are upset," he said, keeping his voice as soft as he would be to a frightened mare.

"Do you expect any other?" she challenged, tinges of fear breaking through her voice. "I am held hostage in a foreign land, wear a gown I would not allow my maid to glance upon, and stand within a hovel that might crumble before the morn."

"Your concerns are valid, but that is not what is bothering you, is it?"

Her finger rubbed at the locket hanging from her neck. "Do you always pry into people's lives?"

"Is that what I am doing?"

Nichola turned toward the downpour, her shoulders as rigid as a sentinel. "I would rather not speak of it."

With the falling rain curtaining the entry, her composure faltered, and he understood. "You do not like the rain?" His question was whispered between them with unexpected tenderness.

She skimmed her fingers along the damp, pitted stone; her shallow breaths audible. "At least the water is not running inside. The floor will remain dry."

He should leave her alone, but her avoidance of his question piqued his curiosity. "What happened?"

Nichola shook her head, but her body began to shudder, betraying the truth of her reaction.

Alexander stepped up behind her. He clasped her shoulders gently. "I know the way of grief, of a hurt so cutting you pray for death." Shaken he'd betrayed such a personal fact, he released her and stepped back.

Never had he revealed the anguish he'd lived through after his father's death to anyone before. How could he admit such a thing, especially to an Englishwoman?

She turned. Grief-stricken eyes searched his with sympathy.

By God's eyes he needed nothing from her! He turned on his heel and started across the chamber. Her ragged exhalation stopped him. He curled his hand around his dagger, torn between duty and compassion.

Compassion won.

Alexander spun on his heel to face her. "Tell me what troubles you!"

A sad smile touched her lips. "Must you always have answers?"

"Not always."

"Is it not enough that you have taken me from my home?"

The soft accusation struck true. She was his hostage, a stranger whose life was opposed to his. "Aye, 'tis enough." He wanted no more and turned to put distance between them.

"Alexander."

At her familiar use of his name, awareness slid through him. And something else he barely recognized, a flicker of hope. "Aye?"

"I . . . Will you look at me?"

Rain eased outside, the slap of water against the stone quieting to a slow, steady thrum. Inside him, 'twas as if a storm brewed. He drew in a deep breath of air until it was as if his chest was on fire.

The soft scrape of slippers on dirt sounded in his wake.

Go away.

"Please," she whispered.

Tension hummed through his body as he slowly exhaled. He wouldn't ask again of her sorrows; already he'd trod on a personal path he had no right to take. He turned.

A tear slipping down her cheek had Alexander drawing her into his arms.

She splayed her hands against his chest and tried to push him away. "Do not."

He ignored her command. Tremors rippled through her slender frame as he held her close. Although she'd deny it, if only for this moment, she needed him.

"I want to help you," Alexander said, damning the truth of his words; but finding with her, he was helpless to do otherwise. He rested his chin against her brow. An unexpected softness coiled within him, filling him with a peace he'd not experienced since his father's death. The thrum of rain echoed around them and for this one moment, everything seemed right.

"This once," he said, "trust me."

"I do not think—"

"Then do not." The pounding of her heart slowed as he held her; pleasing him. Then, like a rose unfurling its petals, the tension within her body eased until she lay within his arms in acceptance.

How long they remained standing together as the storm unleashed its fury upon the land he didn't know. Or care. He ran his fingers through her hair and murmured encouragement, damning whoever had hurt this part of her. And whoever had left her distrusting men.

The warmth of her tears traced down his tunic. Alexander realized he wanted her trust and more. A bond that never could be. For the moment they'd found common ground, but it was far outweighed by the reality of their countries at war; of his vow to his father; and of the fact that he'd abducted her.

But he'd not worry about issues out of his reach. Not now when she was within his arms.

Alexander tucked her head against his shoulder as he would a frightened child. "They say that when the rain falls, it is a fairy's favorite time," he murmured, his hand threading through her hair to the end, only to begin again. "They dance on the puddles, and frolic on the beads of water as the raindrops cascade to the earth."

Thick, auburn lashes lifted to reveal the aftermath of tears, and doubt wedged in her gaze. "Fairies?"

"Aye," he said. A lock of her silk strands slid across his cheek. "The wee folk who live in fairy hills scattered about Scotland." He arched a surprised brow. "Do not tell me you have never heard of them?"

She paused as if trying to decide if she should believe him, then shook her head. "No . . . I . . ." Nichola looked down, but Alexander caught her chin with his finger and gently lifted her face toward him.

"Did your mother never tell you stories afore bed? Tales to fill your dreams as you slept?"

Her lower lip trembled. "She died when I was six."

He gave her a gentle hug, remembering the loss of his own mother at the birthing of his youngest brother, Duncan. Of his inconsolable grief. And that of his family. "I am sorry."

"My thanks, but many years have passed since."

Maybe, but by the ache in her words she still grieved her mother's death. "And your father?"

"They died together."

Her quiet admission broke his heart. "You lost so much."

"It was a long time ago."

"But the emptiness within you still exists." A lesson he'd learned first hand. Years eased the aches of your heart, but time never truly healed the grief. "Your brother raised you?"

"Yes."

That would account for their close bond. "He is a man lauded by King Edward. A man that takes care of his own."

She stiffened in his arms. "Wealthy you mean." Suspicion coated her gaze. Though only a hand's breadth apart, it may as well have been a league.

Mention of her brother had brought back the reality of how much separated them. Alexander released her and stepped back, ignoring the twinge of regret. 'Twas for the best.

She looked off into the distance. "When are you going to send the ransom demand to my brother?"

No reason existed to keep the information from her. "When we reach my home, Lochshire Castle."

Nichola turned toward him. "And how long will that be?"

"Three, four days at most."

"How long until we are on Scottish soil?"

"We crossed into my homeland late this morning." He nodded. "The church we are in is Scottish. It was destroyed during a skirmish many years ago by the English."

"I see."

At her cold tone, he bristled. "I have made little secret of our destination."

Nichola laid her hand upon a stone pillar etched

with time-worn cracks; her fingers trembled. "No, you have been truthful from the start."

Though she hadn't declared it with words, she again viewed him as the enemy; a man she could never turn to, nor lean upon for strength.

"I will be retrieving food from the pack." Alexander strode outside. Rain pelted his tunic and trews. In seconds his body was soaking wet and with each step his boots sank deeper into the mud. As if he bloody cared about his sodden state. Or Nichola's opinion of him.

But he did.

Furious that she could make him care, he whirled to face the ruins of the church. Never before had a woman caused him to have doubts over a decision made. Never before had he needed a woman this much.

He closed his eyes and exhaled. But clearing his lungs did little to unclog the turmoil inside. Shaken, he stared at the rain, which continued to fall: heavy drops that offered no forgiveness.

Seated before Alexander as he guided his mount around a bog, Nichola chided herself at her actions yesterday within the ruins of the church. How could she have turned to Alexander, allowed him to hold her as if he was someone she could trust?

A tight ache built in her chest as she remembered leaning against his muscled frame, seeking support. And if she was honest, wanting more. To taste his kiss, to feel his hands gentle upon her skin. How with a mere touch, he could make her forget her fears and think only of her needs. She shivered. Thank Mary he'd spoken of her brother.

In a normal setting, she would have pushed him

away. But lost within the tragic thoughts of her parents' death, Alexander's unexpected compassion had lured her to accept his comfort. He'd held her so close, his heart beating so strong.

For the first time in many years, she'd felt safe. Protected. And when he'd looked into her eyes, desired. She'd wanted him as well.

How easily she recalled touching his muscled body as she'd treated him back at the inn. The power he kept leashed, that of a warrior, a man confident in his abilities. A shudder swept through her.

"You are cold?" Alexander's deep burr whispered across her neck.

Nichola closed her eyes against the pleasant sensation. "No." Not cold, but so lonely that she ached. He could never know that. Or the fact his presence brought the promise of contentment to her life, which she'd not experienced before.

A promise that was never to be.

The rich fragrance of damp earth and dew-laden grass filled each breath as she glanced toward the clearing sky. Early-morning sun slipped through the thick canopy of leaves slick with rain, the rays warm upon her face. Within the dense forest, the fog clinging near the earth since dawn was beginning to fade.

At any other time, she would have appreciated the serene setting. But the beauty of the land unfolding before her served a potent reminder that they traveled deeper into Scotland. With a man who stirred emotions in her heart.

A man who was her enemy.

Overhead, a raven cried a sad, mournful sound. Nichola scanned the boggy land, cradled by the forest. They were alone. Even if they came upon someone, now within Scotland, she doubted they'd help her escape. So what could she do to gain her freedom?

If she slipped his dagger free, she could hold Alexander at bay until she rode away on his horse. She frowned. After watching him fend off the drunk, he'd easily recover his blade. When he slept she could steal his horse. No, with his warrior instincts, she would never be able to slip past him without alerting him.

Short of being dead or ill, 'twould seem she'd never find a way . . . wait. That was it! If he believed her unwell, he would lower his guard.

Guilt rose at her deception, especially considering his compassion toward her yesterday. Nichola refused to allow those emotions to fester. If he hadn't abducted her, she wouldn't be forced to take such a drastic step.

Slumping against his chest, Nichola moaned.

"Go to sleep. We will be traveling for a good while yet."

She moaned again from deep in her chest, putting more emphasis into it.

He caught her chin in a gentle hold and turned her face toward him. "You are ill?"

"Yes." The truth. Her deception was making her sick.

His fingers skimmed her brow. He frowned. "It is cool."

"I—I feel as if I will"—Nichola gave a rough cough—"retch."

"Mayhap the food from the inn was spoiled."

At the thought of the greasy, poorly herbed meat he'd taken with them when they'd left the inn, fare they'd eaten during a brief rest earlier this day, her stomach indeed grew queasy.

"I do not know what . . . oh—" On another groan she bent over, hoping to erase him of any suspicions.

"Whoa." Alexander halted his mount. "You are very pale."

Beneath his intense gaze, she tried to appear even more grim.

The cleft in his chin deepened with concern. "There is a burn but a short distance ahead. We will rest beside it until you can travel."

He'd believed her! She tampered her joy. Once they'd stopped, she still must figure out how to slip away.

Leaves rustled overhead as they rode down the shallow incline toward where a narrow ribbon of water gurgled over rock, then disappeared from view.

The sun's rays sparked over the rush of water like the sprinkle of diamonds, reminding Nichola of his story of fairies. She couldn't think of that. He'd abducted her, she owed him no loyalty. But with his saving her from the thieves at the inn, she couldn't help another twinge of remorse.

They neared the stream's edge, a rich bank laden with moss and grass. Alexander halted his horse and dismounted. He turned and carefully helped her down.

"My thanks." Without meeting his gaze, she laid her hand over her right temple as if it throbbed, the other cradled low over her belly. "If I could sit for a short while and rest," she whispered.

"Aye." He guided her to where several large boulders lay nestled along the water's bank.

She sat, careful to keep her movements slow.

"I will bring you some fresh water."

Nichola nodded.

Alexander retrieved his water pouch. He emptied the contents into the grass, then knelt at the stream's edge to refill it.

With his attention diverted, she searched their surroundings. To her left, she spied the broken length of a fallen limb.

Inspiration bloomed.

Nichola checked on Alexander, relieved to find him hunkered down at the water's edge, still refilling the water pouch.

Do it.

She hesitated at the thought of causing him harm.

He abducted you!

Taking a deep breath she rose. Her heart slammed against her chest. Nichola waited for him to turn, to catch her moving.

He continued filling his water pouch.

With care, she lifted the branch in her hand, thankful to find it firm and not rotting as she'd feared. She stepped forward. The moss absorbed the sound of her steps; Alexander hadn't looked in her direction.

Her hands began to tremble.

Do not weaken. He only wants the coin your ransom will provide.

She inched closer. Two more steps and Nichola stood an arm's length behind him. With a prayer for forgiveness, she raised the limb and took aim.

He pulled the leather pouch out of the water and started to turn toward her. "That should do—"

Closing her eyes, she swung with all her might.

Wood thunked as it slammed against his skull.

Nauseated, she peered out, desperate to know if she'd succeeded in rendering him unconscious.

Eyes wide with disbelief, he wove and tried to stand. On a curse Alexander tried to step toward her, but his legs buckled. He crumbled to the ground.

Horrified, Nichola stared at his unmoving body. What had she done?

Run!

She made to take a step away, but her conscience had her watching him to ensure she'd not severely injured him. Seconds passed.

He didn't move.

Nichola dropped the limb and crept closer. Blood oozed down the back of his neck. She clamped her hands over her mouth and staggered back.

Oh, God, she'd killed him!

Chapter Five

Nichola sagged to the ground on her knees. "What have I done?" She'd not meant to kill him, only to knock him out. Her heart ached as she lifted her head and stared at him.

Alexander's body lay sprawled on the moss, one arm slung carelessly over his head. His other hand curled peacefully on his chest. If not for the blood matting his hair and seeping down his neck, one would think him asleep.

Move. Stand up, damn you! Curse me. Anything. Please.

Water churned along the moss-edged banks. Leaves rustled overhead in a delicate ripple. A rabbit darted into the clearing, then sprinted into the cover of the woods.

Alexander remained still.

Nichola scanned the woods. She couldn't leave him here, but with his well-muscled frame, she wasn't strong enough to drag him away from the bank. Even if she could, how would she bury him?

She pressed her brow against her knees. The ache in her chest exploded into great, heaving sobs. Dark splotches stained her gown—the wanton dress yet another reminder of Alexander.

She wished the moment back, that she'd never picked up the broken limb. Other opportunities to escape would have presented themselves. Fear had provoked her to make an ill-conceived choice.

Is that what had happened to her brother, Griffin? Had his confrontation with Lord James tragically stumbled into murder? The forest blurred through the tears. Before, she would have dismissed such an explanation. Now, she understood all too well how an act of innocence could decay into a lethal misstep.

The freedom she'd sought lay before her, except now, her path was laden with naught but regret.

With the back of her hand, she swiped away the tears and pushed herself to her feet. However much it went against her every belief, she must leave him here.

A large tear wobbled on her chin. He may not receive a burial fitting of his status, but she'd not leave him without his dignity. She would cover his body.

At least he'd have that.

On shaky legs, she retrieved one of the two blankets from the saddle roll and knelt by Alexander's side. Instead of covering him, she pressed her hand upon his cheek, needing to touch him one more time.

"I—I am so sorry."

Her hand shook as she traced the cool lines of his warrior's face, seeing only compassion in the hard angles; wanting to remember him as a man who could touch her heart.

What was it about him that'd made her care? He'd abducted her. Thrown her entire life in chaos. Yet, his passing incited grief; a depth the like of which she'd not experienced since her parents' death.

Nichola leaned over and gently kissed his brow.

"Good-bye, Alexander." Her hands shook as she draped the blanket over his battle-honed body.

She pushed to her feet, ran to his horse and picked up the reins. And looked back toward him. *Please God, let a kind soul find and properly tend to Alexander's body.*

Nichola set her foot in the stirrup and pulled herself up onto the saddle, the worn leather empty without Alexander's formidable presence.

Wood snapped nearby.

Her pulse rammed in her throat. She scanned the dense thicket, expecting an enraged Scot to emerge and accuse her of murder.

A roebuck's flag flashed in the distance, then disappeared.

Look at her falling apart at the breaking of a stick. Her fingers tightened on the reins. And why wouldn't she? She'd just killed a man. Now, she was stealing his horse. If anyone spotted her with Alexander's body nearby, however unintentional her act, she would be hung.

A cold shudder swept through her. Her breath hitched as she stole one final glance toward Alexander. "Good-bye," she whispered. On a sob, she urged his steed south.

The horse didn't move.

On a shaky breath, Nichola nudged her knees against his sides. "On with you."

The horse swung its massive head toward her with an indignant snort. A wide brown eye stared at her with interest. Then he flattened his ears back, his expression as stubborn as his master's.

The reason why he refused to move dawned on her with dismay. Often knights trained their horses to remain by their side. The bay recognized her as a stranger and was waiting for Alexander. He refused to leave him.

Nichola nudged the horse's sides harder.

He sidestepped.

She yanked at the reins.

He whinnied and tossed his head, nearly jerking her from the saddle.

Would this nightmare never end? Without the use of Alexander's horse, she would have to travel on foot. Without another option, Nichola tossed the reins to the ground and dismounted; the task difficult as her gown caught on the saddle several times before she was able to dismount.

On the ground, she loosened the second blanket and food stores Alexander had secured from the tavern. She paused. Where was the water pouch? Then she remembered. Alexander had it in his hands when she'd hit him.

As much as she wanted to avoid going near Alexander's body, she would need water as she traveled. Her breath hitched as she ran back. At the stream, she stared for a long moment at Alexander's prone, blanket covered form. Grief swelled in her throat until she struggled for each breath. On a cry, she snatched the full water pouch, turned and started walking south.

Away from Alexander.

Forever.

As she traveled throughout the morning, Nichola scanned the dense forest, broken only by swaths of heather strewn fields. Until she reached English soil, she needed to stay as hidden as possible. She dared not trust anyone.

She had no experience in the woods much less knowledge of how to survive on her own. The few forays into the forest as a child to pick herbs with her mother hardly gave her the experience she needed now. The upkeep of Rothfield Castle allowed little time for such details as well.

And what if the need arose to protect herself?

Alexander's dagger.

She groaned. In her haste, she hadn't even thought of taking that. She dismissed the idea of returning for the weapon. What good would it do? She didn't know how to use the knife for defense, much less to catch game.

Her only hope was to keep her bearing straight and press on. She would make it home.

She had to.

But with each foreign sound that echoed through the dense stand of the woods, doubts of her success increased.

Alexander shifted. Pain hammered through his skull with a smithy's accuracy. He opened his eyes. The piercing rays of the sun sent a fresh burst of pain through his head. He snapped his eyelids shut, refusing to risk opening them and invite further misery. His thoughts stumbled and slid around in his mind. Had a mace bashed his head? Was he amidst a battle?

He gripped his dagger and listened, braced to move out of the way of danger. No grunts of horses colliding reached him. No scrape of blades. No screams of men as they died. If he hadn't been felled in battle, what then? Where was he?

Water gurgled a short distance away. Birds chirped in the trees. A gust of wind sent the leaves into a chaotic dance.

A slight shuffle sounded nearby. Then a warm

breath feathered across his cheek. A velvet caress brushed his forehead, then nudged his shoulder.

At the gentle touch, memories flooded his mind. Nichola being sick. Him tending to her by the stream. Refilling the water pouch. Then . . . darkness.

The soft, cool dampness of moss against his back registered in his mind. Then the weight of a blanket became apparent. Nichola had covered him. Whatever had happened to him, she'd not run, but had remained to tend to him.

"I am awake." Whispering didn't prevent another bolt of agony from skewering his brain. "A moment, lass." After a slow deep breath and preparing himself for the intensity of the sunlight, Alexander opened his eyes.

And stared straight into the hairy muzzle of his horse.

"Nichola?"

The bay nickered softly. With a soft snort, his horse dropped his massive head and nudged his shoulder.

What the devil? Alexander gritted his teeth and shoved to a sitting position. The blanket that was draped across his chest rolled onto his lap. The woods came into dizzying focus. A frown settled on his brow as he scanned his surroundings. He didn't see her.

"Nichola?"

Alexander tensed. Had someone attacked him and stolen her? Maybe one of the men from the tavern had followed them and while he was busy fetching water, they'd clouted him. His pulse raced as he searched for any sign of a struggle.

Nothing.

Why did his head ache? Tenderly, he probed the back of his head where the throbbing was most intense. His fingers skimmed over a large bump covered with a sticky ooze. No, not ooze. He drew his hand away and stared down at his fingers.

Blood coated his fingers.

He noticed a curved limb lying inches away.

Had Nichola . . . no. She wouldn't hit him. Aye, he'd abducted her, but he'd reassured her many times over during this journey that she was safe. A fact proven yesterday at the church ruins when she'd turned to him for comfort. Until he'd mentioned her brother's name. Then the warmth in her eyes had faded and she'd stared at him as if the enemy.

He wanted to believe she hadn't ambushed him. Sadly, no other explanation fit. It accounted for why he'd not heard anyone's approach. And why, he, a seasoned knight with many a battle behind him, had been caught off guard.

Anger churned inside him like bubbles inside a boiling cauldron. So this was her repayment of his trust? So be it. When he caught her—and he would— he'd not let down his guard toward her again.

Nichola shoved a low-hanging limb from her path, ducked beneath it. Leaves shook angrily as the branch whipped back into place. She trudged on. Every muscle in her body protested, but at least exhaustion was dimming the pain.

How long had it been since she'd left Alexander? From the sun sitting high in the sky, a handful of hours had passed, but it felt like days.

In more ways than one.

No, she wouldn't think about his death. She was free and headed toward England. Toward home. That's all that mattered. All that could matter.

The distant rush of water rumbled ahead.

Good. She'd refill her water pouch and rest awhile. Not too long. Just enough to catch her breath. But how she yearned to lie down by the bank and sleep.

The leaf-strewn ground ahead of her fell away to a steep hill. Tiredness blurred her vision as she started her descent. On her next step, her slipper caught on the root of an oak.

Nichola screamed and tumbled downward. Rocks bit into her legs. Thin branches whipped her face. Shrubs scraped her body. She clawed in vain at the mass of leaves and rich earth, anything to halt her rapid descent. She was moving too fast.

A large boulder loomed before her.

She was going to hit it! Nichola crossed her hands over her face. The breath was knocked out of her as she slammed to a halt.

Mary's will. Everything hurt. But as long as she felt pain, she was alive. She tentatively moved her limbs. And by God's hand, she didn't believe anything was broken.

Slowly, her vision cleared. She stared up at the large bounder. Moss draped down the sides, which had saved her from a much worse fate and possibly death.

Another wave of dizziness swept over her. She closed her eyes. The cool, fresh scent of the forest filled her lungs with each breath she took. The churn of the river surged nearby.

She was so tired. What would it hurt if she took a short nap? Her eyes drifted shut. No. The price of her freedom was too dear. She had to keep moving.

Wiping the dirt from her eyes, she crawled to her knees. A twig slipped from her hair and landed on the ground. Exhausted, she rested against the padded stone.

How was she going to make it to England when she

could barely move her legs? If only she'd been able to ride, this would have been so much easier.

Thoughts of the stubborn horse made her think of Alexander, in spite of her vow not to. Grief swelled in her chest. He had treated her with naught but respect. 'Twas her attempts to flee that had brought on her troubles.

A contrast from her original impression of him. When he'd stood in her solar, all she'd seen was a formidable man carved in ice. A man bred to kill. Now, she saw him as a steadfast man of compassion. Though he was her enemy, his intent for his cause was honorable.

And now he was dead.

Leaves clattered overhead drawing her attention. She glanced up at the slivers of sunlight. They slipped through the flutter of leaves, illuminating the forest with random sprinkles of light.

Entranced by the dance between sunlight and leaf, she basked in their almost magical interaction. The shimmers of light flitted like fairies upon the leaves.

Fairies?

She frowned at her fanciful notions and brought her gaze back to the sun-dappled ground. Such was Alexander's belief. She touched the pendant at her neck. Before her parents' death, life had held a magical appeal. In the innocence of her youth, she had believed in miracles and unexplainable wonderment.

An ache burrowed in her chest. No, magic and fairies couldn't compete with harsh reality.

Nichola gathered her thoughts. She needed to focus on her present situation, not waste time on the past she couldn't change. Or foolish notions of fairies.

After taking the last drink of water from the pouch, she secured it around her waist and stood. On trembling legs, she rounded the large rock and halted, stunned by the vivid landscape before her.

"It is beautiful," she whispered, as if to speak out loud would taint the setting before her.

Water cascaded from a ledge of rock pouring into a churning pool, the water so deep near the center that it darkened to a black hue. Heather dusted the edge of the basin, entwined with bog myrtle, buttercup, and sprinkled with an occasional meadowsweet.

Her minimal knowledge of flowers and plants made her incapable of naming the many varieties that framed the water's edge, but that fact didn't dismiss their beauty or their amazing scent. She inhaled their bounty, appreciating the soft mix of fragrances.

Her own private pool. And she desperately needed to bathe. She imagined the cold, refreshing water embracing her; soothing the aches that tormented her every inch. Oh, to be clean again. To scrub every speck of dust and grime from her skin. Heaven on earth.

With a sigh, Nichola pushed the inviting thought aside. The sun was beginning to set. She needed to travel south as far as possible before dark. At the waters edge, she knelt to refill her water pouch.

The low, steady thrum of hoofbeats echoed behind her.

She stood and whirled. Nichola scanned the ridge. Griffin! She sobered. Was her brother even aware of her abduction? Even so, how would he know to search for her here?

Her pulse raced as she searched the trees for the rider. She glanced skyward to take a bearing. Whoever it was, they came from the north, from the direction she'd fled.

Someone had found Alexander's body!

The image of a rabid, half-naked Scot in war paint,

wielding his claymore as he rode hard to avenge his kinsman's murder flashed in her mind.

A horse whinnied from beyond the ridge.

Nichola stumbled back. She couldn't let anyone catch her! She backtracked to flat ground, then ran. Her breaths came fast, her legs screaming with every step.

The pounding of hooves increased.

Limbs scratched her face, arms, and legs. She didn't stop running. Didn't dare.

"Nichola!" Alexander's outraged yell boomed through the forest.

She whirled. Alexander! Happiness burst through her as she started toward him. He was alive. She hadn't killed him.

"Nichola!"

At the anger in his voice, her happiness faded. What was she doing going to him? After hitting him on the back of the head with a limb, he would far from welcome her.

She searched her surroundings for a place to hide. He was too close for her to try and cross the river, or climb up and hide behind the waterfall.

In the distance stood a thick hedge surrounding a large, ancient oak.

The steady thrum of hoofbeats closed.

Saint's breath! Nichola sprinted toward the hedge. She shoved the dense shrub open and crawled inside. Limbs and briars tugged strands of hair loose, leaves slapped her face, but she inched deeper into the thicket.

Sticks snapped beneath his mount's hooves as he approached.

Touching her pendant, she peered through the breaks in the leaves.

Alexander rode into view. He halted his mount atop

the hill she'd tumbled down moments before. Like a vengeful god, he surveyed all within his domain; his intense gaze filling her with dread of retribution.

She shrank deeper into the thick growth. Through the dark, heart-shaped serrated leaves, abundant with clusters of green blooms, she watched Alexander guide his bay down the steep incline.

Tiny pinpricks of sensation shimmered up the back of her hands and arms. She shifted away from the dark, hair-covered stem of a tall weed.

At the base of the hill near the boulder she'd slammed into when she'd tumbled down moments ago, Alexander halted his horse. A frown carved his face as he scanned the torn up earth, then his gaze swept the area.

Nichola shivered. *Please do not see me.*

Tiny leaves fluttered beneath her nervous breath and scraped across her hands. Her skin tingled. She owed the irritation to her own nerves, to her fear of discovery.

The scar on his left cheek tightened. Again he scanned the surrounding forest.

Her heart pounded so loud she was afraid he would hear its frantic beat.

The tingling sensations intensified. They fanned over her skin spreading up her arms, then around her neck and up her face. Sweat moistened her brow. Her throat grew parched.

Nichola focused on the soothing flow of water; the rainbow of color surrounding the banks of the waterfall. Neither kept her mind away from the growing need to scratch her arms or quench her thirst. She must remain still. Her freedom depended on her silence.

Go, she silently willed him.

Alexander stood in his stirrups. His bay shifted

beneath him. He absently stroked the horse's neck as he scanned the surrounding woodland.

"Steady lad," Alexander soothed. Nichola had passed through here. The freshly torn up earth and uneven heaps of leaves where she'd fallen offered proof.

With a grimace, he smoothed his fingers over the throbbing lump on the back of his head that still screamed like a raging woman. And had swollen to the size of a duck egg.

The slight rustle of leaves from a clump of thick shrubs at the base of a large oak caught his attention. He studied the intricate weave of branches and leaves. Within the mix, he saw naught but shadows.

A hare, badger, or another small animal might be hiding within, but his senses told him otherwise. The dense foliage provided excellent cover for a person to hide.

Leaves again shook within the dense tangle, confirming his suspicions of exactly who hid within.

He straightened in the saddle, a smug smile settling on his lips. *Now lass, we will see who has outfoxed whom.*

Alexander nudged his bay toward the thicket. Several feet away, he made out a tangle of nettles woven through the brambles; their jagged leaves heavy with clusters of greenish blossoms.

"By God's eyes," he muttered. "She has not been ignorant enough to hide in there?"

The branches shook again, this time more intensely.

He winced, all too aware of the misery she has unknowingly inflicted upon herself. Once during his youth, he'd slipped inside some brambles to hide from his brothers. The hours he'd suffered from his exposure to the seemingly innocent weed had taught him to take heed when seeking shelter in the woods. A fact she would learn this day.

"Lass." His firm tone vibrated in the forest. "I know you are in there. Come out."

Silence. The bushes moved with a vigorous shake.

He shook his head, frustrated at her stubbornness. "Nichola."

"Go away."

At her irritated voice, another smile curved at his mouth. "You have stinging nettles all about you, lass," he explained. "If you remain there, you are doing naught but punishing yourself further."

"As if you are not going to."

"No," he said with a solemn tone. However upset he might be, never had he touched a woman in violence. Even after her brazen act, the thought of striking her repulsed him. "I will not be touching you. Your bout with the nettles will serve enough of a punishment."

The bushes shifted. "Do you swear it?" she asked, her voice a mix of nerves and desperation.

"Aye."

The outline of her face came into view, her gray eyes ridden with doubt.

"The longer you remain in the bushes, the more you will suffer."

With a vicious rustle, Nichola shoved her way from the thicket; her newly stolen dress torn, scrapes running up her arms, and a rash darkening her exposed skin.

God's teeth! In one quick move, Alexander dismounted and rushed to her side.

At his approach, her eyes widened and she stumbled backed. "Do not beat me."

Disgusted by her lack of trust, he gently caught her by the arm. He led her first to his horse. "Do not move." Alexander retrieved a rounded cake of crafted soap, then guided her toward the pool below the waterfall.

"What are you doing?" she asked.

At the water's edge, he released her and held out the cake of soap. "Clean off as much of the nettle's venom as you can. Once you are through washing, I will apply a mix of herbs to help the pain."

Nichola hesitated, her hand moving to scratch at the skin along her forearms.

"Take it," he said, irritated she'd fight him on this. With the redness growing on her skin, she had to be in agony.

Doubt simmered in her eyes. "Why would you help me after what I have done to you?"

He ignored the tremor in her voice. "A question I have asked myself several times since I found you."

Her fingers trembled as she accepted the soap. "My thanks." She walked toward pool. At the water's edge she removed her slippers, lifted the hem of her tattered dress and stepped gingerly into the water's edge. A groan of pure relief fell from her lips.

"When you remove your clothes, toss them back to me."

She spun to face him, her mouth open in disbelief. "It is indecent."

As she stood there staring at him, the water her shimmering backdrop, it was all too easy to imagine her wet and naked. Alexander clenched his teeth. He didn't need to be thinking of that.

"While you are bathing," he said, "I will rinse any venom from the plant off your clothes then hang them to dry. With the nettles venom in you, you will soon be too weak and ill to complete the chore yourself. Go on now. The soap is made with sage and rosemary. It will help the itching."

"I will not strip and—"

"Enough!" He took a menacing step toward her.

"You will do what I tell you or I will wash you myself."
Nichola sputtered with outrage, and he cursed his
body as it hardened at the image of her soapy and
naked in his arms. Blast the lass for tempting him so.
And himself for being so weak when it came to her.

After hitting him with the branch, she should instill
naught within him but distrust. But as his body kindled with desire, 'twould seem it'd betray him as well.

She gave a slow, wary nod, her hands rubbing her
arms. "Turn around."

"And trust you not to clout me again?"

A blush swept up her face. "You have my word I will
not hit you."

He grunted. "If I hear a footstep coming near my
direction, I will scrub you myself." Alexander turned,
ready to dismiss her from his thoughts. And his life.

The scrunch of wet fabric stoked the randy images
swirling through his mind. The slide of fabric allowing him to easily envision her peeling her half-torn
garment from her smooth, creamy flesh, and the
bounty of curves spilling free.

"Blast it," he muttered beneath his breath.

"Do not look!" she all but shrieked.

A vision of her arms trying to cover her ample
swells from his view had him growing harder. "Blast it.
I will not. Now on with you."

Without warning, the water-laden dress slapped on
the ground inches away from him.

Nichola was naked. Except for her necklace, not a
stitch covered her slender frame. If he turned now,
he'd see every inch of her. From the tumble of her
auburn curls, to the slim column of her neck, to the
curves of her tempting breasts. Down her narrowed
waist to the apex of her womanhood.

His breathing became shallow. His body hardened

to a painful state. The softness of her skin beneath his hands invaded his memories.

On an oath, he bent and lifted the garment. Her scent of woman and lavender rose from the dress. He fisted his hand on the low-cut gown. God in heaven, a man had only so much strength.

Water sloshed behind him.

He willed his mind to empty. Instead it painted a torturously clear picture of her slender legs slowly being engulfed in the chilled rush of water. How the shimmer of droplets would linger on her pale skin, and her nipples growing into hard, stiff peaks.

Sweat beaded on his brow as he willed himself not to turn and look his fill. He shifted, trying to ease the agonizing pressure of his manhood within his trews.

A quiet splash of water behind him signaled she'd begun to wash.

He groaned. Careful to not injure himself in his aroused state, he crouched at the water's edge. He should have searched around and stolen another, more modest, change of clothes for her as well. Until he acquired a replacement, this garment would have to do.

Alexander focused on rinsing out her gown. Unbidden, images of her skin lathered with a slick layer of soap formed in his mind. Of the warm scent of her skin. Of how his fingers would skim across her slippery flesh, and her moan of pleasure as she begged him to make love to her.

He shook his head. *Get a hold on yourself, lad.* But with the randy thoughts pouring through his mind, he may as well have been wishing to find a fairy hill.

Disgusted at his lack of will when it came to her, he squeezed the water from her tattered gown. He rose to leave, but lost to temptation as he stole a quick peek at her through his lashes. What did she expect? He wasn't a saint.

A groan of pure lust ripped through him.

Full breasts jutted proudly above the water as she stood lathering herself. The curve of her waist a fantasy in itself. And the downy softness of her auburn hair encasing her essence.

He turned away, desperately wanting a quick douse in the icy water to temper his own raging need.

"Alexander?"

Her soft voice slid through him like warm wine. "Aye?"

"I am ready to come out."

"Then out with you." He regretted his curt tone, but if she knew of his lusty thoughts or ungentlemanly act, she'd remain in the safety of the water. He strode away and hung her garments upon the branches of a nearby bush to dry.

Water splashed in his wake.

He would not envision her walking from the pool naked. Of the beads of water clinging to her body, and of how sweet they would taste as he licked each drop from her flesh.

"I need a blanket to cover me."

"It is on my horse." His body hummed with unspent desire as he headed toward his mount. Alexander drew a deep breath as he unlashed the blanket from the roll, visions of her naked burning through his body with aching efficiency. A sin he suffered greatly for.

With the wrap under his arm, Nichola watched as Alexander strode to the water's edge. Thankfully, he kept his gaze averted. A hand's length from the bush she had hidden in, he stopped.

"Put the blanket on the rock to your left," Nichola said. A shudder rippled through her. The soap and cool water had helped ease the itching, but her body still burned as if on fire.

A wave of tiredness swept over her and she now understood his urging for her to hurry. She wove on her feet. All she wanted to do was rest.

"Nichola?"

"Please, just set it there." The concern in Alexander's voice threatened to break down her resistance. She wanted nothing more than to turn to him, to lean against his strength during her misery.

As much as she wanted his comfort, she was more afraid of what such an action would yield. Already she'd stepped beyond the bounds of viewing him as her enemy. Not that she'd forgotten he was her abductor, but their time together was unveiling a proud, honorable man. A man who inspired trust—something she could never give him.

Alexander kept his back to her as he set the blanket down. He walked away, leaving her alone.

On a sigh she reached out, took the blanket and draped it about her; the coarse wrap was rough upon her tender, itchy skin. Despite the heat coursing through her, her teeth chattered as she walked over the soft, leaf-strewn ground.

Curious as to the green leaves Alexander was mashing on a slab of stone, she moved closer. As she approached, she noticed that every so often he tipped the flattened rock to catch the juice in a small, hollowed piece of dry wood.

Nichola halted by his side. "What are you doing?"

"I am making you a poultice with plantain. The herb often grows alongside the stinging nettles. The juice will help calm the itching and burning of the nettles upon your skin." He looked up and his cobalt eyes locked on hers; desire simmered in his gaze.

Heat stroked her body, but it had nothing to do with the offensive weed that'd left her body on fire.

He turned away and the magical spell was broken. Alexander continued to mash the leaves.

A sense that she'd narrowly escaped a disaster descended over her. She tugged the blanket closer. Or had she avoided anything? Hadn't he been the one to turn away? She drew in a steadying breath, the need for calm far from achieved.

Exhaustion. That was why she was reacting so strongly to his presence. That had to be the reason for her emotional state. And prayed it was the truth.

Alexander added another mound of the wide plantain leaves to the mashed pile and ground them together. Again, he was careful to pour off the juice in the rough wooden container as he squeezed it out.

She huddled under the blanket, mesmerized by his meticulous attention to detail in this task. She'd believed him a man of action, a warrior impatient with life. This patience of his was unexpected, which disturbed her further. He wasn't a simple man as were her brother or ex-fiancé, both with their focus on money and drink.

He tossed the rock with the mangled leaves aside. "It is ready." He held up the rough wooden container with the extracted liquid.

"Thank you," she replied, her voice not as steady as she would have liked. She didn't want to see him on this personal level, as a man who cared, a man who offered to help someone in need. Why couldn't he just be a simple rogue whom once this ransom plot was over, she could forget?

Doubts of that happening grew.

He stood, slowly, his eyes darkening with intent. "Remove the blanket."

Chapter Six

At Alexander's advance, Nichola stepped back and tugged the blanket tighter. Wool scratched her inflamed skin.

His cobalt eyes darkened to an inky black. "It is foolish to disobey me, you will only cause yourself further suffering. The juice needs to be rubbed all over."

"A task I am capable of doing," she whispered. Already he'd aroused feelings no other man had ever inspired. For her own sanity, she needed him to keep his distance. "I will do it."

"Not as efficiently as I."

"But—"

He kept coming, closing a step for every one she retreated. His eyebrows wedged into a dark frown and the cleft in his chin deepened. He appeared every bit the warrior, until she caught the softness in his gaze.

No matter how admirable his actions were, she didn't want to see his caring side. He was her enemy. "You can apply the salve where I cannot reach," she finally agreed. A part of her dreaded such intimacy. Even nauseated, another part of her wondered how his hands would feel upon her skin. Mary's will. Did she have no shame?

Alexander passed her the wooden container holding the freshly pressed liquid. "Go behind the boulder," he said gently. "Do not tarry."

She gave a ragged nod.

"If you try and run, I will catch you."

A tremor shook her body. "As if naked and wrapped only in a blanket I would choose to flee?"

"I will not underestimate you again."

She frowned at where he'd hung her tattered garments—in the opposite direction from the boulder.

Her knees trembled as Nichola headed toward cover. Shielded by the boulder, she released the blanket. She leaned against the moss covered rock and closed her eyes at the cool softness that offered blessed relief to her searing skin.

Her stomach roiled and she almost doubled over. She gave a soft groan as she sank to the ground.

"Do you need help?"

The concern in his voice tempted her to admit that she wasn't sure if she could complete the simple task. "I am almost done," she replied out of preservation.

Nichola scooped the salve into her palm. Sweat beaded her brow. Her vision blurred.

You can do it—or he will.

With trembling fingers, she applied the cool liquid over her body, except for her upper back. She reached over and managed to curl her fingers in the blanket. Her hand shook as she drew it around her body

Blackness threatened.

She clutched the wool wrap, crawled back up to her feet and braced herself against the boulder. *She could not pass out!*

"Nichola?"

Bracing herself, she staggered forward. Halfway around the rock, Alexander caught her. His gaze raked the length of her. Worry furrowed deep lines in his brow.

"By God's eyes!" He scooped her into his arms and strode toward the small encampment at a dizzying speed.

"Put me down."

"Why did you not ask for help?" The softness of his tone did little to diminish the censure in his voice.

"I am naked," she mumbled, the effort to talk a feat unto itself. Blackness encroached around the corners of her vision.

He gave a disgusted snort. "As if I have not seen a woman in all of her splendor." He sat on a stump with her sheltered in his arms. "Did you apply the salve?"

"Yes, except fo—for my back."

"I will see to that then." Alexander carefully angled her against his chest. With a gentle hand, he loosened the blanket and began spreading the ointment.

A sigh fell from her lips at the cool balm against the burning of her skin, but the wool blanket draped around the rest of her body offered its own brand of torture. Damning the consequences and out of sheer desperation, she caught the edge of the blanket and tugged down.

"What is wrong?"

"The blanket. Hu—Hurts."

"I should have thought to give you my tunic."

His sincerity touched her. As he gently removed the blanket, she heard his sharp intake of breath before looking away. She tried to be embarrassed by her nakedness as she lay against him, but with her head pounding and her body caught between freezing and a raging inferno, she couldn't muster the energy to mount a protest.

Another wave of nausea hit. The forest around her blurred in a painful haze. "Please, make the burning stop."

At the pain in Nichola's voice, Alexander wished this day over. Or that he could bear her pain. He could do neither. But he would make her as comfortable as possible.

That, he could give her.

He smoothed back a wisp of hair that had fallen across her face. "It will take time for the effects of the nettles venom to fade." With her still in his arms, he rose. He removed his boots.

"What are you doing?" she asked on a groan.

"Your body is too warm. The cold water will bring you relief." He scooped up the soap and waded into the icy water, ignoring the throbbing in the back of his skull from her earlier blow."

"Your clothes—"

"Will dry." She stared at him, helpless, needy, but beneath, he saw the trust. Moved she would choose to believe in him, ashamed to find her belief warming his heart, he grimaced. Her offering him her trust would only complicate things further. He trudged deeper into the mountain-fed stream.

"But—"

He shook his head. "I am going to wash you again. It will ease the pain. Once your body has cooled and you are dry, I will reapply more balm. For now, it is more important to bring your fever down."

Gratitude flashed in the gray eyes that stared up at him. Then she laid her head against his chest, her teeth chattering; the skin pressed against him burning hot.

When the water reached his waist, he carefully set

her down before him. Pain glazed her eyes as she stared blankly at him, her body continuing to shake.

Blast it. If he had paid attention to her at the stream while filling up his water pouch, she never would have had the chance to clout him, much less escape. But she had.

Despite her foolishness, she did not deserve this punishment. The nettles venom wasn't lethal, but would leave her very ill for the next day.

Alexander rolled the soap in his palms until it foamed. Aye, he couldn't help but appreciate her lush curves as he lathered her body; how her nipples hardened to taut peaks against the cold water, but now she needed his aid, not randy thoughts slipping through in his mind.

But they did, images of her slick body wedged against his, of his mouth skimming over her smooth skin, her heat wrapping around him as he lay her down upon the soft moss and claimed her as his own. Cursing silently, he gazed off into the distance, forcefully suppressing his lust and busying himself with his task.

After he'd cleansed her entire body, he moved Nichola to where water cascaded from the cliffs into an almost black pool. When the depth of the water reached his shoulders, he dipped them both within the freezing water.

As they stood there, his own body began to shiver and slowly numb. He ignored the discomfort. The icy water would lower her fever and offer her another layer of relief.

She closed her eyes and curled tighter against his chest.

Her simple act swept him away as surely as the soap swirling downstream. He stared down at her slender body leaning into him for warmth and her looking fragile. Protectiveness surged through him, a base need to protect her storming his senses as if a well-planned siege. The intensity caught him off guard. He'd made love with women before, but never had anyone touched him as Nichola had.

Trusting eyes, bright with fever, stared up at him.

He wanted to hold her to him, whisper assurances he would protect her always. Struggling to accept the impact of what she made him feel, he continued to hold her.

After awhile, he stroked his fingers across her brow, which was cooler to the touch. Satisfied the water had done its work, he carried her ashore and set her upon a flattened rock. He lay a dry tunic over her.

"Stay still." He kept quiet, conversation would drain her further. Though her fever had left, without the cooling effects of the water, it would return. And when it did, he prayed she didn't fall into a delirium.

But as she watched him, dullness shading the normal vibrancy of her eyes, and he worried it was already too late for his prayers to be answered.

Alexander retrieved the remainder of the plantain salve he'd culled and reapplied the ointment. Then he selected the softest tunic he'd packed and drew the garment over her head. On her slender frame, it fell below her knees.

His heart tightened. She appeared as if she were a lost pixie. "Rest. I will fix you a drink that will aid you to sleep."

She managed a slight nod.

Disturbed by her deteriorating condition, he busied himself to fill his mind with thoughts other than her. He built a small fire and retrieved a small pot he carried in his pack. After picking enough chamomile leaves from a nearby plant to brew a cup, he steeped the fragrant leaves within the boiling water. All through the task, he found himself glancing toward Nichola.

As the steeped herbs cooled, he quickly changed from his sodden clothes. Finished, he carried over the steaming brew and knelt before her. Her teeth chattered even as fever flushed her cheeks and the rash on her exposed skin had spread. The poor lass, she looked hopelessly miserable.

Alexander held the warm tea up to her lips. "Drink it slowly."

She wavered before him.

He caught her shoulder and steadied her.

"I—I just want to sleep." Her voice slurred.

"You will. This will help."

At last she finished the tea. He set the cup down and drew her against him.

Her trembles increased.

Unable to do more, Alexander murmured soothing words in Gaelic he remembered his mother had offered to him while he was ill as a lad.

The next few hours passed in a blur. At times she rambled, at others she thrashed around in his arms. Finally, as the sun faded from the sky and blackness engulfed the earth, Nichola fell into an exhausted sleep.

Careful not to wake her, he placed her on another blanket he had spread out. In the moonlight she appeared so fragile. As if she'd break at the slightest touch.

He pressed a kiss upon her brow. "Sleep well."

Unsettled to find kissing her such a natural thing to do, he walked to the bank of the waterfall. Moonbeams wove through the rush of water, flickering and teasing the erratic swirls as if fairies skimmed over the surface in a mischievous dance.

But the lightness he yearned to feel never came.

Guilt edged through him. 'Twas wrong to be caring for the lass. To do so went against everything he stood for. Against his vow to avenge his father's death sworn upon his grave.

Sorrow clung to him like the drops of moisture to the low-hanging leaves as he returned to where she slept. A pace away he halted.

He stared down at her as if seeing her for the first time, wanting her more with his every breath. How could an innocent like Nichola have made him want her so much?

Crickets started to sing, their cadence filled with a sad lilt. Against his better judgment, he lay down and drew her into the curve of his arms. For this one last night, to offer her succor, he would hold her.

"Alexander."

At the sound of a voice, Alexander instantly came awake. Without lifting his head, he slitted his eyes and scoured the forest for danger, his hand slipping his dagger free from its sheath.

The first shafts of sunlight slipped through the forest casting inky shadows where his enemy could hide.

He watched.

Waited.

And saw naught but the dew upon the grass and the first golden rays of sunlight shimmering through the leaves. The chirp of the morning birds backed by the steady churn of the water further aided his belief they were alone. And safe.

"What is out there?"

At Nichola's whispered question, his body instantly

hardened. He grimaced and he secured his dagger. She lay at his side watching him. Her clear eyes assured him she had recovered from her bout with the stinging nettles. A quick check of her body revealed that only a hint of a rash remained. Pink tinged her cheeks at his overt perusal.

He touched his fingers upon her brow, trying to ignore the softness of her skin. He withdrew his hand. "You body is cool."

She looked up at him, confusion shining in her eyes. "I feel better."

The delectable heat of her body pressed to his side clouded his thoughts. He shifted away from her. "I am thankful. You were very ill."

She searched his face. He saw the desire she was struggling to define, a yearning he should ignore. Needing to touch her again, he brushed several strands of hair from her cheek and swept them behind her ear, savoring the satin warmth of her skin.

Her mouth parted with innocent invitation. "Alexander?"

The huskiness of her voice undermined his good intention. He cursed his weakness for her as he covered her mouth with his own. Nichola melted beneath him, returning his kiss. Aching at her sweetness, he lowered his hand along the silky curve of her neck then beneath her gown to cup her breast. He caught the sensitive nub between his fingers.

At Alexander's intimate caress, Nichola arched against him, lost to the pleasure spreading throughout her body, giving into the heat his touch instilled. For a foolish moment she allowed herself to drown in sinful pleasure, to bask in his caresses as his fingers wandered mercilessly over her in a sensual destruction.

The pads of his fingers wandered lower to the flat of

her stomach. Heat trailed upon her skin in his wake. Her body tightened in anticipation, and heat pooled at her core. A heat she'd never experienced before.

On a groan, his hand slid to the edge of her woman's curls.

She pulled back, horrified by what she'd allowed.

"This is wrong." But even as she cast out the words, she ached with wanting him.

"It is right," he whispered in return, his mouth trailing kisses in a slow sweep along the column of her neck.

His husky burr weakened her resistance. Her body swayed forward, craving his touch. Shame whipped through her. How could she feel this way about him?

She tried to pull free.

He caught her shoulders. "Nichola, listen to me. I—"

"Let me go!" she ordered, desperate to save the last shred of her dignity. "I want nothing to do with you."

Irritation slashed through his eyes. He lowered his gaze to where her body lay flush, to where her legs had twined with his, and even now her woman's place pressed intimately against him.

"It would seem," he said in soft challenge, "your body says otherwise."

Embarrassed, Nichola shoved to her feet. She hugged his tunic against her; the material draped haphazardly to her knees. "I want nothing from you."

Alexander rose to his feet. "What are you afraid of, lass, me or yourself?"

She took a step back ashamed she'd allowed him to touch her so wantonly, that even now, her body burned where his fingers had skimmed over her flesh.

With a lightning quick move, he caught her hand and hauled her against him.

"Do not!"

"What?" His mouth glided over hers, urging her response. "Tell you how you shivered beneath my caress?
How you arched against me when I took your nipple
into my hand? Or that even now, you are wet with
wanting?"

Her breaths were coming fast. She wanted to deny
his charges, but when she should be repulsed from
her enemy, her body screamed with the need of his
touch.

Afraid that if she said nothing—given her intense
feelings for him—they'd be making love in a trice, she
attacked. "I am not your whore to take any liberties
without permission, but an English noblewoman."

He lifted his head, fury darkening his gaze to black.

"I am your prisoner," she pressed. "Not only have
you kidnapped me from my home, but after our night
together in the inn, however innocent, my reputation
is in shatters. No man of honor would want me now."
And any chance to marry for money and salvage their
home was lost. "I wish to God that I had killed you
after all."

As soon as she'd spewed the words, she regretted
them, longed to admit they were a lie. If anything,
he'd taken pains to ensure her comfort. But from the
anger gouging his face, it might be too late to apologize. But, she had to try.

"Alexander, I—"

"You are correct, you are my prisoner." He released
her, the coldness of his stare chilling her. "I have
never harmed a woman in my life and I will not begin
now. Neither will I take what is not freely offered."

Nichola opened her mouth to speak, to explain,
then stopped. His interest in her was the ransom she
would bring.

In the end, she would return to England, and he would remain in Scotland. In all honesty, her wanton reactions to his advances had prompted his boldness. What man would deny a willing woman?

At her stoic expression, Alexander folded his arms across his chest. His prisoner. Aye, she was that. But when he'd held her throughout the night, his thoughts had strayed traitorously far from thinking of her as such.

He turned and stalked toward the branch where he'd hung her gown. Making love with her would have been a grave error. He snatched the ragged dress and brought it back to her.

"Put it on." It wasn't a request.

Her gaze never wavered from his as she took it. Nichola inched back with the ruined gown cradled in her arms as if a shield.

A muscle worked in his jaw. "Be quick about it." At his surly order, she scurried behind the large boulder. Fine, 'twould do her well to fear him.

While she was changing, Alexander repacked his mount. He stripped his mind of thoughts of her passionate kisses of moments ago. Or how if she hadn't stopped him, they would be making love. What had he thought, that she'd find interest in a knight? He gave an indignant snort. She was a rich, English heiress. And he, the middle son of a noble, without an inheritance, and a graveside vow to his father.

He secured the last cinch on the saddle with a hard tug, stowed the tunic and secured the blankets. It was time to leave. The sooner they departed, the quicker they could send for the ransom and he could rid himself of her.

Alexander led his bay over to the burn and let him drink. After, he rounded the corner to find Nichola standing by the rock wearing the tattered dress. Her regal bearing at odds with the seductive cut of the gown; the coldness of her gaze in direct conflict with the heat he knew pulsed beneath.

The punch of desire hit without warning. Alexander clenched his teeth as he waved her over. He would keep his distance, emotionally and physically.

But as she started toward him with her siren's body and a sovereign's bearing, he wondered if he'd just committed his own self to a personal hell.

Chapter Seven

The next two days of travel were grueling to Nichola's tired body and troubled mind. As they rode, she at last gave into exhaustion and sagged back against Alexander's broad chest. He didn't move or acknowledge her presence. Over the last two days of hard travel, she'd grown used to his aloofness. Except for his questions about her thirst, hunger, or comfort, he'd ignored her.

As if she didn't matter.

Or exist.

After wishing him dead, what had she expected, his forgiveness? No, but that he could dismiss her so thoroughly after he'd touched her so intimately still hurt.

A gust of wind swept past. The tall heather-strewn grass bowed beneath its force. The bay picked his way up a steep incline, the angle forcing her body against Alexander's well-muscled frame.

Warmth spread through her. Too easily she imagined his fingers moving over her skin in a soft caress; the heat his touch inspired. Warmth pooled deep inside her. Embarrassed at how he could affect her when she needed to keep him from her thoughts, Nichola leaned forward, away from Alexander.

He guided his steed around a patch of brambles. "What is wrong?" he asked, his voice cool.

"Naught."

"Then sit still. We will arrive at Lochshire Castle before midday."

Nichola scanned the horizon. The sun's angle was nearing its apex. Naught but trees, fields, and jutting rock lay before them. But soon they would arrive at his home where she would be imprisoned until they received her ransom. Payment that would never come. And then what? Uneasy, she shifted.

"Do not think about trying to escape," Alexander warned.

"I am sitting here quiet, as you requested."

He gave a snort of disbelief. "The day you heed my orders, as you should have from the start, I will know you have been stricken with a serious malady. The truth," he ordered, "and I will know if you are telling a tale."

Nichola hesitated. She should remain quiet, but she had to know. "At your home . . ." The steady clip of hooves clattered over patches of broken stone.

"On with it."

She turned and glared at him. "It is difficult for me."

He arched an unsympathetic brow.

"The rebels within your home. They will . . . treat me well?"

"Well?"

Oh, he knew what she meant. She'd seen the flicker of understanding. "They will not hurt me?"

With a shrug he scanned their surroundings. "You will be safe as long as you do not give them reason to treat you otherwise."

"And what would be a reason?"

His cobalt eyes locked on her. "Trying to run away."

"As if given the same circumstance, you would not try the same?"

"Lass, if given the same circumstance, I would have escaped."

Heat raced up her cheeks. She angled her chin in a stubborn tilt. "I will not apologize for trying to regain my freedom."

"I told you before, you will not be harmed. Once the ransom is received, arrangements will be made to deliver you safely back to your home." His mouth settled into a hard line as he studied her. "Unless you have a reason why I should believe otherwise?"

How could she have hinted at her lack of funds? "It is but nerves that lead me to ask."

He gave a noncommittal grunt, which assured her that she had far from convinced him. Alexander guided his horse along a narrow path that cut through a stand of pines. The dense cover chilled the air. The soft echoes of his mount's hooves moving through the forest carried on the wind.

The trail grew steeper, winding up as if it would take them to the edge of the earth. The scent of wild herbs growing around her filled the air. Any other time, she would have savored the raw beauty of this setting.

As if she'd ridden through a magical door, the thick blanket of foliage gave way.

She gasped in wonder. Spread out as far as she could see extended a large lake embraced by dark, fertile land and weathered hills. On the end of a peninsula jutting from the southern curve, arose a well-fortified castle. A drawbridge, now lowered, connected the only road leading out.

She barely made out tiny spots that moved along

the wall walk. A shiver crept through her. Castle guards. Men who would ensure her any attempt to flee would fail.

Alexander halted his bay. He gestured toward the fortress below. "My home, Lochshire Castle."

And from its impenetrable defense, impossible to escape. Her spirits plummeted. "It is magnificent," she said with grudging admiration. And it rivaled the splendor of her home. Except for the touch of savageness, which she attributed to the men who carved the stronghold from this unforgiving land.

"It was built by the Normans and passed down through my family ever since."

"It is yours?"

Shadows flickered in his eyes. As quickly, they were gone. "No. Lochshire Castle belongs to my oldest brother."

"How many brothers do you have?" she asked, needing to know what she was up against.

"Three."

"Sisters?"

"None."

"Oh."

"Even if I had sisters, they would not help you. Neither will my brothers."

"I never thought they would."

He arched a skeptical brow. "That is exactly what you believed."

"I have other things on my mind besides escape," she said, annoyed he could read her with such accuracy. "And with the pittance I know of the womanly arts, I doubt I could seduce one of your brothers, much less convince them to aid in my escape."

That much was the truth, but it was her innocence that added to her irresistible appeal; a fact his brothers would surely notice. Alexander's hand tightened on the reins. His brothers would keep their distance. Once he locked her away in a chamber, he'd warn them of her conniving ways. Although she was a virgin, she could be very persuasive.

A fact he'd learned well.

He nudged his mount toward where the path cut down the hillside, offering a clear, breathtaking view of his homeland. Pride filled him as he looked upon Lochshire Castle. His home had withheld many a siege over the years and would withstand whatever the English could serve.

"What are their names?"

"Who?" Alexander replied, deliberately being evasive.

"Your brothers."

Though she denied it, her intent was too clear. Whatever she might believe, once locked inside his home, she wouldn't escape. But he couldn't see any harm in telling her about his family.

"I am the middle brother. Seathan, the eldest, is the Earl of Grey and lord of Lochshire Castle." He noted the standard was flying atop the tower; his brother was home. "My youngest brother is Duncan. You will like him, most women do."

She arched a brow. "You are jealous of him?"

He thought of Duncan's glib charm and face of a Greek god, which had women swarming to him like bees to honey. "No. It is his nature."

"I thought you said you had three brothers?"

He nodded. "Aye, Patrik is my brother as well, but by adoption. Except for blood, he is kin in every way."

"I am surprised your family would adopt rather than sponsor him."

"Patrik's father saved my mother's life in a raid,"

Alexander explained, remembering the details passed down by his father of the brutal attack by the English. "After Patrik's parents were killed, there was no question about where he belonged. He became part of our family."

Empathy creased her face; her sensitivity toward a man she didn't know surprised Alexander. "How old was he at the time?"

"Seven years," he replied. And Patrik had come to them with savage resentment toward the English; for their vicious assault had served not only to destroy his family's home, but had also vanquished the lives of those he loved as well. Now a man grown, Patrik had learned to temper his hate. But at times when the English were spoken of, Patrik's bitterness resurfaced.

Who could blame him? Watching your parents being murdered would taint the stoutest of men. But a lad—a lad it would devastate.

"Will your brothers all be home?" she asked, fear lingering in her voice.

"No more questions."

She stiffened against him.

If the castle's staunch defenses didn't quell her thoughts of escape, meeting his brothers would. Each of the brothers alone was considered a formidable match, but the four combined were a lethal force. God forbid any fool who dared to insult one of them. Each brother took the slander personally, and together they sought retribution.

He guided his mount to a slow but steady pace toward the shore. Every time their bodies touched, Nichola recoiled from him. Alexander muttered a curse.

She shifted forward, irritating him further. "You lean away from me any more, lass, and you will fall off."

"As if you would care."

Her sputtering indignation almost pulled a smile to his lips. Almost. "I would not want you harmed," he said, his voice gruff, irritated she could affect him so.

"That is all I am to you, not a person or a woman, but goods to be bartered."

The image of her naked and in his arms came to mind, his body hardened. "What would you like me to think of you as?"

She hesitated.

Impulse urged him to turn her face toward him so he could see the truth in her eyes. He left her alone. 'Twould be unwise to journey down this path. Already he wanted her too much.

"I want nothing but to be free," she finally replied, but he heard the unspoken desire, a longing he unfortunately understood.

Silence fell between them. Near the bottom of the steep trail, the dense stand of trees opened to a slope of rolling green. An area his ancestors had purposely cleared to allow guards a clear view of any adversary. And give ample time to raise the drawbridge and prepare their defense.

As the fortress rose before them like an ominous sentinel, Nichola tried to squash her apprehension, but doubts grew. Saint's breath, what was she going to do?

"Sir Alexander returns," a guard's voice boomed as they approached the drawbridge.

A tower guard hailed them as they rode toward the portcullis.

The clunk of hooves on timber gave way to a soft clatter as his horse walked across the stone beneath the gatehouse. Shadows faded as they rode into the bailey.

As with her own home, people were busy going about their daily chores. The smith was stoking a fire, the coals glowing hot. Grooms swept out the stables. Knights trained in the practice field. A girl carried a heaping basket of rushes walked toward the keep.

Except this was far from the peaceable environment she called home.

Or would ever feel welcome in.

The door to the keep opened. The girl carrying the basket of rushes slipped inside, and an elderly man with a bearded face hobbled out.

Nichola scanned the interior for men who bore a resemblance to Alexander. Her mind conjured giants of men, their faces carved in perpetual scowls, their eyes filling with hatred when they landed upon her.

"Edmund," Alexander called.

The old man who'd exited the keep turned. A smile splashed across his face warm and bright. He hobbled toward them.

She tensed. This couldn't be his brother. An uncle perhaps?

Alexander guided his mount to meet him halfway. Two strides away from the man, he pulled his bay to a halt, swung to the ground and embraced the elder.

The old man slapped him on the back with a hearty thump. "Alexander, me lad. We expected you a few days ago."

"You missed me?" Alexander teased.

"Like a festered thorn in my foot," the old man replied with a wink.

Alexander laughed, his easy warmth with the elder a sharp contrast to his coldness toward her over the past few days. But then, she was his captive.

"Did you have trouble with the English then?" the man asked as he stepped back.

A scowl touched Alexander's gaze as he glanced toward her. "Naught I could not quell."

"There's me boy. The bloody English." He spit on the ground. "The lot of them have not the backbone of a fen-sucked lackey." The old man glanced toward her with interest. "Another lass is it? I thought you left to abduct Lord Monceaux?"

"A long story," Alexander replied. "I will explain later—in private."

From his friend's comments, it seemed Alexander's bringing home a woman was a common event. With his ability to devastate a woman with a simple look, she shouldn't be surprised, or care, but the fact hurt.

"Where are my brothers?" he asked as he wound the reins in his hand.

"They are—"

"Alexander," came a deep, rough shout from the entry of the practice field, where the scrape of blades still echoed with a fierce clash.

The old man smiled. "On their way to be greeting ye I would be saying. They would not want to miss your return. It is good to have you home, lad." With a nod, the old man turned and hobbled away.

Nerves roiled inside her as she glanced toward the practice field. Through the mill of armor and curses, three men strode toward them. From their garb and the high sheen of sweat, they had been practicing with their swords.

The tallest of the three shoved back his mail hood and padded coif. Hair, black as Alexander's, clung damp to his head and fell to his shoulders. Though the sun had only reached its apex, a hint of a beard already shadowed the hard angles of his face. The man's walk held an air of absolute authority. As he neared, green eyes narrowed upon her with interest, then his gaze flicked back to Alexander.

The ball of nerves in Nichola's stomach tightened.

From Alexander's description, this must be his eldest brother, Seathan, the Earl of Grey.

She studied the other brothers. Both had removed their headgear as well. They were of the same height and breadth as Alexander. The sandy-haired man on the right walked with an almost catlike grace, while the blonde-haired man on the left strode with a more relaxed, confident gait.

From his youthful appearance, she would pick the man on the left as the youngest brother, Duncan. The cleft in his chin combined with the hint of dimples when he smiled at Alexander confirmed her suspicions.

The man on the right with the sandy hair and unfathomable eyes must be Patrik, his adopted brother.

"I had meant to meet you at your arrival," Lord Grey said as he reached them. He caught Alexander in a fierce hug, then stepped back. "But I had to teach Patrik a lesson about wielding a blade."

Patrik gave an indignant snort as he embraced Alexander, then backed away. He turned to Seathan. "I almost cut off your bloody hand."

Seathan arched a brow with an amused, but dangerous look. "How soon we forget who knocked whom on their arse?"

"Another round," Patrik challenged. He clasped his sword's hilt, the fierce light of competition heating his gaze.

Though playful, the hint of seriousness entwined within Patrik's words piled atop Nichola's unease. As if within her enemy's castle she could ever relax? Their practice was to keep their skills honed for their next attack upon the English.

"I see you have brought home a new lass," Duncan said, striding past the feuding pair as if well used to their bantering.

His warm, beguiling smile fell upon Nichola, demonstrating exactly why women would be drawn to a man like him. If she were to give a name to his appeal, she would call it charm. He all but oozed with it.

Lord Grey scowled at his brother. "Duncan, it is unwise to try and sway Alexander's mistress."

Mistress? Heat crept up her cheeks at the reminder of her disheveled state. Why would they believe otherwise? Alexander had been sent to abduct Griffin.

Oblivious to her plight, mischief sparked in Duncan's eyes. "From the look of you lass, it would seem my brother's care falls far short of what a beautiful woman deserves. And I have not a tight hand with my coin as Alexander. If you tire of him, I will aid you in shedding the oaf." He gave her a wink. "As well as ensure your bed is kept warm."

If possible, her cheeks grew hotter.

Alexander glared at Duncan. "Do not touch the lass." His warning fell between them.

"Enough," the eldest brother commanded.

Nichola silently thanked his intervention. To have them quarrel over her would have made her humiliation complete.

"You can discuss the woman later," Lord Grey continued. "I will dispatch the runner with the ransom demand." He glanced toward the gate, a frown growing on his face. He looked at Alexander. "You have already secured the Baron of Monceaux in a guarded chamber?"

"No," Alexander replied, again debating the wisdom of abducting Nichola. 'Twas too late now for regrets. "I will explain once we are inside." He walked over to his bay and caught Nichola's waist. He saw the fear in her face, but the determination to do what she must to survive as well.

Pride filled him at her strength. Nichola had the resolve of a Scot. But she was English. And his captive. A woman who he could never claim, nor keep.

Seathan arched a dark brow. "About Lord Monceaux?"

Alexander nodded.

Concerned looks passed amongst the brothers.

"See to the lass," Seathan said. "Then we will meet on the wall walk."

Alexander lifted Nichola to the ground, her skin soft and warm against his hands.

Duncan stepped forward. "I will care for the lass."

"No one will touch her," Alexander stated.

"Leave it be, Duncan," Seathan warned. "There are more important issues to discuss than bedding a lass."

His brothers headed toward the keep.

Nichola tried to pull free of Alexander. "Please do not bring me inside," she whispered.

Tired of her distrust, Alexander tugged her forward. "Move."

In silence, she walked by his side and behind his brothers who all towered over her. Alexander could all but hear her mind churning as he caught her desperate glance toward the portcullis.

Alexander scowled at her. "It is too late."

Guilt flickered on her face and she dropped her gaze.

He drew her closer. She tried to distance herself, but Alexander kept her by his side.

Fresh rushes scented the air as they entered the keep. The mix of onions, sage, and meat from a stew simmering over the flames in the hearth made his stomach growl.

Servants called to Alexander as they saw him.

He returned their friendly welcome, then followed his brothers up the winding turret stairs.

At the entrance to the wall walk, Alexander guided Nichola before him.

Seathan blocked her path. "This has naught to do with her ears. Put the lass elsewhere until we are through."

Alexander met his brother's hard stare. "Our discussion is about her."

Skepticism edged his gaze as he looked first at her, then back to Alexander. With a grimace, he stepped back.

On a nervous breath, Nichola swept past him. Even in a gown no more than rags, her bearing was that of a lady.

Alexander's smile was automatic, his respect for her, to hold her own under the most stressful situation, grew another notch. Would she never quit surprising him? His smile faded. With the meager time she would remain here, he would never find out. A good thing he assured himself.

So why wasn't he convinced?

Or relieved?

Alexander led Nichola onto the wall walk. A gust of wind greeted him, the scent of water and the hint of grass and heather a familiar welcome. The view across the loch, embraced by the rugged mountains, stole his breath. It was always such as this, from the first day his mother had led him up here as a lad.

Seathan halted beside him and leveled his gaze on Alexander. "What happened?"

"Upon my arrival at Rothfield Castle," Alexander began, "I learned Lord Monceaux was not in residence."

Irritation flashed in Patrik's eyes as he stepped

forward. "What? My source within the keep assured me Lord Monceaux would be in residence through the next fortnight."

"So you came back with a woman?" Seathan asked.

"Not just any woman." Alexander turned to Nichola. "May I introduce you to Lady Nichola Westcott, the Baron of Monceaux's sister."

Surprise flashed in Seathan's gaze a split second before the fury. "Lord Monceaux's sister?"

"Aye, I abducted her for ransom instead. With the siblings close, I had thought—"

Seathan held up his hand. "Secure her within a chamber."

Confused by his brother's anger, Alexander frowned. "But she is—"

"We will finish speaking of the ransom once you have returned," Seathan stated.

A potent silence fell between them, fractured by the wind and a stray voice from the courtyard below. Duncan cleared his throat. "Lady Nichola, you will forgive my ignorance. Had I but known, I would not have made a disparaging remark on your person."

She nodded, her face pale.

"I will take her to the tower chamber," Alexander said.

Seathan nodded. "And the other information?"

"It is secured on my mount," Alexander replied. He'd retrieve the maps marking the positions of English defenses around Berwick after he'd secured Nichola. "I will bring them when I return." He took Nichola's arm.

Panic filled her gaze as she stiffened beneath his touch.

Why wouldn't she? Guilt crowded his mind as to the cause of Seathan's ire, reasons he'd dismissed as unimportant when he'd abducted her. But as Alexander guided Nichola toward the exit, he glanced back one last time at his brother.

And wondered if in abducting her, he'd pushed his brother's temper too far.

Chapter Eight

"You will be allowed every comfort within reason," Alexander said as they climbed the steps to the tower chamber.

Nichola remained quiet, disturbingly so. If possible, her face had grown more ashen, and her eyes held a hint of defeat. Throughout their entire journey she fought him at every turn. At this moment she'd become fragile.

Because he'd taken her from her home and a brother she loved.

With the rebels need for coin, he'd had no other choice. In hindsight, he recognized desire had swayed his good sense. When he'd first watched her from across the solar, he'd wanted her. Except he'd not counted on his feelings becoming involved. Or her becoming hurt.

He'd achieved both.

At least he could offer her comfort. Perhaps she envisioned the tower room to be barren and unwelcoming. The chamber had belonged to his grandmother who held the second sight. A room where he'd spent many an hour listening to her tales of fairies and their mischievous acts.

A chamber she'd told him was magical.

An impressionable lad during his youth, he'd sworn he'd heard the fairies flitting among the shadows. After his grandmother's death, the chamber and any magic it held was sealed away. Except for the airing each spring, the room remained untouched.

When he'd announced Nichola would be kept in the tower room, Alexander hadn't missed his brothers' surprise, but no more than his own. 'Twas sacrilegious to allow an Englishwoman entrance to the chamber of a woman they'd so loved.

So why had he suggested it?

More disturbing, why had no one objected to Nichola's presence in the tower room? 'Twas as if the assertion itself were crafted by magic; he had made the statement and his brothers had agreed.

Alexander frowned. No, little magic guided his decisions. Concern by Nichola's weariness had evoked his offer of such comfortable surroundings.

Near the top of the turret, he halted and turned to her. Sunlight from a carved window above cut through the dull, torch-lit gray to haunt her pale face. The urge to hold her overwhelmed him. He kept his distance. If he touched her now, wanting her more than was right, his good intention might unravel into forbidden intimacies.

"The tower room is far from a cold dungeon," he explained.

"Is it?" she asked, her voice absent of the flare of temper he'd grown accustomed to.

Blast it. Alexander drew her hand between both of his. "Lass—"

She tried to pull her hand free. "Do not."

He held tight, thankful for her resistance, however weak. "What is wrong?"

Nichola stared up at him, her expression wounded.

That he'd somehow quelled her spirit made his heart ache. On a muttered curse, he gave into temptation and drew her into his arms, her shudders leaving him floundering.

"I am sorry, lass." More than he wanted to be. He cupped her face in his hands, wanting to kiss her, to shelter her from her troubles. Her eyes watched his, their lackluster unsettling. "I promise you, you will be treated well here."

She remained silent.

Alexander stepped back. She was upset. Mayhap from shock. Or the impact of meeting his brothers. And they'd traveled a good distance since they'd begun their journey. Sleep and a hearty meal would help ease her mind.

"Come." He led her to the top of the turret steps.

She followed him without protest.

They arrived at the entrance to the tower room. He removed the bar from the door with a soft scrape. "You will be locked inside as I explained."

Her lower lip began to tremble.

Maybe he shouldn't lock her in? He tensed. Since when had he lost his spine? He was a warrior. He'd served far worse fates to his opponents during daily sword practice.

Alexander shoved the door open. The rich furnishings within could be termed anything but those befitting a prison. She would see it as such, regardless of the finery. Or his words of assurance.

"It is best if you accept your lot," he said in a firm voice. "You will be here for a short time, weeks at best. Look around, lass. Your confines are far from brutal."

"A prison, however you drape it," she said with a cold finality, "is one and the same."

"Think of it as you must. You will remain within this room until your ransom arrives." He drew her inside, pleased when she twisted and tried to break free. The loss of her spirit was something he could never forgive himself for.

"Please do not leave me locked in here alone," she pleaded.

"You will be safe."

She shook her head. "Do not do this." Her voice rose to a frantic whisper. "At least leave the door unbarred. With the castle's fortifications and rebels at every turn, what chance is there that I could make it past the gatehouse?"

He shook his head. "Had you not tried to escape before, I would have allowed you the freedom to move about. Your actions have left me no choice." Before he could soften, be swayed by the panic ripping through her gray eyes, Alexander stepped back, closed the door, and dropped the bar into place outside the chamber.

The echo of her fists pounding on the other side reverberated in the hallway. "Do not leave me locked up here alone! Alexander, please!"

The desperation in her voice tugged at his conscience. He smoothed his fingers over his scalp where his head still throbbed from her last attempt. Turning on his heel, he walked down the hall with sincere regret, Nichola's fierce pleas to leave the chamber unlocked unheeded in his wake.

"Alexander!" Nichola continued to beat upon the hewn door. Her breath hitched as she paused to listen.

Silence.

He'd left her alone!

She slumped against the door. *Stay calm.* As if calm

was an option? She was imprisoned in the tower until they received payment from Griffin.

Ransom that would never come.

But at this moment, worries of empty coffers far from competed with her greatest fear. Her heart pounded as she pondered on these emotions. It felt as if the walls within the chamber were slowly closing in on her.

Nichola caught the pendant at her neck and squeezed until the metal bit into her palm, shaken by confinement of any manner; in a thunderstorm, more so.

Except she hadn't told Alexander of her deep-seated fear. Already he could leave her in emotional shambles by a mere touch. She refused to give him anything more to use against her. Her survival from this moment on depended on her own wits.

Panic fluttered in her chest. Taking a deep breath, Nichola looked around. Sunlight spilled in through a single, arched window and cast the room in a calming, dreamlike glow. She stepped cautiously forward and laid her hand on the warmed pane; the heat a welcome balm to the chill inside her soul.

For several seconds she stood there, absorbing the warmth. Quiet seemed to settle around her, to ease her fears. Slowly, her breathing grew even.

Nichola crossed to the small, but well cared for bed. The coverlet, the color of moon-kissed daisies, beckoned her to touch. Fascinated, she ran her fingers over the finely embroidered cloth, impressed at the detail of each stitch. Whoever had crafted this bedspread had done so with love.

Curious, she padded to a small table, where a myriad of items sat as if awaiting the return of their owner. She stopped, stunned by the many personal items: the bone comb etched with a bouquet of heather, the intricately carved jewelry displayed with a tender hand; each piece seemingly woven around a beautiful gem.

She turned in a complete circle, taking in every nuance of the chamber. This wasn't a prison at all; the room belonged to someone of great importance in the brothers' lives.

From Alexander's grim reserve, she'd expected a stark chamber cast in shadows. So why had he given this lush room to her? She was far from welcome.

Or a guest.

Perplexed, she moved around the chamber, drawn to the lingering aura of whomever had once lived here. A woman obviously. Where was she now? Would she soon return?

Unsure why, she sensed the room's owner would not be coming back, ever. She frowned. That was a foolish thought. How could she know such a thing?

A glitter of light caught her eye. Within a sturdy bowl on the table lay four halved, shimmering stones. She picked up the halved, gold encrusted rock.

Intrigued by the stone in her palm, Nichola studied the contrast of the rough gold shell to the milky white interior. More interesting, caught within its center was a petrified, mossy-type plant.

She laid down the rough half stone then picked up another. This delicate beauty swirled with deep reds as if inside the gem blazed an eternal fire. She moved the stone within her hand. Strange, heat from the gem seemed to seep into her skin.

Nichola picked up the third stone, its color inside the deepest, darkest blue she'd ever seen. A sense of calm filled her. The rapid beat of her pulse slowed further. Like a silent balm, the last of her tension ebbed.

A yell from the courtyard pulled her from her thoughts. Through the open window, the sky began to darken with a hint of night, and a whisper of wind slid into the chamber, scented with the fragrance of heather.

She stilled. Moments ago the window had been shut. Her hand trembled as she returned the dark blue stone to sit amongst the others. A trick? Had Alexander rigged the window to scare her? But why?

She started to walk toward the window, but with each step her legs grew leaden and her head swam as if in a fog. Nichola rubbed the back of her neck. She was tired and her mind was imagining all kinds of things. That must be it.

Turning, she managed to reach the bed and all but crumbled onto the mattress, not surprised by the room's other adornments, to find the downy softness of a feathered bed.

If she'd wanted to move, she couldn't. Sleep. It embraced her, beckoned her with an easy grace. When Alexander had departed moments ago, she couldn't have contemplated the thought of ever finding a sliver of peace imprisoned within the tower chamber. Now, as if she'd drunk a magic sleeping potion, she could think of nothing else.

With the heaviness of exhaustion embracing her, she curled up into a ball beneath the coverlet, embroidered with a gentle hand. And without reason or cause, for the first of many a day, lost herself to a deep and peaceful sleep.

"Christ's blood, the baron's sister!" Seathan hurled at Alexander the instant he stepped back onto the wall walk. "What were you bloody thinking?"

Alexander's fingers tightened on the map in his hand

as he took in his other brothers' reactions as well; Duncan and Patrik glared at him. "Lord Monceaux was not in residence. Aware the siblings are close, logic bade her brother would pay the ransom without hesitation."

Seathan shook his head with disgust. "Aye, he will not hesitate, but not to pay the ransom. When he learns of his sister's abduction, he will bring his knights north and attack Lochshire Castle."

Alexander stiffened. "I considered this, but with the few knights in residence and King Edward's demands for support from his nobles, many have barely enough arms to protect their castles—much less attack."

"What of her status as a maiden?" Seathan demanded. "Or the consideration that with their parents' death, she is all the kin he has left? Think you the baron will allow the fact his sister's reputation is in tatters to go unchallenged? Or with his having King Edward's ear?"

"I had . . . Our need was for coin. Her ransom assured that." Alexander blew out a hard breath, cursing himself. Instead of weighing the dangers of abducting her, he'd become lost, intrigued by a spirited woman. He deserved the censure his brother meted out. Neither would he forgive himself.

Patrik muttered a curse.

Duncan scanned the shoreline with a frown. "We will keep watch for the baron's men."

"It is unnecessary for the time," Alexander said. At least he could offer that. "I ensured we were not followed."

Seathan's jaw tightened.

"Your concerns may be for naught," Alexander continued. "Even if the baron is away, with their close bond, the steward will ensure payment is made immediately."

"Mayhap," Seathan said, sounding far from convinced. "Nevertheless, the deed is done. Until the coin is received, we will keep extra guard upon the walls."

Shame washed through Alexander as an uneasy quiet settled between them. Since his father's death, never had he allowed a woman to sway his thoughts. Now, without wanting to, he found himself caring for her, feelings that had no place in his life.

Now. Or ever.

Steadier, Alexander unrolled the map and pointed to a forest marked in the south-central portion of the parchment. "Here is where King Edward is positioning his troops."

His brothers crowded around him.

Seathan grimaced. "I have received word he has brought in archers from Wales."

"They are a nasty lot," Patrik added. "I would rather not tangle with them."

Alexander nodded, well familiar with the archers' lethal skill. "I feel the same, but with them accepting English gold for services rendered, we have no choice."

"The bugger," Patrik grumbled. "After Berwick, the English bastard expected us to crumble and submit to him like a dog with its tail between his legs." He spat on the hewn stone. "He can rot in Hades."

"Aye," Duncan agreed. "That is where he will bloody end up once we are through with him. However small our rebel force, only a fool would believe we will surrender."

"And King Edward is not a fool," Seathan added.

"Far from it," Alexander agreed. Memories of King Edward having proclaimed himself as their feudal lord came to mind. When met with resistance and in a self-justified move to bring Scotland to heel, he had ordered Berwick razed.

English troops had greedily complied; they slaugh-
tered the men, raped the women, and disposed of
their children with the swing of a blade. While the
dying screamed their agony, the merciless bastard had
ordered the town torched.

As the king's soldiers marched away, fire had consumed what English hands hadn't destroyed. Naught
remained but smoldering heaps. The blackened rot
that had once held laughter and love now embraced
the stench of charred flesh.

Convinced that he'd squelched the Scots' resistance,
Edward had returned to England, confident after his
brutal show of force he'd subdued the Scots. But in his
strong handed approach, he'd made a grave error.
From his lust for supreme power over Scotland was
born a vengeance within the Scots. While blood
pounded in their hearts, they'd not forget Longshank's
slaughter of Berwick.

Alexander flexed his hand. Aye, the Scots had
taken a step back. Not to concede, but to regroup.
With William Wallace uniting both peasant and noble
of a torn Scotland, Edward's savagery wouldn't go
unheeded.

Or unpunished.

"Fool or not," Seathan continued, pulling Alexander from his musing, "we will need to take care in our
upcoming assault upon the English."

Grim, Alexander nodded. A battle they would win.
For to lose could sacrifice their freedom.

Chapter Nine

Hours later in the great room, Seathan refilled his goblet with wine. After, he passed the wine around to Duncan.

"Alexander. Alexander?" Duncan said, louder this time as he nudged the bottle against Alexander's hand.

Alexander grimaced at his younger brother, whose dimples winked with notorious delight.

"Is it a fog dimming your brain?" Duncan laughed. "Or are potent thoughts of a lass shrouding your thoughts?"

Alexander snatched the wine, embarrassed to be caught thinking of Nichola. And so easily read. "I have a bloody headache from looking at your horse's arse of a face."

"Ouch, it is the lass then," Duncan said.

"She is of no concern to you or any of us," Alexander stated, wishing it were that simple. Had she stopped crying? Was he wrong to have left her so upset? Or would he ever forgive himself for locking her in the chamber?

He met each of his brothers' gazes, then refilled his

goblet. He passed the bottle to Patrik. "What matters is Nichola's ransom will allow us to purchase arms."

Duncan winked. "Nichola is it?"

"Enough," Seathan ordered.

Patrik slid a curious glance toward Alexander before turning to Seathan. "Will we demand the same amount as we'd decided on for Lord Monceaux?"

"More." Seathan's jaw tightened. "Our informant assures us Lord Monceaux will be desperate to have his sister back."

The brothers nodded in unison, but the camaraderie Alexander should feel in the achievement of their goal never came. All because of a stubborn, auburn-haired woman secured within the tower room.

An English lass who, by rights, should be locked away from his thoughts as well.

"With new arms in our hands," Seathan said, "we will rout the English bastards from our soil."

All heads nodded, cups clunked in a toast, and the brothers drank in unison.

Alexander lowered his goblet, knowing his brother was no longer angry about Nichola's capture. Subdued, he walked to the open window.

The fresh scent of summer and the cool taste of the loch filled each breath. The full moon overhead illuminated the courtyard below, void of people, except for the guards who made their rounds along the wall walk.

A night like so many in his past. He traced the bottom of his goblet along the stone sill. Except since Nichola had entered his life, nothing was the same.

At the scrape of parchment behind him, Alexander turned toward his brothers.

Seathan rolled up the map he'd brought back from his trip.

Alexander tipped his goblet and finished the last of the wine, appreciating the warm slide down his throat. "Once the ransom is paid and a place to meet decided, I will escort the lass back. Then I will ride to our meeting place to buy arms."

"I will ride along with you," Patrik said.

Alexander shook his head. "My riding onto English soil will be dangerous enough. Meet me where the arms are to be delivered." And he could share the last few days with Nichola—alone. However lacking in judgment on his part, he would savor their remaining time together.

Patrik shook his head. "I will take the lass home. You have already risked your life once, and your familiarity with her might breed other unneeded problems."

He gave Patrik a hard glare. "I said I will be escorting her back."

At his sharp tone, Patrik's face darkened. "To her home or to her bed?"

Alexander forced his temper to calm. "I am off to bed." He refused to discuss his relationship with Nichola further.

Duncan refilled his cup to the brim. "It is early. The moon has not set."

Alexander shrugged, his mind surprisingly unclouded by the quantity of wine he'd drunk. For once in his life, a night of drinking held little lure. Not even the thought of finding a wench to pleasure him kindled a scrap of interest.

Without further explanation, he turned away and started up the turret steps toward his chamber. Though exhausted and having drunk several goblets of wine, he doubted he would find the ability to sleep.

When he reached the third floor, he halted. Alexander

stared up toward where the tower chamber lay. Had Nichola fallen asleep? How long had she beaten upon the door? Was she still clawing at the sturdy wooden frame in desperation? Or had she crumbled into exhaustion, with only whimpers falling from her lips and her spirit shattered?

At thoughts of the latter, he sprinted up the tower steps, echoes of his footsteps feeding his fear. Outside her chamber he halted, thankful to be greeted by silence. As quickly, the reasons for the quiet had him tearing out the bar.

Alexander tossed the honed wood aside. He jerked the door open and entered, anticipating finding her lying in wait to attack him as he entered.

Or worse, her body crumpled on the floor from utter exhaustion.

He hadn't prepared himself to find Nichola curled in a ball beneath the covers of the bed, with moonbeams in her hair, and her face a portrait of complete peace.

She should look out of place, especially in a room that'd once belonged to his grandmother; a woman he'd loved, a woman for whom magic existed.

Except, surrounded by the tumble of crystals piled in a bowl, numerous pillows scattered about, and enveloped by the lingering scents of lavender, rosemary, and chamomile, Nichola appeared as if she belonged.

Completely.

He closed his eyes as relief gave way to stirrings of desire. Alexander fought back the urge to claim her as his own, to peel away the coverlet along with her clothes and make love with her.

He opened his eyes. His blood pounded hot. It must be the wine. Or perhaps it was his desperate need of sleep. *She is English and has no right to fit in so well.*

Instead, as he continued to stare at her, it seemed as if she'd been conceived by fairies and set within his life.

A place she could never remain.

He closed the door behind him, crossed the room to her bed and knelt by her side. As if by its own will, his finger stroked the satin curve of her cheek, his words below to his brothers of escorting her to England already haunting him.

He exhaled an unsteady breath, the softness of her skin against his own making him ache. As difficult as his journey was to abduct her and bring her to his home, the task to return her and leave her behind forever would be doubly so.

The fullness of her lips tempted him to taste them, to again savor her sweetness. He started to rise. No, he must leave her be.

The breath of the night swirled around them, warm with the dew of the heather, restless in the moonbeams. On a groan, he gave in and leaned forward.

"Nichola."

Alexander's whisper wove through her sleepy haze. A tender touch upon her cheek lured her to respond, but the need in his voice had her angling her head toward his caress. His fingers slid through her hair, and she sighed. Then his mouth, as gentle as a butterfly, covered hers.

She sank into the kiss, soft as silk, slow as a lazy summer breeze. His warm growl of appreciation rolled through her, and he deepened the kiss.

As if of their own will, her arms reached out to wrap around his neck and pull him closer. The mattress firmly stuffed with feathers sank beneath his weight, and she stretched out against his muscled length.

His hands cupped her face and he pressed feather-light

kisses over her brow. "You are so beautiful." He kissed her cheek and moved slowly downward until he reached her lips. "I love how you respond to me, how your body arches toward mine." His lips hungrily consumed hers, his teeth nipping at her mouth.

She moaned from the glory of it, and he took advantage and slipped his tongue into her mouth. Then he worked his magic with his tongue, fierce and hot.

"I want you," he breathed, whispering kisses along the column of her neck, igniting fires within her until she trembled from the heat of it.

His hand cupped her breast.

Nichola jolted awake. Confused, she stared up into Alexander's face. The few fragments of her sleep fell away.

The last few moments were far from a dream!

Flustered, she shoved his hand away, remembering how he'd left her in this chamber to rot. "Out of my bed!"

Alexander caught her hand in his and lifted it to his mouth, his gaze relentless on hers. He slowly kissed the tip of each finger.

"Admit you want me."

The need for his touch clawed through her. She could never admit that or forgive him. "I want you— to leave."

The shaft of moonlight spilling into the room revealed the dangerous glint of challenge in his eyes, that of a warrior set out to conquer. Without warning or mercy, his tongue swirled around her index finger. Cobalt eyes watched her as he gently sucked on the tip in a long, slow pull. Her body tightened with need, and shamefully, her nipples hardened.

His gaze flicked downward. Satisfaction warmed his

eyes as they met hers. Alexander scraped his teeth gently
to the palm of her hand and nipped at the center.

"Tell me you do not want me now?" he asked with a
mind-destroying whisper.

She swallowed hard. "How dare you think that you
can seduce me." Instead of the scathing demand, her
words breathed out in a husky whisper. Mary help her,
she did want him.

He rolled on top of her, caging her beneath his
body. "Your decisions are your own."

They were, but with his body framing her own, his
hard length pressed gently against her, the mere act
of putting thoughts into a sensible order fled.

Like a wolf who'd cornered his prey, he pressed a
kiss at the hollow of her throat, when she trembled,
he captured her mouth.

She willed herself not to respond. But he used his
clever mouth on her, his hands taking, touching,
seducing her when she should be refusing his advances; making her want when she should purge
him of her mind.

In a slow slide, his hand skimmed downward and
again cupped her breast. His fingers teased the sensitized swell; slow, luxurious circles until finally he captured her taut nub.

Passion, hot and thick built within her. Ripples of
heat streamed through her until she couldn't remember the reasons why she should push him away. Drowning in the heady sensations, she arched against him.

"Alexander," she whispered, unsure of what she
asked, but aware he would understand her needs.

Like an unruly god, Alexander pulled back and
stared at her, his breath rough, his eyes hot with need.
"You want me then," he accused, passion thickening
his rough burr.

Nichola stared at him in stunned disbelief. "A game?" She wiped the back of her hand against her lips as if to remove his taste from her mouth. "You have done this to prove that I wanted you?"

His eyes answered for him.

Hurt. Yes, she hurt. But she wouldn't show him that. He deserved nothing—in sharp contrast to what she'd almost given him.

She lifted her chin with an indignant tilt. "With your mastery over women, did you find it a challenge to learn you could seduce a virgin?"

On a curse he stood. Her eyes blazed as he glared down at her.

Nichola's courage wavered. She edged toward the other side of the bed, then slid back another degree, thankful when her feet touched the floor.

In one quick movement she stood, the bed wedged between them, little defense against such a powerful man. Her body trembled with nerves as she watched him, afraid he would finish what he'd begun. And with the needs crashing through her, God help her, if he touched her, she would let him.

The anger churning on his face reminded her of a storm.

She braced herself.

Instead of advancing, Alexander prowled the room like a predator. At the door, he halted. His harsh expression faded. Regret, simple and complete, swept across his face.

"I was wrong to come." He whispered the words as if torn from his soul, his sincerity making her foolishly want to forgive him.

He spun on his heel and exited the chamber. The door banged shut. Outside, the bar slammed into place. His footsteps, hard and fast, faded down the corridor.

She slumped down to sit on the edge of the bed, shaken by what he'd almost taken. She cradled her head in her hands. No. At what she'd almost given him.

The rattle of chains echoed from outside.

Nichola walked to the window. Torchlight collided with moonlight casting macabre flickers over the courtyard as the drawbridge lowered.

Hooves clattered from the stable.

A man riding a large bay raced out. The rider galloped beneath the gatehouse and across the drawbridge. Then she caught a faint shimmer of man and horse as they disappeared into the night.

Alexander.

Nichola's breathing hitched as she leaned against the cool stone wall. He'd wanted her; she'd witnessed the battle in his eyes as he'd stared at her, honor against lust, decorum against desire. In the end he'd chosen honor.

And left.

She wanted to be angry at him, but for what reason? He'd taken nothing but what she'd offered. As for her confinement within the chamber, he was ignorant of her fear of being locked within a room or her terror of thunderstorms.

With her body still aching for his touch, she didn't need for him to be noble. Not now. Not when her feelings toward him had grown dangerously tender with each passing day.

Numb, Nichola crossed the room and lay on the bed, the softness of the feather bed far from easing the pain in her heart. She stared up at the ceiling painted with the images of fairies, but thoughts of sleep were the farthest thing from her mind.

* * *

Alexander rode through the night as if chased by the hounds of hell. Wind whipped against his face, its taste cool, the hard lash welcome. When his horse began to lather, he reined his bay to a walk. He allowed him to pick his way down a steep bank toward the loch.

At a shallow beach, he drew his horse to a halt and dismounted. Without hesitation, he stripped off his clothes and dove into the dark, cold waters. With each stroke, he damned himself for touching Nichola again. With each kick, he wanted her. With each kiss, he had crossed barriers he and circumstance forbade.

Furious to be caught in such an emotional mire, he dove deep, until it felt as if his chest would explode. He kicked to the surface and gasped air in desperate gulps.

"She means bloody nothing!" His shout, an echo of mutilated anger, shattered over the water's surface.

Though his limbs trembled from exertion and his mind spun from lack of air, he still hadn't purged himself of Nichola. Muttering a curse, he swam long, mind-exhausting strokes, until the moon began to slide from his view and his limbs grew thick and weary.

Exhausted, and doubting he would ever rid himself of thoughts of her, of the silky taste of her, he finally swam to the sandy shore. He wiped his brow as he walked up the shallow bank to retrieve his clothes. Alexander halted.

They were gone.

Tension rippled through him. God's teeth. He'd been so lost in thoughts of Nichola, he'd let down his guard and ignored the possibility of an attack by the baron in retribution for his sister's abduction.

As quickly, he dismissed the act as the baron's doing; he would have taken his mount. He'd interrupted thieves. He scanned the area as he edged toward his bay. And if he was right, they were still out there.

His bay nickered and flicked his ears toward him.

"A good bloody lot you are," he muttered as he reached his side. And froze. His weaponry was stripped from its sheaths as well.

Positive he was being watched, Alexander covertly scanned the blackened forest for sign of the intruder. If an arrow wasn't trained at him, he might, just might, be able to escape.

He raised his foot to the stirrup.

"Move another inch and you are dead," a deep, raspy voice threatened.

Alexander debated the risks of jumping on his horse and making a run for it. Either way, naked and defenseless, the odds weren't in his favor.

"What do you want?" he called out, stalling for time as he decided on the best plan to escape.

"The woman."

Nichola? His heart stopped. He'd been followed from England? But how? He'd double checked his trail as they'd rode. He'd not seen a sign of anyone in pursuit. As if he would have, he thought with disgust. He'd been so distracted by Nichola the entire journey that a fool could have danced a jig on his head and he wouldn't have noticed.

"What woman do you speak of?" Alexander asked, buying time.

An arrow whizzed past on the left, not three feet away and embedded into a tree with a solid thunk. "The English woman you abducted for ransom."

"I . . ." The request for her ransom had only been

sent last eve. Unless someone attacked the runner and seized the message, no one would know.

Another arrow whipped past, this time from another direction. It landed to his right. "You will be answering us."

Alexander ignored the low-growled threat as he eyed two familiar notches, a thumb's length apart, cut into the shaft of the arrow caught in the fading light of the moon. He'd helped his brothers secure the feathers on the wooden shaft but a month ago.

He glared into the concealing brush that hedged the forest, then toward the brush where the other man had called out. His brothers thought to have fun with him, did they?

"I have abducted no one," Alexander called out.

A harsh snort of disbelief answered his reply. "If you have a need to take your next breath, you will be telling us the truth."

"Where have you left her?" the other man demanded.

Alexander almost smiled, but he kept his face passive. "The wench came willingly."

A drunken chuckle fell from the man to his left. "Not for that scrawny attempt you call your manhood."

Muffled laughter broke out from the other brush.

"Stay back," the voice hitched as Alexander strode forward. "I have another arrow nocked and aimed at your heart."

Alexander charged.

"Certes!" Duncan yelped. His murky figure darted from the brush.

Alexander caught Duncan and tackled him to the ground. Entwined within the shouts came the muffled fray of laughter.

Leaves and rock poked into his back, but Alexander only cursed and laughed harder. A fast ride and a demanding swim had done nothing to ease the tension of wanting Nichola. But this, where his fists could release the unspent energy coiled in his body, was another matter.

A knee in his thigh had Alexander groaning. Before his brother could gain the upper hand, he flipped Duncan on his back and pinned his hands.

"I have him," Patrik yelled as he tackled Alexander from behind. He fell forward with Alexander beneath him, the words spilling out with drunken glee.

"About time, you arse." Duncan sat up and wiped his mouth, spitting out leaves and a spot of blood before he stood with a whoop and dove over to help Patrik.

"Hold his other arm, will you?" Patrik shouted. "He has split open my lip."

"Nothing but what you are deserving," Alexander growled, satisfied when he managed to shove Patrik off. He plowed his fist into Duncan's chin and sent his brother flat on his back. Gratification lasted only a second as Patrik piled on top of him with a hearty shout. Alexander rolled over, then grunted as Duncan jumped atop him as well.

"Get off me," Patrik yelped. "Christ, you are both as heavy as a foul-breed ox."

Neither man moved, but each began to chuckle, which collapsed into deep, rumbling laughs.

"You will make me spill the last of the wine I have tucked within me trews," Duncan charged, and fell off them both as he chortled with laughter.

"You have the wine? Why did you not say so before." Patrik shoved Alexander aside and snatched the bottle from Duncan's hands. He opened the top and downed a healthy draught. Patrick glanced over as he wiped his mouth with his sleeve. "How did you know it was us?"

"Duncan's arrows," Alexander said matter-of-factly as he accepted the bottle. He took another drink. "I helped him make the shafts. I always carve two notches, a thumb's length apart, into each shaft I make."

Patrik glared at Duncan.

"How was I to know he would look at the shaft?" Duncan retorted. "Bloody eyes of an eagle."

"Never forget that," Alexander said with a laugh.

They laid back, taking turns until the wine bottle lay empty.

With a foul curse, Duncan tossed the empty container into the brush. It landed with a muffled clink. On a long sigh, he folded his arms under his head. "Look at the stars."

Alexander stared at the bright shimmers of light so alive within the blackened heavens. "Aye. It is a fine night."

"If only it could stay this way," Patrik said with such sadness, that Alexander glanced toward him. Patrik met his gaze. "Once the uprising begins, there may never come a time like this again."

Alexander laid his head back on the cool of the earth, his throat tight with emotion. Aye, war spared none. Before the first fall of snow, he, or any of his brothers could lay dead, cut down by the English. But each man who entered war understood the cost. This time here, now, was the most precious.

Time he would savor.

Duncan picked up a handful of leaves and tossed them into the air. They spiraled down in a lazy swirl. "Are you afraid of the upcoming fight?"

"Aye," Alexander said in a solemn reply. "Only a fool would not be. But it is our only choice." Grunts of agreement from his brothers followed his statement. Then amicable silence fell between them.

Patrik pushed a stone near his foot. "You checked on the woman?"

Alexander shrugged, not wanting to be reminded of Nichola, of their kiss, or that he'd almost taken her innocence.

"What is wrong?" Patrik asked. "You have not started to care about the lass, have you?" Though quietly said, his words held a warning of the necessity of keeping her at a distance.

"I would never do anything as half-witted as that." The last thing Alexander wanted to discuss was his feelings for Nichola. He damn well understood what was at stake. And his part. He sat up and glared at his brothers. "Blast it, where are my clothes and arms?"

The tension between them eroded. "Ask Duncan," Patrik said with a laugh.

Duncan jumped to his feet. Leaves crunched underfoot as he slowly began to back away.

"Halt," Alexander demanded.

His brother took another step back.

"I told him not to put them there," Patrik said, the humored delight on his face, even in the waning light, clear.

"Where?" Alexander growled at Duncan as he stepped toward him.

"In the nettles," Patrik supplied.

"You promised not to say a word," Duncan yelled, but little regret played in his expression. With a holler of delight, he bolted into the forest.

Alexander raced after him. Sticks poked at his feet, limbs slapped against his naked flesh.

Duncan's laughter echoed throughout the woods.

With a curse, Alexander tackled his brother several yards away from Duncan's horse. He flipped Duncan over and pinned him to the ground.

"You are going into the bushes after them," Alexander ordered with devilish delight.

"It was in jest!" Duncan tried to pry him off. "I used a stick to shove them in. Is your brain fogged? I can not go in there. I will be itching like a madman for the next day."

"A fate you deserve."

"Patrik, where in bloody hell are you?" Distant laughter met Duncan's request.

Duncan twisted beneath him. When he couldn't budge, he grinned up at Alexander, the gentle, fun-loving smile he used to charm. "I will ride home and fetch you another change of clothes."

"Ha. As if you would ever return. I know your tricks too well." He caught his brother by the scruff of his neck. "You are going to go in there and retrieve them now or I will toss you into the nettles myself."

His face paled. "You would not."

He arched a brow, remembering Nichola's plight, finding immense satisfaction in his brother sharing the same fate. "No?"

"Get off me," Duncan grumbled. "I will get your bloody clothes. Not that you will be appreciating my efforts."

"You shoved them in," Alexander said as he hauled his brother up with him as he stood, "and you will be getting them out."

"Not even appreciating a bit of humor," Duncan muttered when his brother released him. He brushed off the dirt and leaves from his garb.

Alexander gestured him forward. "Move."

His younger brother glared back toward where Patrik sat, rolling with laughter at his plight. "The braggart will get his own." He stomped off, muttering something about trust and badgers.

With a shake of his head, Alexander followed, his mirth complete as Duncan yelped and cursed as he shoved through the nettles and plucked Alexander's clothes from the briars.

"Next time you will not be so quick to steal my clothes," Alexander said as his brother threw him his garments, then handed him his weapons.

Duncan glowered at his other brother. "Not with Patrik knowing about the prank."

With a grin, Alexander tugged on his clothes. "Sounds like Patrik is deserving of a wet down."

Duncan picked a thorn from his skin and glanced toward where Patrik sat laughing. "It does now at that." The irritation on his face shifted into mischievous satisfaction. He nodded to Alexander. "The time is ripe."

Alexander set his weapons down.

Both men charged their brother.

At their approach, Patrik scurried to his feet, his hands out wide and began backing up. "You would not be touching me now. It was all in jest!"

They didn't break stride.

Patrik bolted. He'd almost reached his horse before Alexander caught his arm, and Duncan grabbed his other shoulder. They began to drag him toward a large rock that hung over a deep pool in the loch.

"Let me go!" Patrik fought them.

Laughing, they dragged him to the edge.

"This will teach you for telling my deeds," Duncan charged. With Alexander's help, and Duncan's boot on his arse, they tossed Patrik over the edge.

A loud splash rewarded their efforts.

Alexander and Duncan watched with supreme satisfaction as their brother floundered in the water.

"You were deserving it, Duncan," Patrik sputtered. He wiped the moisture from his face as he tread water.

"And crawling through a batch of nettles is far from payment for seducing Johanna, the woman I had my eye on."

Alexander arched a brow at Duncan. So that was what this was all about.

Duncan shrugged. "The lad is slow when it comes to women."

In sure, powerful strokes, Patrik started toward shore. "You will pay for this."

"Not tonight." With a wink at Alexander, Duncan sprinted toward his horse.

Chuckling, Alexander ran to his bay and mounted. He urged his horse into a gallop. In seconds he caught up with Duncan. The echo of hooves mingled with Patrik's curses behind them as he and his brother raced toward home.

Lochshire Castle came into view, along with the tower where Nichola slept, and Alexander's laughter faded. The desire he'd fought only a short while ago to control returned with a gut-twisting vengeance.

Alexander cursed and urged his mount faster. But the slap of reality, of how she could affect him, nearly stole his breath. He'd known better than to touch her. Like a green lad he'd deceived himself into thinking he could take but one kiss without wanting more.

She was a virgin; a woman who would expect more than a quick tumble from her lover. A woman like her would want forever. He could never offer her that.

But as he rode through the gatehouse and into the courtyard with Duncan at his side, Alexander glanced toward the tower window and wondered if such a folly ever could be?

Chapter Ten

In the great hall, the familiar rumble of men eating, talking, and preparing for the new day surrounded Alexander. He stared at the roasted meat speared on his dagger while his brothers attacked their fare at the trencher table, both seated on either side of him.

Images of Nichola locked within her chamber haunted his mind, and Alexander's appetite fled. He tossed the chunk of venison to the dogs beneath the table. They scrambled for the meat as he wiped off his blade and slid it into his sheath.

Seathan shot him a questioning look. "What is wrong?"

Alexander stood. "I will be working alongside Blar making crossbows."

"As you have worked alongside the atilliator for the last four days?" Seathan sipped his wine, his gaze intent. "And you have pushed yourself hard, returning to the keep late in the night after the tables have long been cleared from the evening meal."

"I am not a lad that needs tending." Alexander wiped the grease from his hands and threw the cloth aside. "Once the fighting begins, we will be needing extra weapons."

Duncan tore off a bite of bread, his dimples deepening with amusement. "It is a tumble with a lass you would be needing to ease your mind."

Patrik slanted a hard look toward Alexander. "Do not be telling Duncan the wench you are favoring. He will have her on her back and her legs spread before you can unsheathe your blade."

"It is my charm." Duncan took a drink of ale. "Which is much more attractive to women than your flea-bitten face."

Seathan rose. "The two of you need to think with your brains instead of your cocks." His gaze fell upon Alexander. "We need to speak."

Alexander hesitated. He didn't want a confrontation. He wanted to submerge his mind in the making of crossbows. In the crafting of precision weaponry, he could distance his thoughts of Nichola. He sighed. Seathan's serious expression assured him they would talk.

Alexander walked by his older brother's side as they left the great hall. Their footsteps echoed up the spiral steps as they started up the tower.

Once they exited onto the wall walk, Seathan glanced at Alexander. "I received a missive last night. The barter for the arms has been made. The price agreed. It will be less than the ransom we have demanded."

He grunted. "The extra coin will be welcome."

"Aye," Seathan agreed.

A light breeze scented with the loch and grass swirled past. Alexander walked by his brother's side, edgy, but curious as to the reason of Seathan's request to accompany him. He could have shared the news of the arms agreement while they'd broken their fast.

Seathan halted before a merlon. "I remember standing here on mornings when I could not sleep. I would come here to be alone, to try and work out problems that seemed insurmountable." He leaned against the carved stone and stared out. "Somehow our father would know when I was troubled and he would find me. Though he did not always give me answers, he would offer advice to help me weigh my final decision."

"Aye," Alexander agreed. "He always discerned when one of us needed a guiding hand. Or required a proper setting down." And he'd been a man who'd sacrificed his life to save Alexander's. He swallowed hard. "I miss him."

Reflections of grief sifted through Seathan's eyes. "As do I."

"He would be proud of how you have guided Lochshire Castle with a steady hand."

"But not alone. You, Duncan, and Patrik have helped when there has been a need, offered support when sought out." Seathan paused. "Until now. You are troubled, yet you harbor your thoughts."

Irritated by his brother's ability to discern what most would miss, Alexander remained silent. What would he tell him, that he despised treating Nichola like his prisoner? That he wanted her for his lover? Or that she moved him as no other?

Maybe he should tell him that she wished him dead, and her harsh words hurt the worst?

Shame scraped up his throat. He'd allowed his feelings to grow toward his enemy. 'Twas unforgivable. Even the knowing changed naught. God help him, she meant more to him than she should.

"There is naught to discuss," he finally replied. He looked toward where the morning sun cut through the fog hovering over the calm waters. "The abduction went well enough. The request for ransom has been sent. Now the arms we need are awaiting our arrival."

"What I speak of has little to do with arms, the mission, or the rebels. You have walked around like an injured badger for the last four days."

Alexander stiffened. "I have kept to my self."

"Aye," Seathan replied with a quiet concern that had Alexander clenching his teeth. "More so than since our father's death."

"By God's eyes, I do not want to talk of—"

"You have not spoken of our father's death, but it eats at you," Seathan pressed. "It shows in your every step. At how you always volunteer for dangerous missions."

Guilt poured through Alexander as the last seconds of his father's life rolled through his mind. On his grave, he'd vowed to take vengeance upon the English. Now, his desire for Nichola betrayed everything he stood for.

"Leave it."

"Your being killed will change naught," Seathan said. "Nor replace our father. It is long past time to air your grief."

"Grief," Alexander spat. "Is that what it is called watching our father die in my arms from an arrow meant for me?"

Green eyes darkened to black. "It was his choice. The decision is long made. And past."

"You asked me here to speak of our father?"

"In part."

"And the other?" Alexander asked, afraid he already knew the reason.

For a long moment his brother studied him. "You are a man who loves to tumble with the lasses. But never have I seen a woman who has left you on edge to where you will not turn to family for help. Lady Nichola has."

"I am worried about her," he finally said, which was the truth.

A humorless smile touched Seathan's mouth. "Worried or smitten?"

"Blast it, I have stayed away from her for the last four days."

"And with each passing one, your mood darkens."

His spine stiffened. Because it was the truth, Alexander bit back his sharp retort. "When the time comes to return her to England, I will do my duty."

"I have asked Patrik to escort her back to England once the ransom arrives."

Alexander glared at him. "I abducted Nichola."

His brother watched him, the quiet strength in his expression making Alexander's gut tighten. He knew that look. Seathan would not be swayed from his decision.

Seathan shook his head. "Patrik will go."

Panic shot through him at the thought of losing even those few precious days with Nichola. "Is it wrong to want time with her? Only the few days it will take to deliver her back to Rothfield Castle?"

"There is no right or fairness in war, only sadness and injustice." Seathan studied him, his sharp eyes missing nothing. "With her reputation already in ruins by the abduction, the time you spend with the lass while she is at Lochshire Castle is of no consequence. As long as she is treated well and is willing in whatever you both do in private. With her brother's wealth, he can easily find a man who will offer to wed her."

He held his hand up when Alexander made to speak.

"You may think my words harsh or unjust," Seathan continued, "but I understand the caring and the heartbreak of letting go of a woman. A sane man, when his mind becomes twisted by his feelings, can become a fool. I have already informed Patrik that he, along with a chaperone, will travel and exchange the woman for the ransom."

Unease rumbled inside. "With his grudge against the English, do you think his escorting Nichola wise?"

"You believe he would harm her?"

That was another issue. Though not brothers by blood, he considered Patrik his true brother. But neither could he forget that the murder of Patrik's family by the English had brought Patrik to their home. He'd like to believe that Patrik would never harm Nichola. Mayhap, 'twas his feelings for Nichola that spurned his protectiveness.

Unsure of the base of his misgivings, Alexander shrugged. "No." But doubts remained.

Seathan nodded. "All I have done is changed the time you will spend with Lady Nichola by a few days at most."

Alexander wanted to object, fought the words crowding his tongue for release, but he understood with humbling clarity his brother's reasoning.

Two years ago, Seathan, the rational, level-headed man who always walked the righteous path, had fallen in love—with a married woman. She'd dismissed Seathan's declarations of love and explained she'd used him to make her husband jealous.

Seathan had returned home, his innocences lost,

and his pride shattered. He'd changed, had become quieter and harder. The laughter that had softened his face during his youth was now almost nonexistent.

But for his brothers, Seathan would offer his life.

If anyone else had informed Alexander he wouldn't escort Nichola back to England, he would have rebelled like a wolf protecting its mate. Not to Seathan. His brother's words held wisdom, insight painfully learned.

Even if he refuted Seathan's decree, what could he offer as a defense? His abduction of Nichola had already invited the baron's wrath, hostility he'd shamefully disregarded. Alexander dropped his hands to his sides. Seathan was right. Besides, escorting Nichola home would only deepen his sorrow.

With his mind made up and his heart heavy, Alexander nodded his agreement.

"Upon Patrik's return," Seathan explained, "you, along with a contingent of hand-picked men, will travel to the western edge of Selkirk Forest where you will meet with the men selling us arms. After they have received payment, they will lead you to the weapons."

"Aye," Alexander replied, his throat tight.

His brother laid a hand on his shoulder. "We are given choices, but not always those we want." Pain flashed on Seathan's face before he could shield the emotion, and Alexander understood, his brother thought of the woman who had hurt him. "I have a task to take care of now, but I look forward to our next round on the practice field."

"As will I," Alexander said, forcing out a lightness he didn't feel.

Seathan walked away.

The echo of his brother's steps down the turret faded, and Alexander rubbed the back of his neck.

Aye, he would do his duty for his country and his clan, but he doubted there would ever come a time when he would forget Nichola.

With a heavy heart, he descended the stairs. At the bottom, the servant he'd assigned to Nichola's care rushed toward him, but his gaze was already skimming up to where her window stood open.

And empty.

He remembered the servant's report yesterday of how over the past four days, Nichola had become withdrawn. News that had disturbed him to the point where he'd almost agreed to Nichola's request to see him. But his last confrontation with her, their kiss, had kept him from making such a dangerous move. As much as he wanted to deny her effect over him, he couldn't.

The young woman halted before him. "Lady Nichola did not touch her food last eve or break her fast this morning."

"Is she ill?"

"She looks peaked, but nothing I say will convince her to eat." Lines of worry dredged in the servant's brow. "I fear if she does not eat soon, she will fall ill or worse."

"I will speak with her." But only for a moment. He refused to make the same mistake twice and allow himself to become tempted by her feminine wiles.

Relief swept over her face. "My thanks, Sir Alexander."

"Bring a fresh tray of food to the room. I will ensure Lady Nichola finishes it."

"Aye." The woman hurried away.

Alexander strode across the courtyard. The stubborn chit. Did she think that with her token rebellion he would cave in and allow her freedom to roam the castle and give her another chance to escape?

He ascended the torch-lit tower, his unease growing with each step. Should he have checked on Nichola before? Was she truly ill? Or was this yet another ruse?

After her last failed escape attempt and now with being locked within the tower room, didn't she realize that he couldn't allow her to slip away? No. The chit didn't have enough sense to quit, all because of her stubborn pride.

He couldn't help but admire that Nichola fought for what she believed in. 'Twas a strength of his as well. But her determination to best him changed nothing. He'd not tolerate her defiance. She would eat. Then he would leave.

But when he stepped inside the chamber, the woman who turned to face him from near her bedside was a ghostly version of the spirited lass he'd abducted. The frail sadness in her eyes almost dropped him to his knees.

His heart pounded as he crossed the room.

"You came."

Her shaky whisper dragged his guilt deeper. Intent on keeping distance between, he'd ignored her servant's concerns. By her appearance, he should have checked on her from the first report, or asked one of his brothers to do so in his stead. But jealous, he'd wanted no one else in attendance of Nichola but his servant.

His guilt mounted higher until it stank like a dung heap. However she'd hurt him, she didn't deserve to waste away. "What in God's name are you doing to yourself?"

"I asked to see you . . . each day," she said, her voice but a whisper. "You never came."

He closed the door. "It is best I keep away."

Did he hate her? Was that why he'd abandoned

her? Or was it because she was his prisoner, a fact at odds with him wanting her?

"Why?" Nichola winced at the tremor in her voice, but was unable to hide it. She'd longed for this moment for days, and she had every intention of being strong. But now that he was here, all she could do was feast her eyes on him and wish they'd met under different circumstances. But she couldn't allow him to see how his presence affected her. How she ached with wanting him.

'Twas the days locked inside this room that heightened her awareness of him. Though beautifully adorned and steeped with enchanting qualities, this chamber was a prison.

"If only for a short while, I would like to go outside. Please," she added, desperation forcing her pride to take yet another blow by having to beg.

"So you can try and escape?"

A part of her died at his question. Aching, she summoned the courage to speak. "As if locked within these walls I could escape, much less survive in the forest on my own if I did? Or have you forgotten the pitifully failed attempt that landed me in the patch of stinging nettles?" Or how he'd cared for her with such tenderness during the hours after?

He grunted. "You would still try."

Yes. If given the chance she would.

A knock sounded on the door.

"Enter," Alexander said.

Nichola watched as the woman who tended her swept into the room. She placed a tray of food on the table and left as the rich smell of warm bread, roast venison, and herbs drifted through the room. She stared at the generous spread. The last thing she needed was to spend time with him alone.

Refusing to be swayed from her desire for a token of personal freedom, she turned toward him. "Will you grant me my request?"

"Break your fast, then we will discuss it."

"I am not hungry." Her stomach issued a traitorous growl.

"You will eat." He moved to pick up the trencher topped with the thinly cubed meat and walked over. He halted a pace before her. The air pulsed around them as a silent battle of wills ensued.

Using his dagger, he speared a chunk of meat and brought it to her mouth. Slow, with intent, he brushed it across her lips. Her lower lip trembled, and his eyes darkened with longing, the way a man looks at a woman he wants and desires above all things.

The way she'd yearned for him to look at her.

Nichola's breath caught in her throat. Her pulse grew unsteady. Her body tightened and heat pulsed through her to her very core.

The moment shifted to something intense.

Intimate.

On an unsteady breath, Nichola opened her mouth and he placed the savory morsel on her tongue. She chewed and swallowed, which, with him observing her every move, was an effort unto itself.

His scent, a potent mix of man and earth, filled her every breath and her blood grew hot. If he leaned forward a degree, their bodies would brush. His hard, lean, muscled length would press against hers. And he could sate his desire as well as hers.

As if able to read her thoughts, he shifted closer, his gaze upon her mouth, then lower. Beneath his burning stare, her nipples grew taut. Need built into a painful ache.

He set the food aside. Slowly, he backed her up until

he had her pressed against the wall, caged within his powerful form. Then he leaned forward and slanted his mouth over hers, his hard body firm against her.

The taste of him stormed her senses, ripping away coherent thought. The ache inside her grew stronger, an instinctive response as primitive as time.

She shuddered. This was what she wanted, needed. More than food, more than her freedom. On a trembling exhalation, Nichola parted her lips.

And surrendered to what she could no longer deny.

Chapter Eleven

Nichola shuddered beneath Alexander's mouth as it moved over her lips with soft determination, claiming her with a predatory intent. She should push him away, refuse him such intimacy; instead, she savored his strength, desire coursing through her body until every inch of her trembled. Aching with need, she wrapped her hands around his neck and drew him closer.

Without warning, he broke free. Desire burned in his gaze with a lethal brand as he stared down at her. Hot. Volatile. As if a mere touch would leave her blissfully singed. The scar on his left cheek tightened. He turned away.

"Finish your fare." Hardness coated his voice, leagues from his lover's touch of seconds before.

Nichola sank against the wall, a sharp longing radiating through her body. Alexander was angry, but she wasn't afraid. She sensed his anger was toward himself, his battle between his desire for her and duty. She should be relieved one of them had sense. Yet, if he hadn't backed away, she would have allowed him . . . everything.

Shame filled her as she moved to the table. Her stomach rebelled at the thought of food, but she'd eat day-old porridge if it would gain her temporary freedom. Between the goblet of wine and sheer determination to escape the confines of her chamber, she swallowed every morsel on her trencher.

She rose. "I am finished."

Alexander gave a brusque nod. He walked over and opened the door. "Only for a short while."

Disquiet swept through her as she entered the doorway. He followed in silence, his footsteps softly mocking hers.

They exited the great hall and the aroma of fresh-brewed ale entwined with the melting fat used by the candle maker greeted them. Happiness touched her as the sun-kissed air warmed her face. She struggled to dismiss his unnerving presence. And failed.

Nichola tried to empty her mind by absorbing everything around her. The well-maintained buildings, the peasants who passed them to purchase wares during market day, the pounding of the smith working near the stables melded with the clang of swords as knights practiced in the bailey.

Alexander stepped up to her side, his sheer size alone making it impossible to ignore him.

"It is a fine castle," she said without looking at him, her body far from stable after his kiss in the chamber.

"It is at that. If you are able, would you like to see more?"

Surprised by his offer, she nodded. She'd half expected that once they'd walked outside, they'd remain but a trice before he escorted her back to her chamber.

His hand cupped her elbow.

Awareness whipped through her at the simple con-

tact. She didn't look up. Didn't dare. The last thing
she needed was confirmation he'd experienced the
same need.

Alexander kept their pace slow as they strolled by
the many shops displaying various wares. The people
within called out greetings to him as they passed. A
few nodded to her, but several others shot her a cool
glare. The true reason for her presence at Lochshire
had reached the residents' ears.

With longing, she looked past the lowered drawbridge to where the ragged expanse of rock and
rolling field cut upward to the steep edge of the forest.
Mary help her, she would find a way to escape.

As they closed on a small but sturdy shop, the odor
of worked wood and sweat greeted her. Alexander
guided her inside, blocking her view of freedom. Her
chest tightened at the sense of being trapped within
the confines. She calmed. Alexander showed her the
castle. Their time within the cramped building would
be brief.

A strapping man surrounded by neatly stacked piles
of various wood, along with other tools of his trade,
worked to shape a bough into a long, narrow stock.

"What is he making?" she asked.

Alexander eyed her. "He is carving oak for the tiller
of a crossbow. Like the Saracens, we use oak, maple,
elm, and horn for the construction of the weapon."

"Horn?"

"Aye. Horn is tough and springy and not as likely to
break as if he used wood."

She skimmed her hand down the stock of a finished
crossbow hung on the wall; the warm slide of polished
wood, flawless in its design, reminding her of the
hewn muscles of the man at her side. Shaken at the

way her thoughts always turned toward him, Nichola lowered her hand away.

"We use beeswax to protect the wood against the rain and cold," Alexander explained.

"You know much about the crafting of these weapons."

The strapping man winked. "And the lad learned it all from me."

At the warmth in his voice, her smile came with ease. The man could not be much older than Alexander. Yet, the teasing tone of his voice heralded him as his friend.

"Me name is Blar," he said with a nod. "If I wait for Alexander to introduce us, you might never come to know me name."

Alexander gave an indignant snort. "I would not trust my geese to this fox."

"Appreciative lad, is he not," Blar said with a chuckle. His gaze slid down her with male appreciation. "And is this lass the reason you have been snapping at everyone? I have wondered at the cause of your foul mood."

A blush warmed her cheeks at his overt perusal.

"Blar," Alexander said, "this is Lady Nichola."

The humor on the strapping man's face faded. "The English lass?"

"Aye."

Coldness smothered any warmth on his face. "This is no place for a lady."

She understood. He didn't want English eyes viewing weapons he'd made, arms that would be used against her people.

"You are very skilled in your trade. My thanks for your time." She turned, thankful Alexander didn't stop her as she stepped past him. Outside, Nichola halted, her entire body trembling. She'd been foolish to allow herself that moment of pleasure. She would never be accepted here.

Alexander moved to her side. "I should have thought better than to bring you here. I had but wanted to let you see where I work during the day."

Though his words held little warmth, his apology touched her as did the fact that he'd wanted to show her a part of him. "The crossbows are of fine quality," she said, unsure of what else to say.

Pride lit his face. "Aye, they are the best in all of Scotland."

She studied his hands. Skilled hands that had crafted the stout weaponry within the shop. Hands instilled with patience. Hands that could bend wood into a desired form, or a woman to his will.

Unwanted needs stirred within her. Alexander did nothing by halves. What would it be like if they made love? Or if he loved her? The questions popped into her mind without warning, shattering her momentary illusion that she was in control of her emotions.

"I had not thought you a craftsman. I took you as a warrior," she said, needing to think of something else, *anything* else besides the sensual feelings he elicited. "I can understand where the demands necessary to create such detailed weaponry would appeal to you. A challenge." Mayhap why she appealed to him?

"I am merely an apprentice."

Which explained another layer of friendship between him and Blar. Friend and mentor. "How long have you worked under his guidance?"

He studied her a moment, then his shoulders relaxed. "A year now. I am only beginning to understand the feel of the wood, the curves, how to cut and work with the natural weakness and strengths of the grain." His tone softened, tempered by his obvious love of the craft.

Although she wanted to remain outside, Nichola turned back toward the keep. Too aware of him, of the pleasure his mere touch could bring, it was a mistake to spend time with him. And the more she learned of the man, the harder it was to remember he was her enemy.

Alexander caught her arm in a gentle hold and steered her toward the drawbridge. "Walk with me."

"Outside the castle walls?" she said, stunned. "I am surprised you have not put me on a tether as one would a hawk."

"You are too weak to give me much of a chase."

"Not so weak I cannot cut you down with my tongue."

The whisper of mirth on his face caught her off guard. After she'd wished him dead days before, she'd never thought he'd again gift her with such warmth.

They walked into the cool shadows of the gatehouse, their steps a soft echo against the crafted walls. Warmth brushed against her skin as she stepped into the sunlight outside. A light breeze sputtered around them as if trying to take hold, only to fade away.

"The wind will be picking up before long," Alexander said as they ambled across the drawbridge. "On a fine summer morning, it is always the same."

She stared at him, the beauty of the day dispelling the last of her emotional barriers she needed to keep against Alexander in place. "Why is that?"

He shrugged. "I cannot explain the why of it. But when the skies are blue as a fairy's eyes and the morning still but for wisps of fog scattered about, it is the same."

As if to prove his claim, the breeze again sputtered around them, this time lasting longer before fading to calm.

"Like a babe kicking its way to life," Alexander said. They reached the shore and stopped. Rocks, battered by wave and wind, lay strewn along the uneven shoreline.

Nichola watched the water. An errant ripple tickled the surface. "I would not have thought you would be interested in anything as mundane as the variances of the wind."

He leaned down and picked up a multicolored rock. Though not of the same quality or beauty, the smooth stone reminded her of the four polished gemstones in her room.

Alexander skipped the rock over the mirrored surface of the water. It skimmed in a rhythmic trail, then submerged. "There is nothing mundane in nature or what it creates. Too many people overlook the everyday treasures before them."

His simple words touched her. How true. Caught up in their own strife, most people passed through life without enjoying it. As Griffin did. Lost in a sodden turmoil, his life lay battered by women, drink, and now possibly murder. What would it take to bring back the caring brother, the family she so craved? Where was her brother now?

Please let him be alive.

She looked up to find Alexander watching her with unnerving intensity as when he'd kissed her in her chamber a short while before. Emotion tightened in her throat.

"There is a bowl in my chamber that holds four halved stones," she said, before she softened and did something foolish like leaned toward him, or told him the truth about her brother or their lack of coin.

"They belonged to my grandmother." Alexander picked up another rock, this one angled with strong lines of white racing through layers of black. He rubbed the rough stone with the edge of his thumb, love for his revered ancestor spilling into his smile.

"The room is hers, isn't it?" The warmth of the chamber, the little touches that made the room so personal, finally made sense. With the cold distance between them when they'd arrived at Lochshire Castle, she hadn't expected him to deposit her in a chamber of such luxury; especially a room of a family member he obviously cherished.

"It was."

"Then why did you give it to me?"

Why indeed. Alexander stared at her then, her question one that haunted him still. "I do not know," he replied with complete honesty.

He drew his arm back and threw the rock. It landed a great distance away with a plunk. Waves moved out in a perfect circle from the point of entry.

How odd to be standing here at her side sharing such intimacies. He should have returned her to her chamber when he had the chance and gone hunting with his brothers. Instead, he'd deluded himself in thinking he could be with her and keep her at a distance.

Except, with every glance, he wanted her more.

Another gust of wind spurted to life. Ripples shuddered over the water to merge with those created from the rock, blurring where one began and the other ended, like his desire blurred the reasons why he should keep away from Nichola.

"Would you tell me about her?"

"Why?"

"I have no right to ask something so personal, but there is something about the room that draws me. I cannot explain why." A steady flow of wind teased at her auburn locks as Nichola turned toward him. Confusion filled her gaze along with the need to understand.

Touched by her admission, though not wanting to be, he explained. "Some say her spirit still lives in the room."

Her gray eyes widened. "The chamber is haunted?"

Alexander smiled, warmed by the memories of his grandmother's mystic life. "No, she believed the room is touched by magic."

"Magic?"

"My grandmother was a woman filled with the zest of life, a healer and optimist who had the second sight."

Her brow wrinkled in thought. "Is the room filled with magic or is it haunted?"

Disarmed by her confusion, he relaxed completely. "In a sense, both."

"You are but teasing me."

He shook his head. "She was a wondrous woman. It is that I am surprised you have sensed her presence. I would not have believed you would."

"Being an Englishwoman, you mean?"

"Part of the reason," he admitted, not wanting to acknowledge that she had felt his grandmother's presence in the room or the magic. Neither made sense.

She turned away, but not before he saw the hurt on her face. He should have remained quiet, allowed his silence to put much needed distance between them.

"I had not meant my words as a barb," he said, his heart overruling common sense.

She shrugged. "Does it matter how you meant it?"

It shouldn't. But it did, because Nichola mattered.

"The sight?" Nichola asked, breaking into his unsettling thoughts. "She could foretell the future?"

"Bits, pieces, an event here or there."

"How?"

"Sometimes through a dream, other times by touching someone's hand. Often, she would walk through the forests where she claimed the fairies spoke to her." He remembered how his grandmother's eyes had glittered with mischief, the delight of spinning a yarn rich on her face as she told of her exploits, or the event she said the fairies had foretold.

"And the colored stones in her room?"

He tensed. "Why do you ask?"

"It is just when I touched them I felt . . ." She hesitated as if not daring to admit what she felt for sounding foolish.

"A power?" he finished with a grudging acceptance. She nodded.

And why should he be surprised? She'd sensed his grandmother in the room along with the magic, something only possible for he and his brothers. Until now. It was logical she would feel the energy of the stones.

"And warmth as well." A rosy hue warmed her cheeks. "It sounds daft to speak of such things."

It was ludicrous to continue his torment of being with her and not touching her. It was ludicrous to talk of family matters with her. It was ludicrous that all the reasons he shouldn't be around her didn't matter when she was near.

This closeness she inspired was dangerous indeed. He and Nichola could never be together. He exhaled a long sigh. "No, it does not sound strange."

Relief swept her face. "It does not?"

Alexander swore he heard the faint strands of his grandmother's amused chuckle and wondered if her spirit had sided with the fairies.

"No," he replied. "The stones she kept within her chamber hold different energies for the healing of a body or the spirit."

"I have never heard of such a thing."

Which only added to Alexander's mounting frustration. An innocent in the healing arts, no way could she have known about the purpose or potency of the stones.

Nichola brushed away a tendril of hair that fluttered across her lips. "In the bowl, one of the stones is halved and has what appears to be moss within. The outside is rough and the color of crushed gold."

"That would be the moss agate." He remembered he'd had the same impression when he'd first viewed the unusual stone. "It holds the ability to makes warriors powerful and shield them from those who would bring them harm. Seathan wears the other half around his neck. A gift to him from our grandmother when he was knighted."

Intrigue sparked in her eyes. "When you were knighted, did your grandmother gift you with something as well?"

From a finely crafted chain he wore around his neck, Alexander withdrew his grandmother's gift from the day he received his knighthood; the half of a dark, greenish blue stone mixed with swirls of a lighter green like a core of a cut tree staggered toward the center. He lifted it over his head and handed it to her.

She held it suspended from its chain. It twirled before her in the morning sun. "It is beautiful. I have never seen anything like this before."

An ache built in his throat as he watched her, her face innocent in its pure joy. "It is azurite. It is said to aid in control over your emotions and reactions, and to give the wearer greater insight."

Gray eyes lifted to his. "And does it?"

His mouth grew dry as the need for her shifted to something dangerous. "Usually." Except with Nichola. Whatever existed between them held its own force. One neither the powers of the stone nor common sense could overrule.

She handed his amulet back.

Shaken to realize that the anger he'd nurtured for the last four days had somehow fled, he lifted the draping chain from her palm and ensured their hands didn't touch.

"Your other two brothers have similar gifts as well?" she asked, her voice unsteady, the awareness in her eyes making his blood heat.

"Patrik was given malachite, which promotes inner peace. My grandmother gifted Duncan with a sapphire, known for its powers of prophecy and wisdom. Sapphire is also called the stone of destiny, because of its ability to aid the wearer in clarity of mind for those who seek the truth."

"The gifts are so unique. So personal. She must have been an incredible woman."

A yearning crept into her eyes, and an emptiness so intense that Alexander fought the need to reach out and embrace her. "She was at that. And what of your family?"

Pain lanced through her eyes. She looked away, and he immediately regretted asking. "Never mind." He stepped closer until he was but a hand's breadth away. "Your family will be worried."

"No," she said on a rough whisper. "They will not."

At the sullen hopelessness of her response, he frowned. "Your brother—"

"My brother," she interrupted, her voice weary. She nodded. "Griffin indeed will be most concerned over my disappearance. I am tired and my thoughts are tangled."

Except her half-hearted reply left him far from convinced. "You are very close then?"

Nichola hesitated. "Yes. He is the only person I have trusted since my parents' deaths."

But the sense that she was withholding something nagged at him. Their informant within Rothfield Castle confirmed her words that the brother and sister were close. Alexander dismissed any concern on that front.

So what was she hiding?

Or was there another person to whom she gave her trust?

Jealousy raked through him at the thought of another man touching her, awakening her passion. Why wouldn't men seek to court her? Besides being wealthy, she was intriguing, intelligent, and beautiful.

As if he hadn't already added enough risks for the rebels by abducting her instead of her brother? With the days passing and the absence of the baron leading a charge against the castle, 'twould seem they'd avoided inviting her brother's wrath. Mayhap the Baron of Monceaux had decided to pay the ransom and avoid a confrontation. Or perhaps he'd sent away too many of his knights to support King Edward's bid to claim Scotland for retribution. Whatever his reason not to attack, Alexander gave silent thanks.

"At six, it must have been difficult for you as a child." God's teeth, why had he said that? He already knew the answer; and her past, future, and whom she chose to make romantic liaisons with, was of no consequence to him.

"It was."

His heart reached out to her. "I am sorry you endured such."

She shrugged, but he saw the sadness she couldn't hide. "Tragedy is a lesson of life we must all deal with."

The pain of his father's death still overwhelmed him, and he was a man full and grown. "But your grief is great." Their time together had taught him that Nichola was a woman of deep emotions. A fact that appealed to him overmuch.

Nichola brushed away tendrils of auburn hair fluttering across her cheek. "We were close."

He easily pictured the shattered youth, her struggle to cling to the fragile bond of unity with her sibling. From the grief lingering in her eyes, she'd never fully recovered from her loss. And now he'd stolen her from her home.

Guilt ate at him, but he couldn't change the way of things now. If given the same circumstance and awareness of her past, would he have left her until her brother's return? Caught between the loyalties to his country and his feelings toward her, at the moment he wasn't sure.

"Walk with me, Nichola," he said, torn by the turmoil, wanting to heal the emotional wounds of the child that had grown into a woman. Those scars he'd added to by her abduction.

"Why?"

"Because I want to be with you." That was the truth. And as much as he dared admit to her.

Irritation sparked on her face. The anger he'd come to know and in a perverse fashion, enjoy. "As simple as that?"

He arched a brow. "Aye."

"It may be easy for you to dismiss the circumstances that surround us, but I cannot."

"Cannot or will not?"

"What do you want from me, Alexander? Since our arrival, you have kept me locked within the chamber for four days. With each rising sun, you have denied my every request to see you, to allow me any time away from my room. Now you grace me with your presence and expect me to accompany you without protest. As if you truly care?"

Heavy silence hung between them.

She tilted her chin at an angle of defiance. "The only reason you are with me now is that I am a challenge. Or that for whatever reason, you have decided now is a time to discover if I am a challenge you can overcome."

He moved to touch her, but she stepped back.

"Do not. Not unless you truly want me." Her face paled as if horrified by what she'd revealed. "Not then, either. Forgive me, I spoke in a senseless haste."

But he'd already heard the words. And her confession of several nights before echoed too clearly in his mind. "And if I truly cared for you?" By God's eyes! Why was he even continuing this foolery? But however ludicrous, a part of him needed to know.

Her gaze grew frantic. "It would be a lie." She whirled and fled.

Alexander ran after her.

When she reached the cleared slope, she veered off between the thick limbs of a line of firs and disappeared into the forest.

Cursing himself, he pushed away blocking limbs. He'd meant a calming talk. Not an intimate discussion.

He caught sight of her racing around the edge of a large rock. She was weak and might injure herself.

Alexander found her a short distance ahead on her knees, her hand pressed against the wall of stone, and her breaths coming out in sharp rasps. He hunkered down beside her, angry at himself for having pushed her to this reckless point.

"Keep away from me," she gasped between breaths.

Instead he scooped her up in his arms and held her against his chest, wanting only to heal, to protect. Her resistance lasted but a few seconds.

Her body sagged against him. "Why can you not leave me alone?"

Her whispered plea almost broke his heart. He laid his chin atop her head as he scanned their surroundings. If he were wise, he'd return her to her chamber and depart. 'Twas unwise to be alone with the lass, especially hidden in this private cove of trees and rock, more so when his feeling toward her was far from saintly.

And if her voice held only anger, maybe he could have. Mixed within the regret, he'd heard the wanting. A need that kindled his own.

She looked at him, her eyes a reflection of the grief and desire she worked so hard to shield. "It does not matter. It cannot."

"No, it cannot." But it did. Alexander gave into the recklessness of the moment, lowered his head and claimed her mouth. As her taste filled him, he could no longer deny the truth. He wanted her, with his every breath, with every passing second of the day. And he'd fought to bank his desire until he ached.

Until now.

He skimmed kisses over her face, savoring the taste of her skin, the silken smoothness that beckoned him.

"Alexander," she rasped, "we cannot continue. I—"

With confidence he deepened the kiss, her greedy acceptance betraying her words of denial. He combed his fingers through her auburn hair, then wrapped the strands around his hand to angle her head.

Her breathy moans had him laying her back against the soft bed of leaves and moss, but her passion-filled whimpers had him covering her body with his.

"You are beautiful," he murmured against her mouth. "Everything a man could ever want." He skimmed his hand along the curve of her neck, down the fluid angle of her supple body to slide over her breast.

Her eyes darkened. "Alexander, I . . ." She moaned as his fingers slipped beneath the soft linen to tease her nipple, arching against his hand as he stroked it to a hard peak.

"I want to taste you," he whispered.

She rolled her head back and forth. "I do not want, ca—cannot let you . . ." Her hands began to roam his chest in a furious desperation. "It would not be proper." She dragged his mouth back to hers.

The fervor of her response poured through him. Impatient to touch the cool silk of her skin, he caught the fabric near her neck and pulled it down. Her magnificent breasts spilled free. His body hardened to a tremendous ache. Alexander cupped his hand over one firm swell and leaned down to lave the tender flesh.

Nichola's eyes glazed with passion.

The dream of sliding into her willing warmth overrode his cautions, his regrets. Here. Now. The passion he no longer could deny would consume them both. And he would let it.

Would die without it.

Alexander teased her sensitized flesh, slow circles until her body began to shake. He caught her nipple into his mouth and suckled, her mews of pleasure urging him on.

"How you want me leaves me humbled," he murmured against her skin. Needing to touch her everywhere, to taste her, he laved a slow trail down the flat of her stomach, inhaling her woman's scent.

He moved his hand to her thigh. Her tender flesh quivered beneath his touch. If possible, he grew harder. However much he wished to strip her and drive deep into her, Alexander kept his pace slow. This time, her first time, he would make love to her with exquisite passion.

Alexander stroked her intimate place again, and Nichola cried out from the pleasure of his touch as his finger caressed her over and again, leaving her shaking, wanting, helpless but to let him take. And if this was a sin, at this moment, she couldn't sort out right from wrong.

With fractured movements, she caught the edge of her gown. She tugged it downward, needing to free herself from the cumbersome garment. Agile fingers helped her. In seconds, he tossed the garment to the side. Before she could draw in a breath, his mouth begun to feast on the other breast while his fingers slid across her dewy warmth.

Delicious waves of heat surged through her body. "Alexander." Her gasp echoed with wanton release, but she didn't care. All that mattered was that he was touching her, her body burning with an unstoppable need that only he could fulfill.

The pads of his fingers slid downward, along her thigh.

"Alexander," she whispered.

Cobalt eyes lifted to hers, hot, raw with sensual promise. "As my lady wishes." His fingers slid into her warmth. At her gasp of pleasure, he covered her mouth. With exquisite torture, he slowly began to move his fingers within her. He claimed her every cry, her body's trembles as a slow pressure began to build until it was if she'd burst.

He moved to her neck, his tongue doing magical things to her body, trampling the cautious part of her that is hesitant to allow such intimacy.

Alexander lifted his head, his gaze focused on her with a penetrating stare. "I am going to watch you as you are pleasured. Hear your scream as you fall over the edge." He increased the pace of his intimate caresses.

She twisted, her body's reactions beyond her control.

"And do you want me, lass? With how wet you are for me, I think you do."

She couldn't speak if her life depended on it. A predatory smile curved his mouth, like a wolf ready to devour its prey. And thankfully, she was his feast.

"That's a lass," he said as her mind tumbled in a frenzied state. Then his mouth, for the love of Mary, his mouth caught her nipple and began to suck, his tongue flicking over the sensitized bud mimicking his finger's action.

Steeped in him, his scent, his taste on her lips, her body began to tremble uncontrollably. Reckless, helpless, she now arched to meet each stroke of his hand, the sweet joining that beckoned with a promise of something grand.

Then the world began to slip away toward a wondrous ache. "Alexander!"

His fingers worked her with relentless fervor as

his greedy mouth continued to take, to miraculously destroy.

Her body quaked. A mind-numbing, sensual haze engulfed her mind as if on the precipice to something grand. "I—I—"

"The roebuck ran this way," a deep male voice yelled nearby.

Chapter Twelve

Sensitized beyond belief and shaking with unspent pressure pulsing through her body, Nichola pushed up on her elbows. The breeze scraped across her skin with a pleasurable ache. She turned toward the voice. "Someone is nearby!"

"Shhh," he whispered.

"I know my arrow hit the roebuck in the chest. Look around. It should be nearby," another man yelled, from farther away.

Embarrassed, she gazed to where Alexander's finger had stilled within her, the pressure inside her making her want to scream. Awareness of what they'd done, what she'd allowed him to do swamped her. Worse, even now, with shame washing through her, she wanted him.

Nichola pulled free of his imitate touch and tugged her gown against her body with shaky hands. "What if we are caught?"

"We will not be." Alexander cursed as he helped her don her gown. He surveyed the woods. "We will go to my chamber."

"No—I—this." She looked away. "It is wrong." However

much she wanted him, with her body aching for him to finish what he'd begun, she couldn't allow further intimacy between them.

He caught her chin in his hand with a tenderness that made her ache. "No, Nichola," he said, his eyes still storming with unspent passion. "We have but begun."

Ashamed, she tried to break free.

Alexander's hold remained gentle yet firm, his gaze relentless. "With you trembling from my touch, tell me you do not want me."

His deep, sensual voice sent another wave of desire rolling through her body.

He drew her palm up and stroked his tongue across the soft center; she shuddered in response. "Tell me."

"I cannot." But Mary help her, she wanted to. And to beg him to lay her down upon the leaf-strewn ground and finish what he'd begun, bringing her much needed relief.

The pulse at the base of his neck throbbed in an erratic beat. He remained still. A testament to his control. "I am sorry to leave your body aching with the wanting. It would not be how I would be choosing." A stick snapped nearby. He glared toward the sound, then he turned back to her. "For now we have no choice."

Heat crept up her face as he spoke with accuracy of her body's distress. Never had she experienced such turmoil, a sense of floating between some kind of a half heaven, half hell, with promises of something wondrous.

No, it wasn't wondrous, it was reprehensible. She'd almost given Alexander her virginity.

In the forest, footsteps crunching on leaves echoed closer.

Alexander cursed, took her hand, and began to

walk toward Lochshire Castle, saving her from the necessity of a response.

Unsure how to undo the intimacy she'd allowed, she remained silent. As much as she wanted him, her innocence would be given to the man she would one day marry. To the man she loved.

A shake of a thick-fir limb was her only warning before a man stepped out from behind the foliage in front of her. She almost screamed, then recognized Alexander's sinfully handsome brother, Duncan, carrying a bow.

He spotted them and halted. His brow raised. Then, a knowing smile blazed across Duncan's face.

Nichola's face grew warmer, the waves of desire still pulsing through dredging her guilt deeper.

Duncan winked at Alexander. "I see you are out on a hunt of your own."

"Leave us," Alexander ordered. Ice coated his words.

"At least allow me a slice of dignity and release me," she hissed.

His hold tightened.

"Duncan," a deep male voice called out. "Where in blazes are you?"

Mischief danced in Duncan's eyes. "Over here, Patrik. With Alexander."

"Alexander?" Brush rattled. A muted curse. Patrik stepped into the clearing. "What is Alexander . . ." His gaze landed on Nichola. He halted. Lines of anger ripped through his face. Cold. Hard. Edged with hatred.

Fear cut through her. She tensed.

Alexander drew her closer to his side, his body partially shielding her from his brothers.

Why was Patrik angry at her? From their brief interaction since her arrival, he'd addressed her with polite deference. Now he glared at her as if she were a rabid animal to be destroyed.

Ignorant of the silent battle between Alexander and Patrik, Duncan crossed his arms over his chest with a satisfied grin. "He was edgier than a wounded boar this morning. But understandably, his duties to care for his prisoner would challenge the stoutest man."

Patrik spread his legs in a warrior's stance, hazel eyes blazing with defiance. "Aye, it is a demanding task to seduce the enemy," he said, the quiet delivery in stark contrast to the cold attack.

"It would heed you and Duncan well to continue with the hunt," Alexander warned.

Patrik didn't budge. "It is a mistake to let this to go further. You are allowing your desire for the lass to cloud your judgment."

The scar on Alexander's jaw tightened. "My decisions are not yours to censure."

"When it comes to decisions that affect the rebels, it is," Patrik replied.

"Be gone," Alexander ordered.

"Who are you angry at?" Patrik pressed. "Me for watching over the rebels' concerns or yourself for losing your perspective of what is important?" He scanned the surrounding forest with contempt. "What? No personal maid to ensure propriety? Or . . . was propriety with the baron's sister ever your intent?"

The blood drained from Nichola's face. He all but called her a whore.

Alexander drew to his full height. "Apologize."

Patrik glared at her, his look of pure venom. "My lady, accept my deepest apologies for any disparaging remarks toward your person." Though given, fury resonated in his words. And insincerity.

Duncan strode between the two, his face taut. "Patrik,

it is a hunt we are on. Leave the lass to Alexander." He gave her an understanding wink.

Nichola silently thanked Duncan's lighthearted intervention. Both Alexander and Patrik visibly relaxed.

"Aye," Patrik finally said. "Let us be on our way." Without a word, he spun on his heel and stalked into the cover of the forest.

Lifting his bow to his side, Duncan ran after him. Twigs snapped as they disappeared back into the forest.

The last of the tension in Alexander's body fled, but Nichola couldn't stop from shaking. Alexander and Patrik had almost come to blows. Mayhap he was used to Patrik's temper, but it disturbed her. She sensed that whatever Patrik's reason, she'd earned a dangerous enemy this day.

Alexander turned to face her, his expression grim. "I apologize for Patrik's harsh words." He took her hand. "As I told you before, Patrik came to live with us after his family was killed. What I did not explain was that they were butchered by English troops. Though anger guides him, it does not forgive his rude behavior."

Shaken, she understood. Patrik would detest anyone English. Right or wrong, with his hate entrenched deep in his soul, he would see any affection shared between her and Alexander as tainted.

"It is past," she said, her words surprisingly calm. If only she believed that was true. Until she departed, she would avoid Patrik. A disturbing thought came to mind. At least Patrik was honest in his feelings toward her. How many within Lochshire Castle nourished the same hatred?

Alexander drew her into his embrace and cradled her body against his. She leaned into his warmth. "I would never allow my brother, nor any other to harm you."

"I know." But Alexander couldn't always be there to protect her. Her heart ached as she thought of leaving him, but she wasn't safe here. The sooner she left the better.

Slowly, embraced against his powerful frame, she relaxed. The soft chatter of the birds overhead threaded with the soft whisper of the wind.

Her body stirred with awareness, more so as his body was hardening against her softness. Nichola searched his face.

Desire flared in his eyes, a familiar look that singed her every nerve. She drowned beneath his blatant stare, overwhelmed with the need he made her feel.

With devastating slowness, he pressed a kiss upon her lips. The tenderness of his touch swept her into his heat. Her worries of moments before faded. She moaned as his tongue teased hers; dueled, tangled until she trembled. Heat stroked her body, flames of desire that burned her with its luxurious heat. It would be so easy to give herself to him now, but this wasn't her life. And never would be.

Still trembling from wanting him, she pulled away. "What we did before—I—"

"Do not."

"What, speak of what is proper?" she demanded, nerves backing her words. Nichola pressed forward, afraid if she didn't push him away, he would claim her mouth again. Afraid if he tried to make love, this time she wouldn't stop him.

"I cannot deny that I want you. I do, more than I would ever want to admit. But Patrik's words are those of truth. I am your enemy. What we did is forbidden."

His eyes narrowed.

Her heart pounded as he stared down at her. His sheer size alone guaranteed if he chose, he could take her.

As if a stranger, Alexander's face grew shuttered. He released her and stepped away from her. "It is time to return to the castle."

She watched Alexander struggle with his emotions, those in direct conflict to what duty demanded, but the coldness of his words after their passionate kiss still hurt. They'd almost made love. Yet, he seemed to be able to shut that out. If she could, she would do the same.

The soft pad of their footsteps echoed between them as they walked. But with every step they took, she sensed him pulling farther away.

A short while later, they reached the gatehouse. Nichola waited for him to guide her toward the keep and return her to her chamber. Instead, when they entered the courtyard, he halted and turned to her.

"You will be hungry."

She shook her head, too upset to eat. "No, I—"

"It is not a question." He led her to the kitchen where he procured a flask of wine and some bread and cheese. Alexander guided her up the tower to the wall walk. He halted before an embrasure overlooking the loch.

Wind cascaded through the narrowed slot, fresh with the scent of water. At the edge of the western sky, silvery tipped clouds slipped into view.

He broke off the end of a loaf of freshly baked bread and handed it to her.

Unsure of his motives, she hesitated to accept the fare. "Why have you brought me here?" Nerves quivered in her voice.

"Because, at the moment, you need a friend."

On a quiet exhale, she accepted the bread. Of all of the answers he might have given, she'd not expected this one.

A friend.

Alexander's loyalty was a trait to admire. His passion, zest for life, was an infectious mix, but building a friendship with him would be dangerous. To allow such a trust between them would only invite further heartache when she left.

Aching inside, she turned and let the wind brush against her face. "Why would you offer such when my stay here will be brief? It would be a mistake."

His gaze assessed her. "Why?"

"Given the fact of my abduction and that our countries are at war, do you believe such a bond could exist?" When she looked into his cobalt eyes and witnessed the sincerity there, she wanted the impossible.

"On the border, where upheaval is a common-day occurrence, the English and Scots have been claiming friendships for years." Alexander unsheathed his dagger and cut a wedge of cheese from the block in his hand. "Often, against the will of outraged family members, they pledge their love and wed."

Nichola stared at him, a wild hope building. She was aware of the border marriages, where one day you owned land in Scotland, the next, due to political upheaval and resultant sieges, the land's ownership shifted to England. Were his words an unspoken promise? Was he hinting that he wished to seek a martial union with her?

Her heart pounded as she considered what a life with him would mean. The days of hard work, the exhaustion at the end, unsure what the next day would bring. Heat rose in her as she imagined the nights making love with Alexander.

"What of my clouting you over the head?" she asked, fighting a bout of nerves.

A tinge of red crept up his cheeks. He shrugged. "You are resourceful."

The grudging respect in his voice left her further off balance. "Even if I or my brother agreed, your people would never accept me." Or you, she silently added. She took a small bite of bread and chewed.

"If I have learned nothing else in the time we have spent together," he said with quiet regard, "it is that you are not a coward."

Nichola leaned against the hewn stone and studied his face. She'd believed him angry on their return trip. Now she saw naught but determination. No, anger still existed, yet, for what ever his reason, he quelled it.

Even if she wanted, Nichola was unsure if she could give what he asked. "Friendship is not easy for me," she said, turning the conversation to a safer topic.

"All I am asking you to do is to try."

His request still confused her, but intrigued her as well. "Just friendship?"

Desire lingered in his eyes. "I am only a man."

Warmth slid through her like spiced wine, rich and sweet as their kiss. She released a shaky breath. There were so many reasons she should refuse. From the intimacy they'd shared this day, he wanted more than friendship. He wanted a lover.

Wisdom forbade her to accept his friendship, to dare such a foolish venture. But the quiet yearning of emptiness inside begged her to give him a chance.

"A truce," she finally offered. Nichola handed him the wine flask.

With a nod, Alexander accepted the sewn-leather bag and took a long drink. Unknown to her, friendship would tempt them both even more. She wanted him as well. If not for his brothers' interruption this morning, he and Nichola would have made love. Bedamned

Patrik's censure. His brother was wrong. Making love with Nichola would not sway his loyalties.

Even now, as he took in the soft curves of her body, his body burned with unspent energy, a hard ache that demanded he press her against the wall and bury himself into her slick heat; drive into her until he found his release. Her taste lingered on his tongue. From how she'd fallen apart at his mere touch; if uninterrupted, she would have welcomed him into her body.

So why had he offered her a bloody foolish thing like a friendship? Perhaps because as he'd stared down at her, he'd seen the loneliness, an emptiness recognized by one who had lived through the same hell. However torn he was by his own loyalties, she needed a friend. What she gave of herself would be of her own choice.

Except he intended to make the choosing easy.

The scrape of blades in mock battle below resounded through the warm day as they finished their fare. He remembered Seathan's challenge. With his body still taut with need, mayhap a hard practice would offer relief.

"It is time I took to the field." He wiped the last of the crumbs from his hands. "Seathan has offered up a match."

A shadow fell over her face. "I see."

She thought he would lock her within her chamber. If he was wise, he would. "You are welcome to come and watch." If his prowess lured her into his bed, then so be it.

Nichola nodded her agreement.

After returning the empty wine sack to the kitchen, he filled a goblet with wine and handed it to her. At her confused expression, he smiled.

"To present to the victor of the match."

"You are sure of yourself."

"I know my capabilities—and the skill of my opponent."

"Not to mention the breadth of your arrogance."

He motioned her forward. "Come."

With her at his side, Alexander entered the list surprised to find Duncan and Patrik sparring with each other in the center of the field, distanced from the other knights who honed their battle skills as well.

Patrik's anger had likely caused them to end their hunt early; now his brother sought to vent his anger in a spar.

A cold breeze swept past. Alexander glanced up. The skies were beginning to darken. "We will be having a storm this night."

Nichola lifted her gaze skyward. She shuddered.

"You are cold?"

"No, it is . . ." She fell silent, the concern in her expression easy to see. "It is naught."

Alexander watched her, curious as to what had happened to put such wariness in her eyes. She'd tell him eventually. The sounds of his brothers' banter had him looking toward where they sparred.

"It is a braggart's swing," Duncan teased Patrik as he dodged Patrik's sword.

"You sound like a fishwife with a loose tongue," Patrik replied, then charged.

Duncan laughed. He easily sidestepped his brother's attack, curled his blade in a small arc and caught his opponent's sword. Their blades locked, shuddering from the strength each man wielded.

Pride filled Alexander at his youngest brother's antics. A skilled swordsman, he was.

"Gwen is a fine lass," Duncan said with relish.

"Gwen?" Patrik's voice charged. "You keep your bloody hands off Gwen."

"Too late," Duncan said with a smug smile. "She is a feisty wench to grace any man's bed." When Patrik cursed, Duncan threw his opponent's blade back and mercilessly attacked, driving the older man back.

"Patrik should have learned by now," Alexander said.

"What is that?" Nichola asked.

"Not to fall for Duncan's teasing."

She turned up to him, a light blush staining her cheeks. "But he said . . ." She shook her head. "Never mind."

"Fear not," Alexander said, her innocence welcome when he'd experienced so much war. "Duncan's claims have a tendency to expand with the telling."

"That I believe."

"But his ploy is for a reason. Watch Patrik. See how every time Duncan mentions Gwen, Patrik grows angrier?"

"Yes."

"Duncan uses Patrik's anger to take his mind off their match."

"Which gives Duncan the edge," she said, her voice filled with understanding.

"Aye. It is best to learn your weakness so you can hone your strengths on the practice field. In battle, the error could cost you your life."

Blades scraped. Duncan maneuvered his sword with a lightning quick slice to bring the tip down upon Patrik's throat.

"Yield," Duncan demanded, his breath heaving, the glint of victory in his eyes.

Patrik muttered a curse.

"What was that?" Duncan demanded, his burr rich with arrogance.

"I said you won this bloody match." Patrik shoved the blade away from his neck. "And if I find you have had your hands on Gwen, I will flay your bloody arse."

Duncan raised a hand with mock innocence. "It is not my fault if my skills as a satisfying lover appeal to her."

"You have had your warning." Patrik turned. His gaze collided with Nichola's, and he halted. Anger flared in his eyes. He looked at Alexander. "I see you have made your way back home."

Alexander stretched his sword arm. "As you."

"Why is she here?"

Alexander gave her hand a reassuring squeeze. "She comes by her own choice."

"We need not English eyes prying about the castle." With a curse, Patrik stormed away.

Duncan removed his mail hood, then slid his padded coif back. Sweat lay in a sheen across his brow. He walked up to them ignoring his brother's upset; his blade secured and his helm shoved back as well.

"You have brought me wine for my victory, lass," Duncan said.

"It is for the winner of the match." When he reached for it, she moved the goblet from his reach.

Duncan stood a hand's length before her. "And have I not won the match?"

"Aye," she said. She hesitated, then straightened her shoulders, and Alexander's interest piqued. He recognized the signs of her taking a stand, and was proud she'd not let Patrik's anger subdue her. He remained silent, intrigued to see what her intent would be with his younger brother.

"You have won, but not a spar with Alexander," Nichola said. "The wine is for the victor of that challenge."

Practiced sadness curtained down his younger brother's face. "Lass," he said, his burr thick with the honeyed smoothness that Alexander had witnessed him using to seduce many a woman. "You have left me hurt by your shun."

"I doubt I have done but bruised your pride."

Warmth filled Alexander at her bravado. Though a prisoner, she refused to give into her fears and dared to stand up to his brother.

"Cede, Duncan," Alexander said. "The lass believes not your sweetened words."

Nichola turned toward Alexander, nerves lingering in her eyes, but a tingle of warmth as well.

His heart slammed against his chest as he watched her, wanting to take her to his chamber and finish what they'd started this day.

From the corner of his eye, Alexander caught Patrik returning. His brother's temper still smoldered, but 'twould seem he'd calmed.

"I came here to spar," Alexander said.

Patrik pulled his padded coif and mail hood into place, his sword in his hand. "I will have a round with you."

"I welcome such." Alexander withdrew his sword in a smooth sweep.

Patrik walked toward the open area of the practice field where he'd sparred with Duncan.

After securing his own gear, Alexander strode forward, the anticipation of the upcoming spar surging through him. When he reached the center of the clear space, he turned and lifted his sword.

Patrik raised his own. "I will not be giving you an advantage so you can be impressing the lass."

"I have no need to impress her," Alexander replied.

"No?" Patrik lunged forward.

Alexander swung his blade to intercept the blow. The blades clanged.

"You are bedding her," Patrik charged, then began to circle him like a rabid wolf who'd cornered its prey. "I saw her flushed face this day, that of a woman pleasured. And the looks you give her." He grunted with contempt. "Like those of a love sore fool."

He didn't love her. He cared, aye. But love? He couldn't allow such a decision into his life. Alexander attacked with a merciless bite. He let his blade convey his thoughts.

Patrik tried to evade his blow, but he wasn't quick enough.

Their swords clashed over and again until sweat poured down both their faces, their breaths labored, and a cacophony of striking steel raked through the air with a furious hiss.

At the next blow, Patrik deflected the hit, rotated, and thrust his sword upward in a quick slash.

Alexander fended off the attack. Barely. He caught Nichola's horrified expression, then focused back on his brother.

"Is she worth it," Patrik demanded as he wielded another fierce swing. Their swords met, shuddering from the strength of impact. Wildness gleamed in his eyes as he shoved Alexander back. "Is the bedding fine enough to make you forget she is English?"

"Leave it," he snarled. He evaded Patrik's next swing, but his brother surged forward, wielding his blade and forcing him to take a step back. Alexander stumbled.

Patrik took full advantage of his momentary weakness. He lunged forward in a punishing assault.

Alexander had no room to maneuver. In a last ditch effort, he repelled the next thrust, dropped, and rolled to the side before jumping to his feet. Only by the sheer surprise of his act did he escape Patrik's blade.

Madness glittered in Patrik's eyes as he drove forward.

"By God's eyes, Patrik, it is practice!" Alexander parried, swung, thrust, then dodged Patrik's blade, only to attack once again.

Patrik brought his weapon low.

He had to end it. Patrik's anger had stolen his rationality. He could not allow his brother to harm him, or himself by forcing Alexander's hand.

Alexander made his move. Twisting his sword, he caught Patrik's own and flung it to the side.

Patrik lost his balance.

Alexander jumped forward, slipped his foot against Patrik's legs and jerked them up, hard.

With a yelp, Patrik's arms flailed as he tumbled back onto the ground. Before he could scramble to his feet, Alexander stood over him, the tip of his blade pressed firmly against his throat as Duncan had held his own against Patrik's a short while before.

Nichola's sharp intake of breath from the side reached him. As did Duncan's calming words to her. "Yield," Alexander demanded, his breathing hard.

Patrik glared up at him. Slowly, the madness in his gaze faded. "I will yield," he said, "but I almost beat you because your mind is tangled with the English lass."

Alexander grunted, unconvinced. His brother had used Duncan's ploy to distract him during the fight. That he'd lost concentration during the spar at the mere mention of Nichola's name said how important she was becoming in his life.

But more worrying was how Patrik's temper had turned to madness during their fight. Until he'd pinned Patrik beneath his blade, Patrik had intended to do him harm.

All because of Patrik's hated of English blood.

He would speak with Seathan. Patrik would not escort Nichola home. Alexander removed his blade from his brother's throat, then extended his hand.

Patrik took it and allowed Alexander to help him to his feet.

"A good match," Seathan said as he walked up, garbed in mail, his sword still sheathed. "I saw the last of it. For a time, I thought Patrik was going to best you."

"His mind is on the Englishwoman," Patrik spat. "The fool has bedded the wench."

Seathan's gaze cut to Alexander, dark with reminder of their early-morning discussion. "The bedding of her is his decision and hers. For our reasons, she's only here for one purpose."

"I understand this," Alexander insisted.

"Here," Nichola said from behind, startling the brothers who had apparently forgotten her presence. Her cheeks were pale. Her hands trembled as she held the goblet of wine up to Alexander. The pleasure he'd planned to see on her face, the expectant delight, was crushed by her look of humiliation.

"Lady Nichola," Seathan said. "My apologies. Had I known of your presence, I would have held my tongue."

Duncan blushed.

God's teeth. He'd not meant for her to have overheard their discussion, or the references to her bedding. He took the goblet and drank deep, but the warm slide of wine tasted anything but celebratory. Alexander handed the cup back to her.

With stiff movements she accepted the vessel, and he cursed himself for allowing her this embarrassment.

"Lord Grey," a knight called from the distance.

They all turned toward a knight who hurried toward them, worry etched on his face.

Alexander recognized the man as one of Sir William Wallace's. His senses went on alert.

Seathan strode toward the man. When the knight halted before him, he asked, "What news do you bring?"

The knight gave a dismissive glance at the woman and turned to Seathan. "It is Sir William Wallace, my lord. He has been imprisoned at the Warden's dungeon in Ayr."

Wallace in an English dungeon? Alexander recognized his own grim feelings on the faces of his brothers. 'Twas unthinkable. If Wallace died, their entire rebellion could be at risk. Whatever the cost, they must free him.

Chapter Thirteen

The men gathered closer to the runner to learn the details of Wallace's capture. Overwhelmed by the anti-English furor of Alexander and his brothers, Nichola tried to step back.

Alexander caught her arm. "Stay."

She looked through the gatehouse at the forest. A few hours ago, she and Alexander had almost made love. But with the runner's news, he'd withdrawn as if they'd never kissed, never touched as lovers do. Now he stood before her as the cold, emotionless warrior she'd first met in her solar.

And she'd been recast as his enemy.

"How did it happen?" Seathan demanded.

"A young lad was being harassed by a steward in the streets of Ayr, my lord. Wallace defended the lad," the knight explained. "The confrontation turned into a brawl, and the steward ended up with Wallace's dagger plunged into his heart."

"And English troops surrounded him," Alexander finished.

Pride glowed in the knight's eyes. "Aye, they did, but several of the English bastards paid with their life."

An image of Wallace defending an innocent youth formed in her mind. Her English peers were quick to slander the Scottish rebels as a band of outlaws fit for nothing but death. But the stories she'd heard of the English troops' dishonorable actions and the decency she'd witnessed since being held within Lochshire Castle portrayed the Scots as a kinder people.

As Nichola gazed at the men, she couldn't help but respect them. They fought to hold their own, their acts of savagery wrought out of desperation to ensure Scotland remained free.

"We will have to break Wallace out," Patrik said, hatred in his voice.

Thunder rumbled, this time closer. Nichola glanced skyward. Angry black clouds swirled with the threat of rain. Not tonight, she silently pleaded. Her emotions were already fragile. After almost making love with Alexander this day, news of Wallace's capture, and Patrik's verbal attack, she doubted her ability to endure the storm's fury.

"They have set a trial date to sentence Wallace for the end of the month," the knight said.

"Patrik," Seathan ordered, "send out several runners to the surrounding lairds. There is to be a clan meeting in three nights at Lochshire Castle."

"Aye." Patrick strode toward the guardhouse.

"Duncan, send a runner to contact Wulfe and ask for his aid. Before the runner leaves, I will inform him on where Wulfe and I will meet."

Duncan nodded.

Seathan turned to Alexander. "Speak with the master-at-arms. Have him select his ten best men and ensure they are readied to travel within the sennight." His gaze slid toward Nichola. A frown darkened his brow. Then he turned to Alexander again. "Return her to her chamber."

Alexander cupped her elbow and Nichola shuddered. His cold expression assured her that Wallace's imprisonment would eliminate any leniency toward her. Believing Patrik's volatile comments this day reflected those of other rebels within Lochshire Castle, when the ransom didn't arrive, would they kill her?

Nichola prayed her brother could somehow scrape together her ransom. She paused. Was Griffin safe? Had he even learned of her abduction? Grief built in her throat as doubts lingered that her brother would care for her enough to try to gather the coin.

Through the years, she'd thought of her and Griffin as a family, had worked hard to keep the illusion alive. Compared to the uncompromising depths of loyalty interlaced between Alexander and his brothers, she and her brother didn't even have that.

How she wished to be a part of such a family, one that would stand behind her, whatever the cause.

Stunned, she paused. What was she thinking? They would never accept her, not that she would ever want such. But a part of her still, foolishly did.

And what of Patrik's quips of Alexander's bedding her during their spar? Though his words had not been meant for her ears, Alexander hadn't denied Patrik's charge. Why would he? Men reveled in their prowess. Alexander was no different.

Thunder again rumbled through the heavens. Nichola slowed. She didn't want to return to the chamber, to be locked inside when her emotions were shattered and a storm approached.

"What is wrong?" Alexander asked.

She glanced up at him. A mistake. Warrior's eyes watched her. The intimacies they'd shared in the forest seemed ages ago. The tenderness he'd shown her, lost. Except at the moment, missing her brother and agonizing over her desire, she hurt too much to care.

"Who is Wulfe?" she asked, to break the silence spilling between them as forbidding as the echo of thunder of the oncoming storm.

He studied her a long moment. "A lord who believes in and aids Scotland's cause."

She thought of Alexander's hesitation, then understood. "You mean an English lord?"

Alexander didn't reply. Why would he? If King Edward learned of the English lord's loyalty to the Scots, he would brand the man as a traitor.

They entered the keep, then headed up the spiral steps. A cold breeze swept past them with an eerie howl, tossing the flames of the torches about in an erratic dance.

She fought for calm.

"Nichola?" The concern in his tone tugged at her conscious, but she refused to look at him, to allow him to see her weakness. What was it he'd said of sword play? That a warrior used his opponent's weakness against him.

The bells of nones tolled the arrival of midday, their deep clangs overpowered by the rumble of thunder.

The morning had already faded? Her heart slammed against her chest. In hours, the day would be consumed by the night. Please let the storm have passed before then.

Another howl of wind surged down the stairway, cold and unwelcome. She focused on thoughts of her youth, of her mother's laughter, her father's intriguing tales of his travels.

But with every step toward her chamber, the walls

seemed to close in. Her chest tightened, her every breath a task unto itself.

Memories of being trapped while the bitter summer storm unleashed its fury overwhelmed her. Her vision blurred. Nausea swirled in her stomach. However much she wanted to keep Alexander ignorant of her fear, she couldn't allow him to lock her inside this night.

Nichola halted a foot from the entry to her chamber, the pain too close, the hurt too raw, the fear from her past too vivid.

"Do not lock me in," she gasped.

Through Alexander's troubled gaze, she saw the regret. Then determination thinned his mouth into a tight line. "It is for the best."

She pressed her hand against the wall and shook her head. "You do not understand—"

"Later, the servants will bring you food." Alexander caught her elbow and ushered her into the chamber.

She whirled to face him, her breaths shallow. "Do not leave me alone with the storm." She made to slip past him, but he blocked her exit.

"I have no choice."

He couldn't lock her in! "Leave the door unbarred." The desperation she fought to keep under control edged into her voice.

"No."

His refusal to listen spawned anger; she clung to the emotion, much safer than fear. "And your words hours ago of friendship? Did they mean naught?"

Alexander's brows narrowed. "Nichola—"

"No!" She stepped back into the chamber, cut by his denial of even a degree of trust. "You never wanted friendship, nor a truce. Admit it," she demanded. "It was only your interest in bedding me that motivated your appeal. A fact that became clear when you sparred with your brothers."

He had the grace to blush. "I am sorry for that. I had meant to clear up their misunderstanding."

She gave a harsh laugh, fear of the storm clouding her restraint. "Did you? And what time would have served you well in telling the truth, before or after the passing of the next moon? Or ever?"

The coldness of her charge left him scowling. "I am a man of my word," he stated, his voice as icy as hers.

"Mayhap, but right now, I am not sure what to believe. Especially from you."

Anger flashed in his eyes. "Believe what you want then." He turned on his heel to leave.

What was she doing arguing with him? She should have kept quiet, at least until she could have discussed the issue with a modicum of calm.

"Alexander!"

He crossed the threshold and shoved the door shut. The bar scraped into place with a hard bang. His footsteps faded away.

A shaft of lightning split the sky outside her window. Thunder shattered the heavens. She threw herself onto the door and pounded until her fists ached.

"Please come back!"

The reverberation of another blast of thunder rattled in reply.

Nichola turned, hugging herself, clinging to her fragile grip on sanity.

Through the open window, a blast of wind whipped into her chamber, cold and moist, pungent with the storm's fury. Beads strung from a thin line near the panes danced with a macabre jig. The skies continued to darken, and shadows within her room grew into menacing creatures of grotesque shapes.

Mary's will. She had to be strong.

Then came the rain. Hard. Merciless in its battering strength.

Caught by the storm's indignation, shaken by its intensity, she could only watch the torrential downpour. When the next bolt of lightning slashed across the sky, Nichola started. She stumbled across the room. Gripping the shutters one at a time, she shoved against the wind's strength.

They slammed closed.

Breathless, she turned and leaned back against the stone wall; cold, wet, and absolutely terrified. The tempest howled outside, while fear clawed in her chest. The nightmare of her past raged with mind-raping vividness.

Again she was the child traveling with her parents on that storm-filled summer night, en route to pay for Griffin's freedom. The covered cart had lost a wheel. Out of balance, and on the treacherous terrain, the cart had flipped over. In the jerky crash, the door had been ripped off and her mother had been tossed out into the storm. She and her father had remained inside, battered, but alive.

Except she had been trapped, helpless to move beneath the groan of broken wood. She'd cried out, in pain, fear, and desperation. Finally, her father had regained consciousness. He'd ripped the heaps of wood and baggage from her, then wrapped her in his cape. He'd bade her to remain inside and told her he had to find her mother. After crawling outside, he'd disappeared into the fierce lash of the storm.

As lightening had ravaged the blackened heavens

and the wind had howled around her, she'd remained there, waiting, watching for any sign of her father.

He'd never returned.

The next morning, hungry and desperate, she'd broken her promise to her father and had climbed outside. Splattered by sun-dried mud, their driver lay dead, his leg twisted in an unnatural position, her father and mother nowhere in sight.

Then she'd seen the nearby cliff.

With a yell of denial, she'd ran to the edge and found the bodies of those she loved sprawled far below. With her throat raw from tears, she'd gathered her father's thick cape, wrapped it around herself and followed the rutted path away from the accident in a shocked haze.

She'd finally stumbled upon a crofter's hut, but she'd barely felt the hands that had cared for her or heard their murmurs of concern. Then from somewhere in the murky mists of pain, Griffin had drawn her into his embrace. She'd broken down in his arms.

Days had passed in a convoluted succession. Her brother had tended to her, helped her heal from the tragedy she'd witnessed, from the horrific loss she'd suffered.

"Griffin," she whispered into the shuttered blackness, her hopeless whisper smothered by the crash of thunder. "Oh, God." She stumbled toward the bed.

Her gown caught. Then a loud rip sounded as the cloth tore, leaving her chemise exposed from the waist down. Nichola stared numbly at the torn fabric. As if a ruined gown mattered now? Cold and wet, she curled up on top of the linen bedding and stared into the storm-fractured blackness.

Sleep wouldn't come. For her, this night of reliving her own personal hell had just begun.

* * *

The following morning, Alexander opened his eyes and rubbed the sleep away. He stretched, wanting to remain in the welcoming warmth of his bed. After debating late into the night, he and his brothers had plotted out a way to free Wallace, which they would present to their clansmen.

Through the shutters, a dismal gray filled the sky amid the steady patter of rain. The storm had lasted through the night, raging like an angry woman. Somewhere, in the midst of the rumbles of thunder, he'd fallen into a deep, exhausted sleep. He'd witnessed rain like this before, the type that lasted for days soaking everything, including the spirits of those within the castle.

Nichola. He sat up, the distress on her face when he'd left her last night haunting him still. How many times had he damned himself for leaving her banging on the door and calling out his name? Then he remembered the last time he'd left her in such a manner, only to return to find her lost in a peaceful sleep.

That she'd not trusted him had set him on edge. Her accusation of him tricking her to sate his lust had pushed him to the edge. Time alone would do her good to release the anger she hoarded like an old woman would coin. And when she lay spent, she would find in the tangle of emotions, the truth.

She wanted him.

He needed no tricks to bring her to his bed. If his brothers' hadn't interrupted them yesterday morning within the forest, she would have already accepted such.

His body hardened at the thought of her lips, of his

hands skimming over her silken flesh. Of her moans as she'd soared toward her release.

"God's teeth!" Alexander shoved up from the bed. The coolness of the morning spread goose bumps over his nakedness. With a grimace he dragged on his trews, linen shirt, and tunic.

He left his chamber to break his fast, but at the turret he paused and stared up the steps. Alexander grimaced. What was he doing softening toward the lass. Wanting her in his bed was one thing, but this stirring in his heart was another. Didn't Wallace's abduction show him how much stood between them?

It bloody should.

With a ripe curse, Alexander started up the steps. He'd check on her. No more.

By the time he'd reached the door to her chamber, his mind had dredged up a myriad of questions. Would she be angry still? Or drugged by sleep, would she forgive their heated words of last night and accept him into her bed?

In his mind, he pictured her staring up at him, her eyes misted with sleep, caught up in a blend of innocence and need. With her stubbornness, Nichola wouldn't forgive so easily. The sensual vision shattered.

Alexander slid the bar from the door, then entered with caution. He half expected her to be hiding behind the door with a broken edge of a chair to bash upon his head.

Instead, she lay curled up in a tight ball on the bed, her face deathly pale. With her eyes glazed, she stared at the shuttered window.

Fear ripped through him. Alexander strode to her side and hunkered down next to her. "Nichola?" Her eyes never wavered, nor did she indicate she was aware of his presence.

What in God's name had happened last night? He glanced around. A tray of food the servant had brought the evening before lay untouched. Everything seemed in its normal place. Nichola's pleas not to leave him echoed in his mind. She'd been desperate, but he'd owed that to her being upset at being held prisoner.

He caught sight of her torn gown. Alexander closed his eyes, torn between fury and soul-wrenching regret. God's teeth, he didn't want to believe anyone within the castle walls would harm her. He knew these people, had grown up sharing their laughter and grief.

As much as he wished to be convinced otherwise, the scene before him claimed his fear real. Sometime during the night, a man had entered her room and raped her.

Swamped with guilt and aching for the brutality she'd endured, he drew her into a gentle embrace as one would a wounded child. "Nichola?"

A small whimper slipped from her, tormenting him, feeding his guilt, and leaving him to damn himself for the horrors the bloody miscreant had served upon her person. Damn him. He'd vowed to protect her. Whoever dared this outrage would die.

She shuddered, then another frantic whimper tumbled from her lips.

Right now, she was of the utmost importance. He would care for her. Later, he would serve pennance to whoever had dared touch the woman he wanted for his own.

Shaken, Alexander brushed his thumb in a soft caress against her alabaster cheek as he realized that however wrong, he had claimed her as such.

"I am so sorry," he whispered, the ache in his chest as painful as if crushed by a mace. He kissed her brow, needing to erase the nightmare she must have lived.

Blast it. She was a virgin. Her pain at the attacker's brutality must have been tremendous.

She trembled in his arms.

"Please forgive me," he whispered.

In answer she shifted her body closer against him, pressing her face against the curve of his neck.

He swallowed hard and smoothed the back of his fingers over her cheek, then curled them under her chin to gently lift her face to meet his.

Gray eyes wounded and filled with horror stared back at him.

Alexander's guilt grew twofold.

Her lips quivered, and all he could think of was erasing her pain, offering her a remembrance of something good. The vows he'd made of not touching her again or allowing himself to care fell away with total disregard.

She needed him.

And by God's eyes, he needed her as well.

As much as he wanted her, now was not the time to indulge in his desires. She needed him to offer comfort, and that he would give her.

"Who," he asked after a long while had passed, his quiet voice trembling with anger. "Tell me the bastard's name." And he would slay him with his bare hands.

Confusion slid through her eyes. "Name?"

He must be a fool. Of course she wouldn't know her attacker's name. She was a stranger to his home. "Describe the man who entered your chamber last night and dared force himself upon you."

A frown deepened across her brow. "The man?" Her question fell out in a rough tumble.

He wiped away the tear with his finger, and it pooled on his skin. "Do not be afraid, lass. Whatever threats he made are naught but an empty promise. He will not touch or harm you again. You have my word on that."

Nichola shook her head as if unsure.

"You have nothing to fear. I swear it."

"No," she said, her voice unsteady. She pulled away from him and sat up. "No man entered my chamber last night."

Alexander heard her words, but he didn't believe them. Whatever her reasoning, she wouldn't protect the bastard. Threat or no, by God she'd learn to trust him here and now.

"You will describe him."

At his demand, her eyes darkened with an almost haunting sadness, a lingering terror. "There was no one."

When she made to move farther away, he held her fast, his hold gentle. "Please, tell me."

She stared at him. On an unsteady breath, Nichola began to explain. At times she paused, at others her voice grew thick with emotion as she recounted the tragic nightmare of her parents' deaths, of her trapment, and of discovering their bodies twisted on the ground below the battered cliff.

As she continued, a budding trust he'd yearned for was plain to see.

"Since then, I have been terrified of thunderstorms," Nichola quietly confessed. "And locked inside this chamber with last night's storm—"

"You fell apart," he finished. And caught up in his own anger, he'd ignored her pleas. Now he understood her unease when they'd stayed overnight in the ruins of the church. Why from the start she'd rebelled against him when he'd imprisoned her within this room.

He rubbed his thumb over the soft swell of her palm. "I am sorry."

She shook her head. "You did not know."

He searched her face. "Why did you not tell me?"

"I tried, but you refused to listen . . ."

Her words fell away, but he understood. Her foolish, stubborn, pride hadn't allowed her to push the issue. "From now on your chamber will be left open."

Wariness crept into her expression. "You would do that?"

"Aye." For her, he was realizing, he would do most anything. And considering their situation, that wasn't good. He released her and stood. Was his desire for Nichola clouding his judgment as Patrik claimed? He couldn't be sure. To ease his doubts, he would have her promise. "First, I will have your vow not to run."

That after offering such warmth he would ask for her word hit Nichola like a slap to her face. "You would ask me to sacrifice my pride?" She watched Alexander pull back, not only physically, but emotionally as well.

Her skin tingled where his fingers had touched, the unspoken promises of his tenderness and caring all too clear. Except he would never allow his feelings to go that far.

Nichola hesitated, stunned at what she'd just divulged to Alexander. Whatever had happened between them, he was still her captor. If he saw fit, he could use her confession to destroy her. As if he needed physical torture to gain the upper hand. Yet, already her feelings toward him had exposed her to excruciating pain.

"Nichola?" He watched her, his caution too easy to read. "I will have you swear it."

Though softly spoken, she heard the underlying

command. She stood, her emotions still tainted from her traumatic events of last night, but no less fragile than what this man could do to her if he chose.

And God help her, he could never know the true power he wielded over her.

She remained silent.

Frustration darkened his face at her continued silence. "What I ask of you is simple."

"No, what you ask is for me to forsake my freedom. I will not barter for what is mine, for you or any man."

Alexander muttered something about stubbornness and a donkey's arse. "Your safety is—"

"My safety? This is not about my safety, but your pride and money. Of how it would damage your reputation if I escaped."

"A lie!"

"Is it? Then tell me, Alexander, explain what I seem to have missed? Are you or are you not ransoming me for coin, whilst sacrificing my reputation as well."

At his silence, pain wrapped around her heart. She stared at the shutters.

"Please leave," she said, her voice like stone. "If you find the need, bar the door on your way out." She met his gaze, the hurt immense. "I would rather you treat me as the prisoner I am than have you alternately comfort then shun me."

He stepped toward her and caught her shoulders.

Nichola froze. If he kissed her now, with her strength depleted from last night's upset, she was unsure if she could keep her resolve and not respond.

"Is that your way to solve problems with a woman?" she attacked, before his lips could settle upon hers, claim her as she secretly wished. "To seduce? Or maybe you gain a woman's cooperation with a smile and bolstered words?" When he hesitated, she plowed forward. "Is not that what the problem is now? Or has that always been the way you handle issues throughout your life—you take the risks, but after, you walk away with no emotions involved?"

When his eyes narrowed, she realized she'd hit the right angle, so she plunged recklessly ahead. "Except this time, I am still here, aren't I? Aren't I?" she demanded when he only glared at her. "Why do you not admit it? You are good at everything but the lasting. When it comes to requiring an emotional commitment for you to stay, you walk away."

She lifted her chin. "Lock the door behind you when you leave, because I for one am satisfied with my lot in life. Though I am a prisoner, once the ransom is paid, I will gain my freedom. But you, you will never achieve more than the smile you wear."

He released her, his cobalt eyes blackening like a tempest threatening to be unleashed.

Her heart slammed against her chest. *Mary's will.* She'd pushed him too far.

Chapter Fourteen

Alexander glared at Nichola. He wanted to deny her charge, but he couldn't. By the saints, how could she have pinned his motives so accurately when he hadn't even acknowledged them?

After his father's death, afraid of allowing another into his heart, he'd volunteered for the most dangerous assaults against the English; taunting death to take him, to pay for his sin of not dying on the battlefield that day so long ago.

When the blades from each battle were secured and the rain had cleansed the land of the blood of the dead and dying, he had hastened to the next challenge.

Never had he wanted to linger in one place.

Until now.

Until Nichola.

Anger flushed her cheeks as she watched him.

However much he wanted her to remain here, she would return to her home. Her people. Her family.

The anger at the confrontation faded. Loneliness burned his throat like charred wood. With his mind steeped in war, he'd believed himself immune from hurt. Now, a woman who should by all rights be his enemy, was tearing his life apart.

"Stay away from me," he growled, but inside he ached with the need to touch her, to hold her and whisper reassurances. As if he could offer her the "forever" a woman like her needed.

She remained silent.

Alexander turned on his heel and stalked from the room. He slammed the door, then glared at the wooden bar angled against the wall. She wanted trust, by God he'd give her this one freedom, but no more. Alexander strode toward the stairwell. Halfway there, he met Patrik.

"I missed you on the practice field." Patrik's eyes slid toward where Nichola's chamber lay unbarred, then narrowed.

"Not a word," Alexander warned. Aye, he had erred in almost making love with her, again in allowing her to become important to him when his entire focus should be on Scotland's freedom. But now his mind was clear.

Patrik turned and followed him into the turret. "We should receive the ransom any day," he said casually.

"A day you will raise your goblet in toast to." He damned the bitterness crawling through his voice.

"Whatever your feelings for her, she will not interfere with our cause. Once the ransom is paid, she will be returned."

At the warning edge to his brother's voice, Alexander halted. Fragments of torchlight from a nearby wall sconce highlighted Patrik's harsh expression.

"Do not threaten me."

"And do not forget the reason she is here."

Alexander drew up to his full height. "Dare you question my loyalties yet again?"

"Should I?"

Alexander's hand shot out and caught the collar of his tunic. "Were you not my brother, I would kill you for such a remark." He shoved him back, turned on his heel and stormed down the stairs.

The angry slap of Patrik's boots echoed in his wake as he hurried to catch up to him. "Alexander."

He ignored Patrik's fury, unsettled by a realization he should have thought of before. If Patrik saw Nichola as a threat, their close community would have seen Alexander's interest in her and believe the same.

By God's eyes!

He'd been nothing but noble to Scotland.

Soon the ransom would be paid and Nichola would be out of his life. A fact that would give her great pleasure.

He exited the keep, ignoring the sounds of Patrik's rage in his wake. He headed toward the atilliator's hut, desperately needing to lose himself in the exacting work of crafting crossbows. To not think of the empty days ahead of him.

He grimaced. He was acting like a love-sick fool, but falling in love with Nichola would be the ultimate betrayal to his father. Loving an Englishwoman went against everything he held holy, it violated the trust his family put in him to free Scotland from England's tyranny. No, he didn't love her, he wanted her in his bed.

"Alexander!" Patrik yelled from behind him. "Damn you, face me!"

He whirled, planting his feet in readiness for Patrik's attack. Aye, he welcomed a fight, anything that would release the unceasing torment and restore them to equal terms. Nichola's presence was not only dividing his loyalties, but causing strife between him and his brothers. With Edward's troops marching north, they couldn't risk any division.

His face raw with anger, Patrik stalked toward him.

"A rider approaches," the tower guard yelled.

He and Patrik froze. Muttering a curse, Alexander turned with his brother to look through the gatehouse entry. In the field across the loch, a distant figure rode at a rapid clip. As the rider galloped up the narrow road to the Lochshire Castle, Alexander noted that the man wore his brother's colors. Then he recognized the knight.

The lust for a fight drained away. He dropped his hands by his side. It was the runner they'd sent to retrieve Nichola's ransom. 'Twould seem his time with Nichola had indeed run out. This day, Nichola would have her wish. As would Patrik.

He shot his brother a withering glare.

Satisfaction settled within the angry lines on Patrik's face as he strode up to him. "The ransom has arrived."

And Nichola would depart.

Patrik's silent taunt echoed between them.

Alexander ached to wipe away the smug look on his brother's face. By God, after they'd almost come to fists over Nichola in the turret, whatever it took, he'd ensure 'twould not be Patrik escorting Nichola home.

Seathan's man rode under the gatehouse. The hoofbeats echoed off the curved stone like an executioner's drum.

With leaden steps, Alexander walked alongside Patrik toward the rider as he cantered into the courtyard. He noted Seathan and Duncan coming from the armory as well.

The runner pulled up his horse before Seathan.

"My lord." He dismounted, his breath heaving, his mount lathered.

A stable lad ran up and took his mount away.

Alexander and Patrik halted by their brothers' sides.

"You have brought the ransom?" Seathan asked as he reached for the leather pouch hanging from his mount.

"No, my lord." The runner shook his head. "The Baron of Monceaux—is dead."

"Dead?" The brothers said in unison.

Alexander glanced toward Seathan, but already his thoughts went to Nichola. The news would devastate her.

"How?" Seathan demanded.

"It is said he came to blows while out gaming." The messenger shook his head. "I could glean naught more without raising suspicion."

Anger clouded Seathan's face. "The details matter little. With the Baron of Monceaux dead, our plans for a ransom have come to naught."

Seathan's rough claim reached Nichola. Her brother was dead. The air around her spun, her body trembled. The world blackened, but she felt only pain. Hard. Hot. Ripping through her until she staggered back against the wall of the keep.

She sagged against the stone wall, fighting for sanity when everything in her life had eroded to chaos.

She stared at the men gathered before the runner. Upset from her discussion with Alexander, she'd sought to escape the confines of her chamber. But as she'd walked from the entrance to the keep, she hadn't anticipated the runner's arrival or his shocking news.

Griffin was dead.

The words clattered through her brain, robbing her of thought and tearing out her heart. Though their relationship had degraded over the past year, it hadn't diminished her love for him.

Now he was gone. Their last words heated. She hadn't even told him that she loved him.

"And what of the ransom?" Patrik demanded.

The ransom. As if that mattered now. At the moment she hurt too much to care. Or fear. Hadn't life already served its worst? What in God's name was left?

"She is the sole heir," Duncan argued, his confident words sliding somewhere through her haze of shattered disbelief.

"Aye," Seathan agreed. "We will not be denied the ransom."

"Her steward will be paying without delay," Patrik added.

A hysterical laugh welled in her throat, but it came out in a gut-wrenching sob. She crumbled to the stone steps. Then came the tears, hot, wet, and released with a savage pain that rose straight from her soul. She hugged her body and rocked herself, keening softly.

At Nichola's anguished cry, Alexander whirled and spotted her crumpled in a heap by the keep door. A sword's wrath, she'd heard of her brother's death!

"Alexander?" Seathan called as Alexander strode toward her.

Alexander gestured to Nichola, and Seathan nodded. He knelt before her and gathered her against his chest. "I am sorry," Alexander whispered, aching with the intensity of grief she must feel. He hadn't even known she was outside. If given the opportunity, he would have spared her learning about her brother's death in this harsh manner.

He glared at his brothers and shook his head when

they made to interfere with expressions ranging from disapproval to sympathy. He would see her through this loss. Let them think what they wanted. This had nothing to do about duty to country, but about caring—in the most basic of ways.

She struggled against his hold. "Let me go." But her demand stumbled out in a ragged whisper.

In reply, he made his way toward the quarried walls of the chapel. He ignored her feeble attempts to struggle free. Thickheaded she would always be, but right now, she needed him. Though she would fight him every step of the way, he would be there for her.

Inside the sacred building, he strode to a roughly hewn bench and sat down with her cradled in his arms. The flicker of candles surrounded them, the air rich with the scent of beeswax tinged with the hint of frankincense and myrrh. The flagstone floor lay swept and scattered with fresh rushes. Each symbol within the holy building offering a degree of hope to all who viewed them. He prayed that along with His presence, they'd bring her a degree of peace.

Alexander held her against him, feeling her each tremor, the wetness of her tears against his neck, and her long, keening cries as though ripped from her soul. He let her weep as tears misted in his eyes, understanding her sorrow too well.

"I am sorry, Nichola."

She gave a soft hiccup. "He is dead. I ca—cannot believe Griffin is dead." A shudder racked her body. A muffled sob spilled from her lips.

Then she drew back, her eyes wide, filled with tears and grief. "Ho—How?"

"In a fight," Alexander replied, omitting that the runner had informed them that the brawl and confrontation had erupted while her brother had been heavily drinking and gaming. She didn't need to know that. He would leave her with fond memories of her brother's bravery and pride, not of those of a drunkard.

She shifted on his lap as if to stand, but he held her firm. "Rest easy. It is time you would be needing."

She tried to push free, her hands unsteady upon his chest. "Let me go," she said when he didn't remove his hands.

"Nichola—"

"Release me!"

He stared down at the determination brimming along with the tears in her eyes. Would she always be this stubborn? Yes. And though it was another characteristic of hers that he didn't always agree with, it was a trait he understood. Alexander lowered his hand.

She stood and slowly turned, taking in her surroundings as if seeing them for the first time, her expression wary and wrung with pain. On a shuddered breath, her lower lip quivered, but she didn't cry. He watched her battle her tears as a warrior would fend off an oncoming assault. With stature. With pride.

And by her own choice—alone.

A muscle worked in his jaw. He was here for her if she would allow him to help. Could she not see that?

He stood, but she stepped back, her gesture clearly stating her wish for him to keep his distance. When he stepped closer, she hesitated before moving to the stand before the cross. On wobbly knees she knelt, then bowed her head, her whispered prayers, intermixed with sniffs and raw little cries that cut straight to his heart.

Time passed. Slow, thick with grief. The candles gutted; their flame wavering, then flickering out.

Alexander rose and relit new candles.

Yellow flames flickered to life, filling the chapel with

warmth. Nichola stood and turned to him, her eyes bright with tears, but her face dry and her expression humbled. Beneath that, determination simmered as well.

She lifted her chin in an arrogant tilt. "I am ready to return to my chamber."

"Let us go for a walk." Alexander held out his hand.

She stared at it, the slide of anger in her expression coming hard and fast. "It is because of you!"

"What?" he asked, her accusation throwing him off guard, not liking where this might be heading. "What is because of me?"

"This." She gestured around the church with unfurled contempt.

"Nichola, I—"

"Do not give me empty words." She took a step toward him. "If you had not abducted me things would have been different." She jerked in a desperate breath, the belief bright in her eyes. "And mayhap my brother would not be dead."

"I—"

"What?" she attacked. "Did not steal me from my home? Did not care whose life you threw into chaos? Or was it," she said stepping toward him, "that you did not care as long as the thrill of challenge remained. Now you have had your thrill—and my brother is dead. Tell me," she said as she took another step toward him. "Do you find excitement in that? And what now? You will have your money in the end and that is all you care about. Isn't it?"

"No," he said, his own anger coming fast. He caught her by the shoulders, hurting, wanting to comfort, to explain. Guilt stilled his tongue. He tried to soothe himself with the reminder that if not him, another of his brothers would have ridden to complete the abduction.

Would they have taken Nichola when Lord Monceaux was absent from his residence?

That he couldn't answer for sure.

And that doubt ate away at him until his mind churned with only regret. He gentled his hold. "I never meant you harm."

She gave a brittle laugh. "No? Though not your intent, you succeeded quite well."

"Nichola—"

"Have you not said enough?" She tried to move from his hold, but he held tight. "Let me go."

"I cannot." He caught her face gently in his hands. "Stay with me. We could handfast this day." The words fell out before he could stop them.

Her eyes widened in total disbelief.

"I can offer you a home and protection. You would never want," he quickly added. 'Twas easy to envision her within his life. There would be times of fury, but he would ensure the emotions always slid to passion. And there would be heat, that for which a saint would sell his soul.

Contempt clouded her face, shattering his visions of her in his future. "How dare you think I would remain here as your wife! The sight of you sickens me."

She tugged at her hand still held in his.

This time he let her go. "I am sorry." He was, more than he could ever express.

Nichola shook her head then opened her mouth as if to speak. With a cry, she bolted out the door and headed toward the keep.

Shattered, Alexander watched her run. What in God's name had he done?

Struggling against the tears, Nichola bolted across the courtyard, not wanting to believe Griffin was dead. Her chest ached, her body shook from exhaustion.

How dare Alexander ask her to be his wife! She couldn't remain here. Worse, wanting him, the security he offered, the tenderness of his touch compared to the emptiness she faced, for a moment she had almost accepted his offer.

Her pulse raced as she ran up the turret steps, then she broke into the sunlight of the wall walk. Nichola halted before the embrasure where she and Alexander had stood only a short while before.

The early-afternoon bell of none pealed. Nichola wrapped her arms across her chest in a protective gesture and stared at the pristine waters of the loch. Somewhere in her saddened haze, the bells of vespers filled the air, announcing that many hours had passed since her arrival on the wall walk. Surprised, she looked up and found the sun now hung low in the sky, shards of amber light mellowing into a soft gold as if to bid the day a final farewell.

She scanned the rugged landscape bathed in the golden light, feeling empty. Through the exhaustion, she couldn't deny the truth.

Mary help her, she loved Alexander.

Nichola hung her head, trying to catch her breath, to digest the feelings she would rather deny. What was she going to do now? With the differences between their countries, a union between them would never work. Even now he supported a rebellion that would most likely lead to war. And her home, situated on the unstable border, would most likely fall prey to the upcoming battles.

Home.

She'd almost forgotten the debts. Her brother's death wouldn't halt the creditors who would demand their due. For all practical purposes, she didn't have a home to return to. Yes, she would go back, to sell off the final pieces of value, but even then, would that be enough to pay off the debts?

Morbid humor rose swift and sharp. If after selling off the last family heirloom and she still hadn't settled her debts, she might be cast into the debtor's prison. Even knowing this, she remained resolute. If she managed to escape, she would ensure Griffin received a burial fitting of his station and welcome the opportunity to clear her family name.

In the distance, a hawk floated with effortless grace upon the current of wind, soaring over the dense forest, then out over the open waters. She wished for such freedom, to be able to leave her troubles behind.

Then she remembered her angry words to Alexander, her accusations that Griffin's death was somehow his fault. She cringed at the unfairness of her attack. If she'd learned nothing else from their time together, it was that Alexander was far from the undisciplined rogue she'd initially believed him to be. His actions were honorable.

She remembered the times on their journey when he'd threatened her. In the end, he'd punished her with naught but tenderness.

Though a warrior, he was a man of integrity, loyalty, and honor. The strong bond of love between him and his brothers was undeniable. The respect the men gave Alexander was unprecedented. Yes, he had abducted her, but his actions were driven by his loyalty to his country. He never meant to offer her personal harm or wish her subjected to such tragedy.

After learning of her brother's death, he'd not taken her to her chamber to leave her to struggle with her suffering alone; he'd understood in her time of grief, she would need the solace of the church. And when he'd asked her to wed, his offer of marriage was sincere.

Nichola splayed her hands over the cool, sturdy stone. She needed to apologize. Gathering her courage, she turned. And plowed headlong into a strong, warm chest.

Large hands caught her shoulders.

She fought to steady herself, expecting to see Alexander. Instead, she found herself gazing up into the tempered hazel eyes of Patrik.

Panic swamped her. So lost in her grief, she'd not considered the danger she'd placed herself in being alone.

He stared down at her, the coldness in his eyes leaving her further shaken. "I am sorry. It is hard to lose those you love."

She nodded, wanting only to distance herself from him. "Thank you." Nichola made to step from his embrace.

He held tight. "Alexander is not about?"

"No, he is . . ." She had no idea where he was. She'd fled the chapel hours ago only wanting escape.

A frown marred his brow. "It is not good for you to be out alone. Although my brothers and I tolerate your presence, I cannot vouch for some of the Scots within Lochshire Castle."

Though his words were softly delivered, she understood the underlying threat. She would agree, at the moment, she definitely didn't feel safe.

"I should be returning to my chamber," she said, fighting to keep her voice calm, not wanting him aware of how his mere presence terrified her.

"I will escort you." He released her shoulders, only to cup her elbow, his grip assuring her he would not take no for an answer.

So she allowed him to lead her to the turret and down the inky, torch-lit steps. Halfway down, his grip on her tightened. The premonition of him shoving her off balance to tumble down the rest of the way made her miss the next step. A scream wrapped in her throat.

Footsteps echoed from below. A guard rounded the corner.

Patrik's other hand caught her shoulder as she started to fall.

"Sir Patrik, my lady," the guard said as he passed.

"Are you well, my lady? You almost fell," Patrik asked with maniacal politeness.

Her heart slammed against her chest. He'd almost killed her. Would have if not interrupted by the guard. "I . . ."

"You need to rest," Patrik said, saving her from a response.

Yes, it was one thing she desperately agreed upon. At the bottom, they walked out into the afternoon sunlight. Relief poured through her.

"What is wrong, my lady? You look terrified." He hesitated, a sly look seeping onto his face. "Pray it is not of me." Malice threaded his calm assurance. "I would seek naught but your safety. For it seems that you are the woman who has caught my brother's eye."

He knew he terrified her, savored her fear. "Alexander is a man with his own mind," she said, holding back her cry for help. "I would be deluding myself to think that your brother's eye is not caught by a comely woman on a routine basis."

"But never before has he treated a woman the way he does you. Or consort with the enemy."

People milled nearby, the day bright and warm with cheer. Inside, her body chilled.

"But the situation does not provide what it appears that Alexander would seek."

Caught off guard, she gasped. "You know of Alexander's request for my hand?"

His hazel eyes darkened to black. "Has he?" Fury backed his words.

"You did not know?"

He started forward with his hand upon her arm. "It is time you returned to your chamber. There is much to be done."

A shudder ripped through Nichola. She stole a glance toward Patrik, who seemed lost in his own thoughts. Mary's will, what had she done?

Chapter Fifteen

"All is well." The guard's call from the wall walk announcing that the keep was secure echoed faintly through the corridor.

Through an open window, Nichola glanced out to where the moon had eased into the sky, its silver light streaming across the loch with an iridescent glow.

A lover's moon.

A fierce ache tightened around her chest. Life had taught her to be wary of men. Even having abducted her, Alexander had shown her time and again that he was a man she could count one. Could love. But how did one accept loving a man who should be by all rights her enemy?

At this moment, with grief crowding her mind, she was unsure of anything.

Though late, she couldn't sleep. If she remained in bed, she would only relive her grief. And she needed to apologize to Alexander for her unwarranted attack on him in the chapel.

Nichola stared down the passageway to the door where a servant, earlier this night, had told her Alexander's room lay. When she'd tried to find him earlier this evening, she'd been surprised to learn he'd left the castle. She'd not pressed as to where, but had returned to her chamber.

With the overly late hour, he would be abed. Once she'd apologized, she would leave. She hesitated, an unwanted thought creeping into her mind. What if he wasn't in his room?

Or worse, what if he was with another woman?

She braced herself, unsure if after learning of her brother's death, she could accept another emotional blow. *Please, God, if he has returned to the castle, let him be alone.*

As she reached his door, the bells of matins announced the hour after midnight. Gathering her courage, she took a deep breath and knocked.

Silence answered, invaded only by the soft scuff of the night breeze.

She touched the pendant around her neck. Perhaps she hadn't knocked loud enough? Mary's will, what if Patrik found her outside Alexander's chamber? Mayhap she should sneak back up to her room where she would be safe. But if she didn't speak with Alexander this night, with the news of Wallace and the rebels upset, she was unsure when she would see him again. Her decision made, she knocked again.

At the insistent rap on his door, Alexander turned from where he stood before the hearth. He glared at the door. The thought of it being the servant wench he'd bedded before he'd ever met Nichola left him empty. He did not want another woman. He wanted Nichola.

Except she didn't want him.

Since she'd fled the chapel, he'd kept his distance from her. She was right. His decision to abduct her might well have cost her brother his life.

Another knock sounded.

He stalked to the door, aware that if the situation were of grave urgency, one of his brothers would have burst within his chamber to deliver the news. Whoever dared interrupt him would soon regret their coming.

With a curse he jerked open the door, prepared to flay the simpleton who dared disrupt his solitude.

Dressed in a long, wheat-colored robe, her auburn hair unbound and cascading down her back, Nichola stood but inches away. A taper was in her hand illuminating her pale face, how her body slightly trembled and her wide, gray eyes staring up at him, unsure.

The string of oaths readied on his lips fell away. His blood heated as the robe hinted at curves he'd touched, the opaque material inviting his imagination to fill in what he couldn't see.

He steadied himself. There could be many reasons she would come to him in the night, but after her charge this day, he doubted making love with him would be the foremost event on her mind.

With her belief he was responsible in part for her brother's death, mayhap he should search her for a dagger. It would not surprise him if she'd come to carve out his heart. Except from her fragile expression, she needed not a weapon to destroy him.

"You should not be here," Alexander said, wanting her nowhere else.

"I . . ." She glanced down the hall then back to him, her desperation and hurt carved in her expression.

"Go back to your room," he said, his voice harsh. He didn't need her here, with her emotions too easy for him to read, and with him wanting her with his every breath.

She angled her chin in a stubborn tilt that made

him insane to have her. "I will. After I have said what I came to say."

For his own sanity, he should have shut the door in her face then. With her close enough to touch and her scent filling his every breath, one of them needed an ounce of common sense. Except even with her stubborn pride guiding her every movement, she appeared as if she would break. God help him. Alexander opened the door wider.

She glided her tongue over her lower lip with a nervous slide. Then she entered.

Alexander's grip on the door tightened, unsure if he should close it or leave it open to prevent him from doing something foolish like kiss her. Bedamned. He wasn't an untried lad. They would talk. He would keep his distance. Once whatever matters she'd come for were settled, she would leave. He closed the door behind her with a soft but firm snap.

Nichola turned to face him.

With the candlelight flickering over her, he could make out her stance, tall and proud, her full lips quivering, and her gaze blurred by pain. When she held out her hand to him, his defenses shattered.

Damning himself, Alexander crossed to her and drew her into his arms. He held her as she trembled.

"I am sorry," he whispered and kissed her brow.

"It is not your fault." She lifted her head, her eyes watching him with sincere trust, an expression he'd never expected to see. Especially now.

"Nichola—"

"No," she said, her breath warm against his neck. "I was wrong to accuse you of my brother's death." She inhaled deeply, the cost of her apology easy to read. "I was angry and I am sorry."

As was he. He cupped her chin with his hands. "If I had known . . ."

"How could you have? We have no control over one's fate."

"No, we do not." If he hadn't been convinced of that before, as he stared at her, grieving her loss, he would be assured of fate's might. He stared at Nichola, her apology laying siege to the reasons he should leave her untouched. Her lower lip wavered, drawing his gaze. He remembered her taste, soft, warm, and destroying. His body hardened.

She raised her mouth to his.

He ached to taste her again. On a groan he gave into his need and claimed her mouth in a gentle kiss; slow, easy, wanting only to reassure Nichola he never meant her any harm.

Her immediate response ignited a fire all its own. When her hands reached up to wrap around his neck and draw him closer, he sank into the kiss as a dying man would seize a drink of water.

Alexander tangled his fingers in her hair. A soft, needy moan spilled from her mouth and the last of his control faded. His hands turned greedy, sliding down the silky skin of her neck, delighting in the feel and at her tremors with his every touch. His body throbbed as his hands skimmed across her skin to push away her robe and expose her chemise. In the candlelight, her soft swells translucent beneath her linen shift jutting proudly before him.

He lowered his head and devoured. He swirled his tongue around the hardening bud, the thin veil of cloth only heightening his desire.

On a whimper, she arched against him. "Alexander."

Her sultry demand whispered through him. He suckled harder, sliding his hand to cup her other breast. She shivered against his intimate touch, and he glided his thumb in a teasing circle over her dusky tip.

Needing to see all of her, he caught the soft material and pushed her robe free. It dropped to the floor with a gentle swish. She stood before him, half exposed, the thin-linen shift beneath translucent in the flicker of firelight, where he'd laved her breasts damp and glistening for his return.

He froze. What was he doing? His body shook as he pulled himself away, his breathing ragged. "Nichola—"

"Make love with me, Alexander. Make me forget this day." She pushed aside her linen shift until it, too, swirled to lay atop her robe. Naked, she stood before him, full breasts gleaming in the candlelight, the dark, auburn triangle at her apex tempting him into delightful insanity.

His hand automatically reached for her, wanting to hold the weight of her breasts, touch the sweet softness that he would never tire of. As if burned, he turned away.

"Alexander?"

He clenched his teeth, fighting the urge to lay her on his bed and drive deep within her body.

Nichola's hand touched his shoulder.

He rounded on her. "I want you, but not this way." Damn this entire situation. Alexander reached down and grabbed her gown and robe. He shoved them in her hands. "Put them on."

She stared at him with disbelief, her lips parted, slick with his kisses.

Fighting to steady his warring emotions, he cupped his hands over hers. "As much as I want you, it will not be as a balm for a loss."

Her eyes narrowed. "Is this what you think my reason is?"

"Yes," Alexander replied, speaking the single hardest word he'd ever said in his life. He wanted her, but if he took her now, he would use her sorrow to suit his own purpose. And he could never do that. Though he hadn't always made the right decisions in life, he would here. "When we make love, you will do so with a clear mind."

"I know what I am—"

"I can see your pain, the grief you wear like a badge. A grief you do not trust to share with me." And that hurt the most. "Yet you ask for an intimacy as great. I may want you, but I will not take advantage of your vulnerability."

Nichola glared at Alexander, unsure if she felt more like a fool or humiliated. Damn him! He was wrong. True, the loss of her brother had left her devastated, but she loved Alexander and needed him as well. Couldn't he see that? Would she be here offering herself to him if she felt otherwise?

"If I wanted someone to take advantage of me," she charged, "I could have found many willing men below."

His eyes narrowed to a dangerous edge.

Good. If he was upset, more the better. They would be on equal ground. "Instead, I am here." She softened her voice, needing him to understand. "It is you I want." His skeptical gaze extinguished her desire. No, obviously he would never believe what she had to say this night.

Her body burned where he'd touched her, ached where he had not. Resisting the urge to scream her frustration, she jerked on her chemise. The fabric tore at her rough handling, but she ignored it. Then she tossed on her robe.

"You do not know what I am feeling." But he would.

Nichola stormed from the room. She'd thought when she went to apologize that she'd make a deranged part of her world right. Instead, it seemed she'd somehow misjudged that as well. Next time, he would have no doubts of her claim.

And there would be a next time.

On the practice field, Alexander lifted his blade. Sweat rolled down his face as he surged forward in his attack. His pent-up frustration over the past two days since Nichola had swept from his chamber backed the bite of his blade.

Aye, she'd not kept from his sight as he would have wished. Instead, she seemed determined that wherever he turned, he'd see her. And he'd noted the undaunted determination on her face, and her desire.

Except, he'd convinced himself that to take her now would be wrong. She only sought comfort. He swung his next blow with the force of his frustration.

"Certes!" Duncan twisted to the side and barely evaded the blow. He took another step back in the training field and angled his blade to deflect Alexander's next swing. "You are fighting like a milk-fed maid."

Alexander ignored his taunts, jibes his youngest brother used to sidetrack his focus. He thrust his sword forward then angled the blade to catch the hilt of his brother's broadsword.

Metal scraped. With a quick jerk, he cast Duncan's weapon from his hands.

Duncan's stunned expression as he stood defenseless before him almost made Alexander laugh. Almost. If not torn between his loyalty toward the rebels and his need for Nichola, he would have enjoyed the moment. Instead, Alexander sheathed his sword, his heart aching.

"I have had enough for the day." Alexander ignored Duncan's curiosity at his curt comment, and Patrik and Seathan's concerned stares as they stood nearby. Let them think what they'd like. With the runner sent back to Rothfield Castle to collect the ransom demand for Nichola, he'd been given but a few days reprieve from her inevitable departure. And the money would come of that he had no doubt.

Then she would leave.

He turned to find Nichola waiting on the boundaries of the practice field. God's teeth, did the lass have a wish to drive him insane? Mayhap he should leave her barred within her chamber? It would serve them both well. But when she'd asked him to allow her to accompany him to his practice, he'd agreed.

Alexander strode to her.

"Congratulations, you fought well." She lifted the goblet to him. Late-morning sun glittered off of the bloodred wine.

Their eyes clashed. He remembered when he'd first envisioned the pleasure of her doing such a task. Now her gesture brought only regret.

"My thanks." He downed the wine in one gulp and tried to ignore her watching him drink, every swallow forced. He handed her back the empty goblet, welcoming the sharp bite of the spiced wine down his throat. "I will return you back to your chamber. I doubt you want to remain outside."

And he wished her to be removed from his view. With his body aching with a need to touch her, remembering her woman's taste warm upon his tongue and the softness of her skin, he needn't linger. With her watching him with blatant desire, 'twould be too easy to forget his reasons for leaving her untouched.

To his relief, she nodded. He ignored Patrik's displeasure as he walked with her. In silence they made their way through the floor of the keep, up the curved steps, until they reached the tower chamber. He opened the door and stepped aside to allow her to enter.

Instead of walking past, she turned to him. "I would ask you to stay."

Her throaty whisper ripped through him, the desire in her eyes destroying him further. God's teeth, he'd kept his hands off her the last two days. It had not been easy, and he was far from a saint. Couldn't she see that he was tired? That he wanted her? That what she was asking of him never could be? Once the passion between them faded, he would always be a reminder of her brother's death.

She reached out to touch him. "Alexander?"

"Do not," he said through gritted teeth.

Instead, Nichola stepped closer, alluring, stubborn, everything he wanted in a woman, and more. "You said you wanted me."

His blood heated, but he remained still. She continued to hurt over the loss of her brother.

She laid her palm against the side of his cheek, trailing down to his mouth. Her index finger swept across his lips. "What if I told you that I loved you?"

The thrill of her words rushed through him a split second before the panic. He caught her hand and drew it away. "You do not need—"

"I need you," she said. "You have kept yourself at a distance. Now you toss my words of love back as if they were easily given." She stepped closer and pressed her body flush against his. "Damn you, Alexander, I love you and need you as well." She jerked her hand free and stepped back. "But I will not beg. If you do not want me, tell me now."

He stood there with his heart in his throat, wanting her with his every breath.

Gray eyes glinted with determination. "Tell me!"

And at this moment, with his feelings for her running deeper than he'd ever meant them to, he could deny her nothing. But in all honesty, he would give her this one last chance.

"My taking you with your heart still fragile from your brother's death would not be fair."

"Fair?" She stiffened. "At what moment does life decide to be impartial?"

"I only meant to spare you more pain."

She laid her hand over her heart. "The pain is here," she whispered. "There is naught more you can do."

"I am sorry for that."

Nichola dropped her hand to her side. "I know. But it is you I need, do you not understand? Make love with me, Alexander. Hold me as if you never mean to let me go." When he hesitated, wanting her with his every breath, she shook her head. "I will not ask again. If you will not accept what it is that I am asking, what I am offering, then I am a lackwit to beg. And Mary help me, never will a man play me for a fool again."

With her heart-felt request, his every good intent to leave her untouched eroded. Taking her hand in his, he led her into her chamber and shut the door.

He turned her toward him. "What you make me feel, want . . ." He stroked his fingers through her silken hair as the full impact of his passion flowed through him. "I promise you, that what I will make you feel will only be good."

"I am not afraid. Touch me, Alexander. I need to feel you against me. In me."

On a groan he took her mouth, hot and hard, her immediate response making him harder. As the late-afternoon sun poured through the window like a river of gold, her taste swept through him, seeping through every pore until there was only him, only her. He promised himself, in this decision she would never find regret.

Nichola tumbled into his seductive heat, drowning in sensation, shaken by the tenderness of his touch, of how he could savor and ravage her mouth so completely. Alexander's hands skimmed along the sensitive curve of her nape, slow, wondrous circles that stole her every thought. She gasped at the sensations, at the sheer impact of the feelings that rushed through her.

The warmth of his breath feathered across her neck as he trailed kisses along the slender column. "I am going to make love with you in the ways I have always dreamt."

He discarded the chain belt around her waist; it clinked on the floor, forgotten. Then he nibbled across her lower lip, sliding his tongue to meet hers as his fingers loosened her gown.

Anxious for his touch, she reached up to help him.

He caught her fingers, his own cupping them in a gentle embrace. "No," he said with infinite tenderness. "Our first time, allow me." He released her. Alexander's gaze held hers as he untied the final draw, then slid her gown from her shoulders. He pushed away her chemise to leave her naked before him.

She shuddered, but it wasn't from the cold. As his eyes trailed down her, the heat that churned in them left her with no doubt of his desire. Hot. Wanting. Intense.

"You are beautiful." He clasped his hands behind

her neck and drew her to him. With devastating reverence, he lowered his mouth upon hers. "Your love is the greatest gift a man could ever ask for."

He lifted her in his arms and crossed the room. Gently, he lay her upon her bed. Then he kissed her, not with the fierceness she'd expected, but with a gentleness she couldn't have imagined, until her mind spun and she could do naught but give.

When she thought she couldn't feel more, his fingers began their erotic exploration, skimming down her arms, caressing the soft dips and angles of her skin. Then he linked his fingers with hers and drew her hands up to his mouth. He kissed each fingertip, before pressing his lips against each palm, his tongue swirling along the sensitive center.

A tremor stole through her body as he kissed along the curved base. Then he took her index finger into his mouth and gently sucked.

"Alexander, I . . ." She moaned.

He released her finger to kiss the tip. "You are an amazing woman. Never doubt that."

She shook her head, emotion choking her. "Never."

He smiled and laid her hands back over her head in a gentle hold. He feathered kisses against her neck as he slowly moved down her body, his tongue and teeth never giving her leave. He laved the curves of her breast, tasting, touching, teasing until she cried out from the sheer pleasure of it.

Then he claimed her nipple with his mouth and feasted. Waves of emotion streaked through her over and again. She twisted, arched, but the pressure continued to build inside her. A shudder ripped through her. Then another.

"Alexander!"

He murmured his satisfaction as he continued his

sweet torture, his tongue relentless in its task. As she gasped for control, his hand moved down to cup her womanhood. Nichola soared higher.

"Open for me," he whispered as he again drew the tip of her breast into his mouth.

Without hesitation, she complied.

His finger slid into her slick warmth. Her mind exploded with sensations. Lost to the dizzying rush, to the sense of speeding up an emotional cliff on a desperate race, she gave him everything he asked for and more.

As he continued to stroke her, Nichola opened for him like rose petals spreading out to capture the sun. Alexander watched her body melt beneath his every touch, her mews of pleasure driving his own need to a frenzied height. He held back. This time, her first time, would be for her.

Her body began to convulse. "Alexander!"

And with her every gasp tangled with sheer pleasure, he watched as she tumbled over the edge. Her body trembling, lost in the fervent trembles of release, she sagged against him. He pressed soft kisses over her face and wished for forever with her.

Stunned by the thought, he steadied himself. It was a foolish wish, that of an innocent lad, that of a man whose focus was on more than war.

She stared up at him with guileless fascination. "I never knew it could be so beautiful."

He brushed a lock of hair behind her ear, shaken by the feelings she invoked, and by the sincerity of his wish to keep her here. "There is so much more that I want to show you, to teach you."

Sadness clouded in her eyes. "There will not be time—"

Alexander pressed a finger over her lips. "For now, what we feel, give one another, is all that matters."

"But what of—"

"Trust me." Even as he said the words, what exactly was he promising? Or could offer? Already the messenger demanding her ransom was en route to Rothfield Castle. Once the money was received, if asked again, would she stay and be his wife? If she agreed, with him riding to attack English soldiers—her own people—if anything should happen to him, would he want her on Scottish soil?

Then she nodded, the trust in her gaze pressing him to follow through. Yes, they would talk, but not with her body warm from her release, they would not pursue the topic further this night. They would discuss any decisions as to their future tomorrow.

She shivered. Then as if remembering her nakedness, in the dimming light, a blush fell over her face.

"No." Alexander caught her hand when she made to cover herself. "Never be embarrassed. You are beautiful."

"You truly think so?"

He saw the doubt. God's teeth. She didn't even know of her own beauty. It would seem she'd humble him on every level. "Aye."

Pleasure wove through her eyes. "I wish to see you as well."

He took her hands in his and brought them down against the flat of his stomach and wished her hands lower. "I would be liking that."

She hesitated.

He arched a brow, intrigued she would choose this moment to show reluctance. "You are not a coward now are you?" At his light teasing, she bristled with the spirit he loved so well.

She lifted her chin. With nervous but determined

movements, she caught the edge of his tunic and
lifted it over his head.

"You are not helping?" she said as she dropped the
finely woven linen to the floor.

He laughed. "Is the lady who bashed me over the
head with a limb asking for assistance?" he asked, positive his concept of aid and hers were far from the
same.

A smile tugged at her mouth. "You would enjoy
this."

"Every moment." He chuckled. Before she had an
idea as to his erotic siege, he knelt before her, cupped
her womanhood in his hands, and drew her to his
mouth for the sweetest kiss.

"Mary's will!" She tried to squirm back. "Alexander . . .
I . . ."

His only reply was to curve one hand around to the
small of her back and press his advantage while he slid
the finger from his other hand into her slick heat.

On a moan, her hands caught his shoulders as her
body trembled against him, but he persevered, flicking his tongue along the silken folds to taste her
essence, loving her untrained response, pure and
needy—for him.

Her movements became frantic. Now when he slid
his finger into her heat again, she arched to meet his
every stroke; then he released her. At her expression
of wanton disbelief, he smiled.

With his eyes on her and his body throbbing to be
inside her, he stood. Slowly, watching her, he removed
the remainder of his garments.

Standing there still trembling from his intimate
touch, Nichola watched him disrobe until the evidence of his desire jutted proudly before her. She
glanced up nervously at him.

"You are . . ." Mary's will, he would break her apart.

"You are ready for me," he said, his voice far more convinced than she felt. "It will hurt only the first time. After that, you will experience only pleasure."

She had her own doubts. How could he believe she could take his entire length inside her? "This is not going to work."

His eyes lit with intrigue, then laughter. "It is a challenge you are making it, lass." He swept her up in his arms, his rippling muscles against her doing little to ease her fears. He gently laid her on the bed.

She frowned, but caught her breath as he gently parted her legs wider. His hot gaze devoured her as he skimmed his fingers up her thigh.

"I am not a challenge," she said between gasps.

"Aye, on every level. And you are a gift, Nichola, one I will always cherish." Then he slid his finger inside.

And she soared. She'd thought that after the last time she couldn't feel anymore, but under his skilled hands her nerves fled. On his next stroke, her doubts diminished in a blazing inferno.

When Alexander positioned himself above her, she hesitated, but as he worked his hands over her body, his touch stripped her of her last fears. Then he eased within her, watching her, his eyes hot with passion.

She'd expected discomfort, but instead, his presence within her ignited a new urgency. He stilled within her dewed entrance and began pressing kisses on the curve of her breast, nibbling until heat kindled inside her. Needing all of him, she pressed against him.

At her boldness, he slid deeper inside her, just a degree only to pull out again. He continued to move, again the pressure began to build inside her. With his next stroke, needing relief, she drove her body up to meet his. He penetrated her inner shield and sheathed himself fully inside her; a sharp pain lanced through her.

He laid still, his breaths ragged. "I am sorry for that. It will never hurt again."

She shook her head and smiled, her body already adjusting to his size. "I feel naught but love."

He groaned, claiming her mouth in a heated kiss and began to move within her.

Nichola basked in his every stroke, amazed by what his every touch made her feel. When his fingers slid down to intimately caress her, his mouth seducing hers, she helplessly raced up and spiraled into an explosion of light.

"Alexander!" She clung to him, taking him as he filled her over and again, amazed that even now, with her mind awash with sheer wonder, he could take her higher. Then, with her name spilling from his lips, he plunged deep and filled her with his seed.

For a minute they lay there, him poised above her, their heat, their bodies, mingled in sweat. If he never moved, she wouldn't complain.

The wild glaze in his eyes warmed to tenderness. He leaned down and kissed her with a sultry heat. "That," he whispered, "is making love."

"Is it always the same?"

Alexander rolled over and drew her to his side. "No." He stroked her face with his fingers, her lips, then lay his palm along her cheek. He kissed her tenderly. "I have never felt this way with any other woman."

Nichola smiled, for once in her life finding herself at a loss for words and not caring. Alexander nestled beside her. He rested his arm over her naked body, but this time she found no shame in his touch.

Only peace.

The haze of sleep claimed her, but throughout the

night, much to her surprise and joy, he claimed her over and again; until her mind was filled with nothing but him and the pleasures of their lovemaking.

As dawn peeked into the sky and he finally slept with her in his arms, she smiled, happy, sated, and never feeling so loved. Then the ramifications of their intimacy crept through her, a consequence she'd not considered.

What if she carried his child?

Chapter Sixteen

The irate grumble of men spewed through the room with an angry bite. Torchlight flickered over the brawny mass of Scots, lairds of their clans who'd joined in the rebellion against the English king.

Alexander scoured the room. Seathan would have his hands filled this night to keep the tempers under control. A task his brother was more than capable of.

On the dais, Seathan stood. The room quieted to an unruly murmur. "My brothers and I have devised a plan to aid in Wallace's escape," he said, his voice strong as his gaze moved around the room in a slow, lingering sweep.

"If he is not bloody dead," a fierce, red-haired laird yelled. "The bastards are slowly starving him, feeding him naught but rancid herring and water."

Anger carved through the tight calm of Seathan's face. "We will free Wallace, and the English will pay for the injustices to our people." Heads nodded. "I have sent word to Wulfe to meet us outside of Ayr."

With detail, Seathan outlined the strategy he and his brothers had plotted out over the past few days. When he finished, debates of their plan began in earnest.

From the back of the room, a commotion stirred. Wallace's man pushed through. "Lord Grey, I have important news."

Everyone turned toward the messenger, whose eyes were red, wrung with grief.

Expectancy hung like a noose over every man's head. The rebels stepped aside. Not a man said a word as the messenger hurried forward.

The runner reached the dais, his breathing coming in sharp rasps, dirt coating his garb; both a testament that he'd traveled hard to reach them.

Seathan nodded. "What word do you bring?"

"It is Sir Wallace," the man said. Shaking with exhaustion, he turned to face the crowd. "He is dead!"

The rebels exploded into an uproar. Curses flew. Angry shouts calling for an immediate attack on Ayr rent the air.

Dazed, Alexander wrapped his hand around the hilt of his dagger and squeezed tight. Wallace was dead? What in God's name were they to do now?

"Silence," Seathan ordered, his face ragged with the keening loss that was reflected on every warrior's face in the room.

Alexander stepped up to his brother's side, his heart raw. "We cannot let our anger destroy our cause. Whatever happens from now on, it must be as a unified front. We will neither let Wallace, nor our people down."

"The English bastards will not win," Duncan added, stepping up beside Seathan.

Eyes hot with hatred, Patrik joined his brothers. "If need be, we will slaughter every last one."

Angry cheers of the outraged men boomed in agreement.

Seathan gave Patrik a quelling look, then he turned

toward the rebels. "To massacre the English for the satisfaction of killing will earn us only King Edward's wrath."

"As if the bloody bastard does not slay our babes in our sleep now?" Patrik demanded.

"If we lowered to Longshank's methods, it makes us no better than him," Alexander threw out to the crowd. Damn Patrik for stirring up the men further. Couldn't he see his outburst was driving the already grief-stricken men into a frenzy? Or was that his intent?

"By God, I will have silence in the chamber!" Seathan demanded. His gaze swept the incensed men within the room. Amidst grumbles and curses, the warriors gradually quieted. "What Alexander said makes sense. To attack without a plan is foolhardy."

"So we wait?" Patrik said with contempt.

Seathan shot Patrik a hard look. "Aye. We will. To allow our tempers to rule would be our greatest error."

"What are we to do now?" asked a stocky man with a grizzled beard.

"First," Seathan said, "we retrieve Sir Wallace's body and give him the burial he deserves."

"Like they would open the gates to Ayr and bloody allow us in," a laird from the back said.

Grunts of agreement rolled through the room.

Seathan shook his head. "No, the odds are they will not let us in without a fight."

"But they might allow his nurse inside," Alexander added, the plan he and his brothers had devised, brilliant in its simplicity.

"His nurse?" another laird shouted in disbelief. "Christ's blood. Why not send in a child of six summers to dicker with the English scum? It would be as effective."

Mutters of agreement backed up his claim.

"The sheriff of Ayr will not be suspecting a woman to aid in our recovery of Wallace's body," Seathan reasoned.

The laird snorted. "It is a man's job."

"And what the English will be thinking and expecting as well," Alexander shot back.

"What of Wulfe?" a man near the front asked.

Seathan nodded. "A runner will be sent to meet him and bring him to meet us at Ayr."

After a pause, Patrik turned to the crowed. "I would be agreeing with the plan."

"As I," Duncan stated.

Pride filled Alexander at his brothers' unity. In strife, they put their differences aside. United as one.

The room hummed with fervor. One by one the rebels agreed.

With the anger of moments ago fading, Alexander thought of Nichola up in her chamber. The sweet warmth of her as they'd made love still thrummed through him. Her innocent touch. Her complete surrender.

He'd not meant to touch her. But what man in his right mind could have resisted such temptation when she'd reached out to him? Even now, hours after he'd left her, memories of their bodies entwined, her slick sheath taking him deep inside her blistered his thoughts. Of how after, she had trustingly curled up next to him and fell into a deep, restful sleep.

His body throbbed at the thought of waking to find her curled up next to him in his bed. However tempted to wake her and make love with her again, he'd left her sleeping in her own bed. Speculation of her being his mistress was one thing, but anyone finding her in his chamber would provide proof.

And tarnish any remainder of her reputation.

As if his abducting her hadn't done as much? A thought that'd come too late. He would rectify his discrepancy. He hadn't told his brothers of his decision to claim her hand in marriage and to have her remain here. Though she'd not agreed when he'd asked her at the chapel, once she calmed, he was sure she would cede. He wouldn't lose her.

Now or ever.

But he'd not speak of a union with Nichola now. Especially not with Wallace's death so fresh.

Alexander awaited the guilt of his decision to handfast with an Englishwoman. The self-condemnation of marrying a woman who should be his enemy. Instead, a sense of rightness filled him. A sense of wanting her remained.

Wallace's death would further fuel the dissent toward the English. Nichola's presence would give the people within the castle a focus for their anger. He frowned. If she agreed, would her remaining in Lochshire Castle as his wife be putting her life at risk?

At this moment, he couldn't be sure.

"And what of the rebellion?" a laird from the right corner asked, breaking into Alexander's musings.

"Our plans to regain Scotland's freedom are unchanged," Seathan replied. "De Moray is en route to my home as we speak. Wallace had gained his employ prior to his arrest."

"How can that be?" a large Scot from the left called out. "De Moray was imprisoned after the Battle of Dunbar with his father."

"I have received news this morn from one of Sir de Moray's men that he has escaped. I suspect with the help of several of Wallace's men. Sir de Moray had planned to meet with Sir Wallace and Wulfe here on the morrow," Seathan explained, "but with Sir Wallace dead, I am confident Sir de Moray will step into the position as our leader without hesitation."

Heads nodded in agreement.

Alexander stared at his brother, stunned by the news of Sir de Moray's escape as well as filled with relief that their rebellion would continue with strong leadership.

Unbeknownst to the English, they had made a critical mistake. The loss of Sir Wallace would but rouse the Scots further. Aye, the English had struck a fierce blow with the death of Sir Wallace, but their butchery would not go unanswered. With Sir Moray to lead them and Wulfe to slip them English troop movements, the Scottish forces would teach the English bastards a lesson.

One they would never forget.

"I will be waiting within the edge of the forest when they bring out Wallace's body," the red-haired man stated.

"As I," a laird from the back agreed.

Seathan nodded. "I will choose several more men from this room, plus I will add my own knights to ride along as well." His gaze moved from man to man. "It is time to pull together." His gaze lingered on Patrik. "Not strike out in anger. We cannot allow our actions to be guided by emotions. To do so could jeopardize the very freedom we strive to reclaim."

At Seathan's bolstering words, lauds to Scotland rang out in fierce shouts.

The angry churn of voices arrowed into Nichola's heart. She pressed further into the shadows at the back of the room where torchlight didn't reach.

William Wallace was dead.

The stories of the mountain of a man, as lethal as he

was charming, spun through her mind. She experienced a moment's regret.

But as dangerous as their deceased leader was, the men within the room presented a more viable threat. More so with the news of Sir de Moray's imminent arrival. And this English lord they called Wulfe.

The rebels' righteous anger would fuel them to lay siege to England with an even deeper hatred. And Sir de Moray's reputable cunning would ensure lethal attacks that would strike fear in the hearts of the English.

All too easy she could imagine the terror, the carnage. Her stomach rebelled at the thought. Lord help them all.

"It is unwise to eavesdrop when a country makes plans for war," a low voice hissed against her ear.

Nichola whirled to find herself boxed in by a large, muscled body. She looked up. Her breath caught in her throat as she stared into Patrik's partially shadowed face, his expression carved with contempt.

Mary's will! "I—I did not mean—"

"To listen in? To slink in the darkness of the corner to garner information to pass on to your English king?"

He leaned closer, his body blocking out any light, his face drenched in shadows. The rawness of his fury smothering her.

Terrified, Nichola pressed back. The cold stone wall dug into her shoulders. "No, that is not the truth." She wet her lips, her mouth suddenly dry, understanding how furtive her actions must appear to him. "I had come to see Alexander. When I heard the angry voices I was curious to the reason why and . . ."

His skeptical grunt made her hesitate.

"To see Alexander?" His mouth curled in a sneer. "You expect he would want to see you now that he has gained your bed?"

Coldness vibrated through her. Alexander wasn't the shallow man Patrik painted him. He hadn't said he loved her, but his actions spoke of a deeply caring man. "It is the truth."

He angled his face. Yellowed torchlight illuminated the temper in his eyes that she'd witnessed in his spars with Alexander on the practice field.

"Treachery is no game," he said.

"I know."

"If I dragged you into the chamber of Scots behind us, exposed you as an English spy, it would be their justice you would taste."

After Patrik had almost thrown her down the turret, she had no doubts he would. Panic swept her. The act of spying in these unstable times dealt her a swift blow. She imagined the noose slipping around her neck, the rough cord as they yanked it tight. Even if Alexander tried to intervene, with the rebels' outrage this night, no leniency or compassion would be offered.

Sir William Wallace's brutal death ensured that.

"Please," she whispered. "I am innocent of your charge."

Nichola glanced back toward the stairway and wished she'd never left the safety of her chamber. After making love to Alexander, for the first time since her arrival, she'd let down her guard and had foolishly followed her heart. "If you let me go, I will naught say a word to anyone. I swear it."

"Patrik," a Scot from inside the room yelled. "What are you about hidden away in the corner?"

Panic surged through her as his calloused hand seized her arm. She tensed.

"A word of this to anyone," he hissed, his face dark with menace, "and I will serve you death beneath my own hand. Do you understand?"

Unsure what spawned his reprieve, she nodded.

He released her and turned, leaving her hidden in the darkness. Patrik shoved his way to the front of the crowd where his brothers and other men argued tactics.

Keeping to the shadows, Nichola fled. Only after she'd reached her room, thankful not to be dragged before the outraged Scots and slain, did she crumble upon her bed. And to think, before she'd worried about something as mundane as carrying Alexander's child.

After the rebels departed from the meeting, Alexander sat on the bench with his tankard. He took another deep swallow as he watched the flames waver in the hearth.

The rich scent of wood blended with the echo of angry voices and the lingering stench of ale, but he ignored them. His head pounded, swollen with the emotions rioting through him, heated by his fierce loyalty toward his country, but aching that Nichola had become caught in the midst of the uprising.

She'd had no choice from the start. Torn from her home, she'd suffered the loss of her brother. Now the group of Scottish leaders had agreed to methodically reclaim Scottish strongholds taken by the English, including Rothfield Castle. After everything else, she would lose her home as well.

For her, the cost of war would be monumental. How could it not be? They awaited her ransom, but after it arrived, then they would attack. Nichola couldn't return home now. Or ever. But the loss of her home, of the people she cared for within, would hurt. He couldn't allow her to return and witness that. Not to mention that in the fray, she could be raped or killed.

"It has been a bloody long night," Seathan said with a sigh.

Alexander glanced where his eldest brother took a seat, a tankard of ale in his hand as well. "Aye, it has at that."

"I still cannot believe Wallace is dead." Alexander walked over to the hearth and leaned against the side stone.

Patrik crouched before the fire and stared into the flames. "Murdered," he said with a dangerous calm. "But they will regret it. For each drop of Wallace's blood, my blade will claim the life of ten Englishmen."

Silence fell between the brothers like a quiet promise. Patrik's fury matched many within Lochshire Castle. Alexander thought of Nichola. Though it was best if she remained here when the rebels began their siege, again he wondered if she was truly safe?

Seathan stood and downed the last of his ale. He set the empty tankard on the bench and glanced at his brothers. "We will all be needing a good night's rest. Once the fighting begins, the days ahead will offer naught but glimpses of sleep."

Emptying his tankard, Duncan set it aside, then stretched. "Aye, it is time to be heading to bed."

"And what is her name this night, Duncan?" Patrik asked as their younger brother stood.

Alexander released a rough sigh. The teasing in Patrik's tone brought a lightness to the room they all desperately needed. He, along with his brothers, smiled. Patrik's extreme behavior of late when talk of the English disturbed him, but often, as now, his anger faded as quick.

"I will not be telling you the lass's name," Duncan replied.

Patrik hooted at that. "And the same you said about

the previous lass you bedded. You dance around commitment with a fine step."

They all laughed as Duncan threw Patrik a disgruntled look.

And for this moment their world was right. Alexander savored this peace, the love of his brothers. All too aware that once the fighting began, the chance existed that they would never stand together again.

The laughter fell away and somber glances passed between them. Seathan nodded. "Until the morn."

"Aye," the other brothers said in unison.

"I am off to console Rois," Duncan said with a wink and headed toward the door to the keep.

"I do not know how he keeps up with their names," Patrik said. On a heavy sigh, he leaned against the wall on the opposite side of the hearth to Alexander.

Alexander nodded. "I doubt he does."

"I think you are right." A contented silence fell between them. "You are not heading off to bed?"

"In a while." Alexander grimaced when he found his mug empty. He wanted to be with Nichola, yet she would be furious when he told her she would remain here even after the ransom was paid. Neither would his brothers be pleased by his decision.

"Here." Patrik leaned over and filled his tankard. He set the pitcher down between them with a solid clunk. "It is a night for ale."

"Aye."

"And women," Patrik added.

"Always for women," Alexander replied automatically to hide his turmoil.

"You are sounding like Duncan," Patrik gently chided. "Except after Duncan's heartbreak when Isabel Adair severed their betrothal to become Lord Frasyer's mistress, Duncan has never fallen in love."

Alexander lowered the tankard, the serious undertones of his brother's words putting him on the defense. "What do you mean by that?"

"It is not a secret of the feelings you hold for Lady Nichola."

"What I feel for her is for me to sort out."

"Not when it comes to our country's freedom."

Alexander slammed down his tankard. Ale sloshed over the rim. He stood and glared at his brother.

"I told you—"

"And what would you say if I told you she was a spy?" Patrik interrupted.

Feet spread apart, hands braced on his hips, Alexander snarled, "She has lost her home, her family, and she is the furthest thing England has of a spy."

"Then why did I find her hiding in the shadows outside our chamber while we, along with the clan leaders, discussed our plans to attack the English?"

Alexander hesitated. He'd not seen her there. "She would never do that."

"I saw her."

From the resolute expression on his brother's face, Patrik spoke the truth. Why would she listen in on their meeting? The thought that she would pass along any inside information left a sickening stench inside him.

He stared at Patrik. "She is our prisoner."

"For now," he agreed. "But once the ransom is paid, what then? She is free to pass along the information she has gleaned to aid those who would set up an ambush and slaughter our men."

"She would never share anything she learned this night." He wanted to believe that, but if she were a spy, neither could he discount that if the English ever caught her, they would treat her as an assumed traitor to them as well. What if they believed her loyalties had swayed toward the Scottish cause during her stay, or they tortured her to see what she knew? What if they learned she and Alexander had been lovers?

Anger burned in Patrik's hazel eyes. "You claim she would never eavesdrop, yet I found her doing just that. Now you say she will hold her tongue against her own country's behalf, that she will allow her people and lands to be seized without revealing naught." Patrik snorted. "Tell me, Alexander, with her brother having had King Edward's ear, can you assure me that these will be her actions once freed? Or are your views skewed by having bed her?"

"Damn you! Her sleeping with me changes nothing."

"No?"

He glared at his brother.

As much as he wished to deny Patrik's claims, doubts remained. If they'd had time together to strengthen their bond of trust, then he would be sure. But their emotions though strong, were fragile. Had she played him for a fool? Were her words of love those to buy time, a cover for actions that would serve England? No, he could never believe that.

"She will remain here," Alexander revealed.

"After the ransom is paid?" Patrik said in disbelief. "With her wealth, position within the gentry and heiress of a major stronghold against the Scots, do you think Seathan would allow such a folly? Keeping her after the ransom is paid would be an invitation for King Edward to lay siege to our home."

God's teeth, he'd naught considered that, but Patrik was right. King Edward would clasp onto her detainment as a direct challenge and attack Lochshire Castle. The number of English troops who would pour down from the hills would wreck havoc upon the untrained men and women remaining within the keep, while his brothers and the rebels were attacking more tactically important English strongholds.

The pounding in his head severed through the warm mists of ale. "I do not know the right answer," Alexander finally said, his heart aching.

"I do," Patrik stated as calmly as if asking for a refill of wine. "She must die."

Chapter Seventeen

"No!" Alexander shot Patrik a furious look.

Patrik bristled. "She is a risk we cannot take."

"A risk to whom?." Alexander stilled the urge to grab his brother's throat. Barely. "The rebels or your hatred toward the English?"

Red mottled Patrik's face. "I have never lied about my hatred of the English. But her spying is not about my personal feelings toward her or her country."

"Is it not? Since the day I brought her here, you have watched her with ill intent."

"Her brother is King Edward's advisor to the Scots. Think you if she sought an audience, King Edward would not grant it? Aye, and he'd listen, greedy for all she would tell him about our rebel plans."

A pounding built in the back of his head. He couldn't believe she would betray him after they'd made love. "You cannot be sure she was spying on our discussion."

"I know what I saw."

"Appearances can be deceiving." Even as Alexander spoke, how would he have viewed her actions if he had witnessed her hiding in the shadows and listening to the rebels' debate?

Patrik paused. "They can be, but I watched her. Her intent was clear. Had her presence been innocent, then when she saw the gathering, she would have quickly left."

"What—"

His brother slammed his fist upon the table. Empty tankards clattered. "Listen to your claims. You are allowing your feelings for the lass to skew your thoughts. We are at war. Wallace is dead. We cannot risk anything compromising our plans—including Lady Nichola. Once the ransom is received, no other choice remains. She must be killed."

Alexander stood. He stepped toward him and halted a hand's breath away. "Whatever her intent, she will not be harmed. Defy me, and it will be my blade you face.

The anger coursing over Patrik's face crumbled into a mask of sorrow. "Christ, Alexander, do you think it is easy for me to reveal her treachery to you? It is the last thing I would wish. I know your feelings for the lass run deep. If I could aid you, keep her from suspicion or harm, I would." A weary sigh spilled from his mouth. "I ask you, if the positions were reversed, what would you be asking of me?"

Troubled, Alexander didn't reply. He set down his tankard. A short while ago he'd looked forward to going to Nichola to make love with her through the night. Now, seeing her brought an uncertain dread.

"I will speak with her," Alexander finally said.

"No," Patrik said softly.

Surprised, he turned toward his brother. "Why not?"

"It is better if she has not discovered that we have caught her spying."

His words made little sense. "But you confronted her."

"Aye, and promised I would not say a word. She believes she has convinced me that she was but walking through the castle when the sounds of the angry men drew her attention."

Alexander jumped on her explanation. "It could be true." Or mayhap she was coming to see him?

Patrik made a grunt of dismissal. "How often since her arrival has she wandered around the castle at night or alone?"

He didn't answer, didn't need to. Since he'd allowed her door to remain unbarred, except for the night she'd come to his chamber and he'd rejected her, she'd not once left the confines of her room after they'd supped.

"It is better if she remains ignorant that we have uncovered her scheme." Patrik pressed his finger against his brow as if it ached, a sensation Alexander could empathize with. His own head throbbed as if battered by a mace.

"We will covertly watch her for other suspicious activities, but for now, we will allow her to believe we think her innocent," Patrik said.

Alexander wanted to disagree, but by her own actions, she had placed herself under suspicion. The thought of her spying on them stripped him raw.

Trust.

How could a bond grow without this essential element?

"—to ensure she suspects nothing."

"What?" Alexander asked, realizing he'd missed most of Patrik's comment.

"I said, you will have to keep your actions normal or she will know I have told you."

He swallowed hard, disgusted at the thought of this deception. "I will tell Seathan."

"He has enough on his mind."

Alexander nodded, too hurt to argue. Helping reclaim Wallace's body, meeting with Lord de Moray and Wulfe wouldn't allow any free time to speak with Seathan.

"We will tell him after we have buried Wallace," Alexander said.

"And it will give us time to see what mischief she is about."

Or time to prove her innocence. However much he believed her guiltless, he refused to allow her to endanger the rebels' plans if there existed the slightest chance of her guilt.

Aye, he would heed Patrik's suggestion, but he didn't have to like it.

Like a man sentenced to the gallows, Alexander climbed the castle steps. As he neared his floor he stopped. If he were a smart man, he would go to his chamber and sleep. He wouldn't be standing here staring up the winding steps, wondering if she lay in her bed waiting for him. Or if her thoughts were drenched with wanting.

God help him, even with Patrik's suspicions of her, he couldn't stop caring about her. Mayhap if he went to her chamber, she would confess she'd listened to the rebels along with her reason.

With a heavy heart, he climbed the steps up to the woman he wanted as no other, to a woman who if Patrik was correct, might expose his country's bid for freedom.

The quiet scrape of her door was the only indication that Alexander had entered her chamber. Had Patrik told him of their confrontation? Nichola lay in bed torn, a part of her hoping he'd come to her this night, another, nervous of how he'd act if he did.

She remained still and watched Alexander's solid form glide through the murky darkness. She held her breath, unsure of what to do, but she refused to hide behind closed lids.

His eyes, she needed to see them, then she would know if he trusted her still. Or if he knew her enough to see the truth in whatever lie Patrik had told him.

He halted by her bedside, but he stood in the shadows and she couldn't make out his face.

"Alexander?"

His fingers reached out to touch her shoulder, to glide up her neck then skim over her lips.

Currents of heat shot through her. "Make love with me."

Alexander hesitated. His fingers trembled. He whispered a curse that had her nerves dancing on edge. Then he touched her, lightly, tenderly, and with a passion that usurped her fears. Her doubts.

He knelt and claimed her mouth. His hungry kiss destroyed her while his fingers moved down her arm in a slow caress.

Fire swept through her body, singing her every nerve until she couldn't think, only want. Him.

His mouth glided down to her neck, his teeth scraping softly over her sensitized skin, while his hand inched up her thin chemise. On a needy exhale, he leaned back and stripped her until she lay naked before him.

She reached up for him, but he caught her fingers and kissed the tip of each.

"No," he whispered.

The moon peeked out from the blanket of thick clouds. Silver beams spilled through the open window to illuminate her body. He lowered his head to her breast. As he laved the soft swell, she gasped. His lips inched over her with a tender assault, merciless in his sensual siege.

She ached beneath his touch, her body urging him to take her, to drive her wild for more. With his every touch, his every kiss, she sensed a desperation, an urgency that had never existed within him before.

Alexander covered her body with his own, pressing himself intimately against her. "Nichola," he rasped, his voice almost a haunted ache. Then he drove deep.

Her body convulsed, his every thrust casting her higher until there was only raw pleasure. She called out his name, wanting this to last forever.

On his next drive, she arched to meet him, taking his entire length, crying out as he withdrew only to impale himself in her again. Pressure built. Shudders tore through her body and she spun into sweet release. But he pressed on, relentless, pushing her further.

Sweat covered her body. Coherent thought fled. Somewhere in their erotic dance, her body began to spiral up again. She welcomed his every drive, the tide of heat that ripped through her.

For the second time in minutes, Nichola exploded. Shaken by the sheer beauty of their lovemaking, she cried out as he found his own release. Tears slipped down her cheeks at the beauty of their intimate bond.

He lifted his head. In the moon-washed light, worry crowded his face. "I have hurt you?"

"No, it was beautiful." Never before had she felt so needed or cherished. "I love you so much." She tried to convince herself that she hadn't felt him stiffen at her words. At his silence, nerves fractured her calm. She touched his face. "Alexander?"

He rolled off of her and lay by her side, not touching her, not moving to a more intimate position. "Go to sleep."

At his rough whisper, goose bumps rippled over her skin. The cool night air that flowed over where his body had lain, where even now his sweat mingled with hers, chilled her further.

"What is wrong?" Doubts stormed her. Did he know she'd been downstairs earlier? Had Patrik informed him that she'd been spying? If so, did he believe his brother?

The beauty of her nakedness of moments before seemed tainted. She drew the coverlet over her. She'd known Alexander less than a fortnight. Though adopted, he viewed Patrik as his brother. His blood.

And what if she told Alexander of her fear of Patrik, her suspicions that in the turret he'd meant to shove her down the steps to her death? Would he believe her? Or, would he dismiss her claim as nerves at being held hostage?

He rubbed the tired lines of his face. "It has been a long day," he said into the silence. "I am glad you stayed up in your chamber this night. It was an unruly scene below."

She relaxed. 'Twould appear Patrik hadn't spoken to him of her presence below. So why did she sense this change in Alexander, an emotional withdrawal?

With slow strokes as if his head ached, Alexander rubbed his brow. "We learned that Sir William Wallace is dead."

Relief poured through her. That explained his emotional withdrawal from her. He was grieving. "I am sorry."

He linked his fingers with hers, gave her hand a firm squeeze, then let go of her hand. "I am sorry as well."

The quiet seriousness of his words again stirred her unease. He'd said he was glad she'd not come down, but what if this was a test to see if she'd tell him the truth?

If she also chose this moment to reveal her fears of his brother, would he believe her words given to cover her guilt? Or would he dismiss her worries, owing any anger toward her from Patrik as due to Patrik's tragic past?

Nichola curled her hand in the blanket and fought for calm. Why was she concerned about an event now hours old? Patrik had obviously kept his word and no harm was done. What mattered was that a man Alexander revered was dead. Instead of seeking trouble where there was none, she should be offering him sympathy, comfort.

She laid her hand upon his, but he didn't move to clasp it in his own. The silence of the night fell between them, the chirp of crickets, the feather of the light, summer breeze sliding into her room. He never made a move to touch her or to make love with her again.

When the bells of matins rang, he stood and quietly dressed.

The shifting of the bed woke her from her restless slumber. She peered over to see Alexander standing and reaching for his garb. Despite his indifferent expression, she sensed him withdrawing.

"Alexander?"

"I have to go."

"Wait." She sat up and came to a decision. She couldn't let this go on. Whatever his reaction, she needed to tell him her fears about Patrik, that she'd gone below and overheard of Wallace's death this night.

Alexander turned, cobalt eyes dark with a sadness

that stole her heart. "Goodnight, Nichola." And without further explanation, he departed.

As the morning sun streamed into her chamber, Nichola dressed with care. She tried to assure herself her unhurried pace was due to wanting to appear her best, but she couldn't deny the truth. The tension between her and Alexander had not been her imagination. He had left yesterday morning before she could ask, but she refused to let another day pass without speaking with him.

Throughout the night she'd battled her doubts and had come to a realization. She'd told Alexander she'd loved him, then she'd let her wariness toward men still her tongue when she should have trusted him with the truth. After Griffin's death, she was afraid of losing Alexander as well.

She wasn't a coward. Whatever happened, she had to try.

Armed with courage, she exited her chamber. She made a somber search for Alexander as she passed through the great hall of the keep, alert for any sign of Patrik. She would avoid being alone with him at any cost.

Only a handful of knights remained at the trencher tables to finish the last of the morning fare. A few men nodded curtly to her, but the warmth she'd witnessed in the days before was no longer reflected in their eyes. Now, grief and loathing lingered there instead.

She couldn't blame them. They'd lost their leader. A man whose name already graced many a legend. Unsettled by their cool looks, she hurried out of the keep.

The practice field was crowded with men locked in

mock battle, their swords clashing, trembling from punishing blows. She scoured the rebels. Alexander wasn't in their midst.

Further unsettled, she walked through the courtyard, the scent of cooking meat reminding her that she hadn't eaten. Mayhap when she found Alexander, they could break their fast in the forest, then make love.

Her body grew warm at the thought. Once he was relaxed, she'd broach the subject of Patrik and what she'd learned that night.

Children playing rushed past. Their shrieks of laughter startled her from her musings. She laid her hand on her stomach. Warmth sifted through her. She might be carrying their child. The thought of a new life brought a rush of joy. If she indeed carried Alexander's babe, she promised if nothing else, their child would know love.

A hard pounding of metal upon metal had her glancing toward the smith who lifted a blade that was glowing an angry red. He inspected it, then shoved the weapon into the fire before returning it to his anvil to continue reshaping the hot steel.

She stopped. Had she thought this just another day? Beneath the façade of normalcy, the Scots prepared for war. A shiver crept through her with lethal precision. How in God's name could she think to bring a child into this world? Now it was too late, she'd already lain with Alexander.

A child, if conceived, would be God's will.

Heavy with thought, Nichola walked on. As she approached the atilliator's hut, Alexander's voice echoed within. She moved to the door and saw the atilliator who Alexander had introduced to her before. Except his harsh expression offered anything but welcome.

The atilliator gestured to the door. "You have company."

Alexander appeared around the corner. Irritation darkened his cobalt eyes. "I will be but a moment," he said to the atilliator. He walked outside and stood before her, his hands on his hips.

"Why have you left your chamber?" he snapped. "With Wallace's death, it is not wise for you to walk around alone."

Nichola touched the pendant hanging around her neck, his cold warning leaving her further unsettled. "I need to speak with you."

For a moment, need flickered in his eyes, then his face grew unreadable. "I have naught the luxury of time."

"This eve?"

"Return to your chamber."

His cold dismissal hurt. They'd made love but a day ago, now staring up into Alexander's eyes, she saw nothing but unwelcome. Had something else happened to escalate the unrest between their countries?

With each passing second as he continued to watch her with a guarded expression, her hopes of even a few more days with Alexander dissolved. Until she stood before him, transformed back into the prisoner whom he'd stolen from her home.

Nichola stepped back, her throat rough with tears. "Alexander, please."

He remained silent.

She hesitated, waiting for his face to soften, to crease in warmth, and for him to ask her to stay. To allow her to explain why she'd come.

Alexander only stared at her as if anxious for her to leave.

She turned at last, pain hissing through her like the

lash of a whip; hard, searing, slicing through her every emotion. She kept walking, slow, steady, and with purpose. With Alexander so cut off from her, so went her motivation not to escape. For whatever the risk, she refused to stay even one more night within Lochshire Castle.

Except for her heart, which would remain here with Alexander, forever.

Alexander watched Nichola walk away, hating that he'd hurt her. Knowing that he'd pushed her away. When she'd looked upon him with love, he'd wanted to embrace her, but Patrik's words of her espionage battered his mind. Why had she not told him the truth the other night?

With a muttered curse, he started after her. He was wrong to doubt Nichola. He would let her speak.

"Alexander," Patrik called, halting his departure. His brother strode toward him, then stopped by his side, frowning at Nichola's departing figure. "I see she came to visit."

Blast it, he needed to go after her. "She is upset."

His hazel eyes narrowed. "You have not revealed that you know of her spying?"

Alexander shook his head, torn, not liking his deceit, nor that she had not offered the truth. "I have not said a word."

"It is important to keep her ignorant."

Alexander wasn't so sure. With Nichola he couldn't play games. She mattered too much. "This is wrong. I need to explain to her—"

"Wrong?" Patrik's quiet voice filled with anger. "Wallace lays dead, tossed in a dung heap, and you are more worried about an enemy in Scotland?" He jabbed a finger in the direction Nichola had taken. "What if she were to escape and tell the English of our plans? How many other of our men might die for her treachery? Is that wrong?"

"She would never tell," Alexander denied, but even as he claimed otherwise, how could he be sure? England was her homeland, where her last ties to her family remained. Wouldn't her loyalties lay with her country, especially as it was the Scots who'd abducted her from her home?

"No?" Patrik demanded. "Are you willing to risk the lives of Scots to test your belief?"

Damn the entire situation. Alexander ground his boot against a clump of broken dirt, watching her retreating figure grow smaller and smaller. He just needed time to allow his emotions to calm. To consider all of the facts.

"Are you?" Patrik pressed.

While Alexander watched, Nichola hesitated at the entrance to the keep. With her hand upon the door, she turned back.

Their gazes locked.

Even from the distance, he heard her silent questions. He wanted to go to her, erase her fears, but with his feelings in turmoil, if he went to her now, he would probably make the situation between them worse.

Her head lifted in a stubborn tilt, that endearing gesture that now broke his heart. Then she jerked the door open and sailed inside with the bearing of a queen.

Patrik stepped into his line of vision. "Answer me, Alexander. Are you willing to risks the lives of your countrymen?"

Alexander glared at his brother, never so frustrated in all of his life. He shook his head. "I will tell her naught." But with his decision made, he wondered if it had been the right one after all?

Chapter Eighteen

Shadows of the oncoming night lengthened outside Nichola's window, stealing the last fragments of the day. Darkness shrouded her room. Silence echoed around her. The candle burning on the table sputtered and pools of shadows stumbled across her chamber.

The emptiness in her heart was complete.

All day she had awaited Alexander within the tower chamber, but he hadn't come. A small part of her had coveted the hope that he would yet come to her this night and explain his aloof manner. Didn't he understand that her heart was breaking? That she hadn't given her love to him easily?

Her hand shook as she finished penning her brief note to Alexander, telling him that she loved him, explaining her lack of finances, and asking his forgiveness that she'd not told him before.

He would be upset when he learned she had withheld her financial destitution from him, but at least he would have the truth. She was a fool to leave him any explanation, but as much as she wanted to walk away and sever all ties, the part of her that desperately loved him believed she owed him that.

She curled the missive, secured it within a piece of ribbon she'd found in the chamber, then placed it on the bed. With trembling fingers, she picked up a small loaf of bread and shoved it into the satchel a search of the room had uncovered.

By traveling light, with any luck she would cross the border and find aid within a sennight. Remembering the scoundrels of the disreputable inn that Alexander had lodged her in during their trip into Scotland, she would take care with who she approached for help.

The bells of matins pealed. She couldn't tarry or waste time grieving about the nights she and Alexander had spent together. Damn him for making her care.

Her hand closed around the small dagger she'd procured from the kitchen. She'd asked for wine to bring to Alexander, a request they would believe as she'd obtained the same over the past few days to reward him with after his training of arms. When the cooks and other servants had been busy, she'd slipped a small wedge of cheese, bread, and a roughly crafted knife into the folds of her gown.

The cool steel was an ominous weight in her hands. With a silent prayer that she would never have to use it, she slipped the weapon inside the small pouch she'd devised and drew the cinch tight.

She was ready to go.

Through the window, a thousand stars sparkled in the cloudless sky. A hint of heather along with the fresh scent of the loch filled the air.

Her heart broke. Surprisingly, she would miss Lochshire Castle. But it was time to go.

Nichola had turned to leave when moonlight glinted off of the dark greenish stone sitting in the bowl on the table. Frowning, she stepped closer. Moonlight was

absent in this corner of the room. Oddly, the mate
to the stone Alexander wore around his neck seemed
to glow.

She worried the side of her gown with her hand,
sure the misery of this day played with her mind. As
she continued to stare, the light within the stone
seemed to grow stronger.

Baffled, she walked over to the small table and laid
her finger upon the rough half. Heat, soft and warm,
wove over her skin. A sense of rightness enveloped
her. Nichola lifted the stone, palm open, unsure if she
could believe what she was feeling. Then she remembered his claim that this room held magic.

Her chest squeezed tight. She stumbled back. No.
He was wrong. This chamber held naught but pain.

Aching, she clenched the stone within her fist and
ran to the door. She paused, steadying herself. As
much as she wanted to race from the keep, she must
move with caution.

It seemed to take an eternity to creep down the
spiral steps, convinced at any moment she would meet
a knight, a servant coming up or worse, Patrik.

She peered round the corner into the great hall.
Several knights slept on the stone floor surrounded
by rushes, their snores loud and rude, accompanied
by several hounds who lay stretched out. Much the
same as in her own home. She swallowed hard. Rothfield Castle. In days that would be lost as well.

Nichola refused to succumb to her misgivings and
stepped into full view. As she moved along the wall
where the firelight didn't reach, a soft scrape sounded
behind her.

Fear slinked up her spine. She searched the darkness, but saw naught but shadows. She released a slow

breath. No one was following her. Her imagination was working overtime.

Halfway across the room, a dog lifted his head, his tail thumping on the floor in welcome. When he decided she wouldn't cast scraps of food his way, he lowered his head and went back to sleep.

By the time she reached the door to the keep, her heart was pounding. She slipped outside, greeted by the cool breeze of the night. She searched the castle walls. Guards stood posted on this side of the wall walk, their heads turned toward the hills beyond. Uncluttered by clouds, the moon, a silver wedge in the night, stole shadows she desperately needed for cover.

A guard called out to another from directly overhead.

Nichola stilled. Had they seen her? Taut moments passed. No one approached her. Sweat beaded her brow as she inched forward in the meager shadows and skirted the courtyard.

Almost to the gatehouse, the quiet pad of footsteps echoed behind her. Positive she'd been spotted, she whirled, a scream building in her throat.

The courtyard stood empty.

Panic tightened in her chest as she scoured the courtyard. For a moment, she swore she saw the outline of a man in the shadows.

A cloud shielded the moon. The fragile wisp slipped past, moonlight illuminated the darkness of moments before to expose nothing but a ragged path.

Nichola exhaled with relief. Footsteps sounded at the keep's entrance and she again tensed.

Ghostly shards of moonlight embraced Patrik as he walked down the steps of the keep and headed toward the turret that led up to the wall walk.

Mary's will, had he seen her? If he had, he would

have challenged her. Should she return to her chamber? No, she couldn't go back.

Patrik disappeared inside the tower.

She crept forward. Several times Nichola glanced toward the top of the wall walk where Patrik would exit. She saw no one. Her senses warned her that he watched her.

Nichola waited for him to alert the guards. To reveal he'd caught her hidden at the rebel meeting, then offer her attempt to escape as proof of his claim she was a spy.

The last few yards to the gatehouse were agonizing. Finally she reached it, thankful to find the drawbridge still lowered. Through her chamber window a short while before, she'd watched the small contingent of troops depart to meet with Wulfe and reclaim Wallace's body, Seathan riding at the lead.

With darkness as her shield, she'd decided to use the main entry as her escape.

"Lower the portcullis and lift the drawbridge," a guard shouted from above.

They were securing the castle! With one last glance around to ensure no one watched, she sprinted through the gatehouse and out into the night.

On the other side, she pressed back against the cool stone of the castle wall.

Chains rattled. The gate creaked. With a muffled clang, the portcullis settled on the ground.

She'd made it outside! The narrowed road straddled the moon-stroked water before her, her only route to escape. She would have to creep along the edge of the road. And pray she wouldn't be seen. With her heart pounding, she inched forward.

* * *

The next morning, Alexander walked toward the turret, Patrik by his side.

His brother frowned at him. "Do you think it is wise to leave Nichola's door unbarred?"

"Seathan agrees she poses no threat."

"She could try and escape."

"She could." Alexander shrugged. "But she will not. It would be foolish to try. Nichola would never make it past the gatehouse undetected."

Patrik snorted. "Has the lass blinded you so much she has won your trust then?"

Alexander spat out an oath. Then he remembered his warning for her to remain within their room at the keep—a dictate she ignored. Unease stumbled through him.

They reached the turret steps. Instead of heading down to the great room, he started up the steps. "Break your fast," Alexander said, "I will be but a moment."

"I will go with you."

Alexander halted on the steps, then started up. What did it matter if Patrik accompanied him? With the cold welcome Nichola would offer him this morn, he would be there but a trice. And his mind would be eased that she was safe.

"You were out late last night," Alexander said as he headed up the steps.

"Out late?"

"I could not sleep and saw you on the wall walk long after we had departed from the meeting."

Patrik shrugged. "With the amount you drank, you saw naught but a guard. I have better things to do with my nights than roam the wall walk."

Alexander frowned. He was sure it was Patrik, but his brother had no reason to lie. He had drank until the room had blurred before him, but still . . .

At Nichola's chamber door, Alexander gave a quiet knock. A long moment passed, but no answer came from within. "Nichola."

Silence.

Patrik lifted a curious brow.

Impatient, he rapped again. "It is Alexander." He waited for her to answer, not wanting to walk in with Patrik in case she was unclothed. More likely, after his treatment of her last night, she had probably wrapped herself in layers of bedclothes.

"Is she not there?"

God help her if she wasn't. "Wait here." He shoved open the door, half expecting to find her hidden behind it with a weapon, or sitting in bed wrapped tight in blankets, glaring at him with unconcealed disdain.

But when he stepped inside, the last thing he expected to find was the chamber empty.

"Alexander?" Patrik called from the corridor.

Unease built in his gut. Where was she? He called to his brother, "She is not here."

"What?" Patrik strode into the room and scanned the empty chamber. His jaw tightened. "Where has she gone?"

"I do not know."

"Christ, Alexander."

He ignored Patrik's outburst and walked to the window, cautiously dismissing his unease. Still grieving for her brother's death, she was surely in the chapel lost in prayers.

Alexander turned and froze. Her bed lay untouched. She would not have tried to leave Lochshire Castle, would she? No, she had given her vow that she wouldn't try to escape. Then he remembered. He had asked, but she had never agreed. Alexander squeezed his hand into a tight fist. He wanted to believe she wouldn't try and escape, but a part of him understood she'd done exactly that.

Patrik walked away from the bed. As his hand disappeared into a pocket, something crumpled.

Alexander almost asked if his brother had found a note, then stilled his question. As if Nichola would assume he needed an explanation for her absence? Besides, Patrik would have mentioned if she'd left him something.

"We will search the castle grounds," Alexander said.

"Sir Alexander," the servant greeted as she walked into the room, carrying a platter of food in her hand. Her gaze shifted from him to Patrik, then around the chamber. "Where is Lady Nichola?"

The maid's innocent question deepened his worry. "Leave the tray," Alexander said. "She will eat upon her return."

The woman set down the platter then left.

"Do you think she would try and escape?"

"I believe her wiser than that." But that's exactly what he thought. If so, when? She couldn't have left the castle this day. Even if she had made an attempt, the portcullis had been raised only for the last few hours and heavily guarded. "We will look in the chapel. Likely she spent the night grieving at the altar. If she is not there, we will split up and continue the search. She cannot have gone far."

Alexander studied the room one last time. He paused. The other half of the stone that hung around his neck was missing. Had Nichola taken it?

He was jumping to conclusions. Many reasons for the stone's disappearance existed, except to him it confirmed that Nichola was trying to escape.

Alexander strode to the door. "Come."

Patrik walked in silence at his side. Their boots slapped on the turret steps as they descended.

They scoured the great hall and the courtyard, but found no sign of her. When they reached the chapel, Alexander stepped into the dim interior.

Candles flickered on the walls. A woman garbed in a swath of pale linen knelt before the altar, her head bowed.

Alexander's shoulders sagged with relief. Nichola. Then the woman turned, and he recognized the seamstress who'd lost her son to an English sword two days hence.

A lump built in his throat as Alexander nodded and backed up. He closed the door behind him.

Patrik studied him, his expression grim. "Well?"

He shook his head. "We will split up. Alert the guards. Discreetly. We do not want to cause a panic in case we are mistaken."

"And when she is found?"

"Bring her to me." After which he would make damn sure she regretted her attempt to escape.

Patrik nodded.

Alexander watched his brother go. He could only pray they found her.

A short while later the brothers retraced their steps and met at the chapel. With every minute he'd search, Alexander's anxiety had built. And from the frown carving his brother's face, he'd not found her either.

"Nothing?" Alexander asked grimly.

Patrik's expression was equally serious. "She is gone."

Alexander allowed himself several moments to curse her rashness and his own stupidity in trusting her. "I am going after her."

"I will go with you."

"No, I will ride alone."

Anger darkened his brother's eyes. "And allow her greater odds to reach English sympathizers?"

Alexander remembered her hiding in the stinging nettles. "She will be easy to track."

"It is best if we bring along several men as well."

"I said I would find her alone." As his voice rose, Alexander saw Duncan who'd exited the keep glance toward them.

Duncan strode toward them rubbing the sleep from his eyes. A pace away he halted. "What is wrong?"

Patrik shot Alexander a damning look. "Nichola has escaped."

"What?" Duncan asked.

"Tell him of her treachery, Alexander," Patrik stated.

Irritated to give Patrik's claim any credence, Alexander stiffened. "Patrik believes Nichola might be a spy."

"A spy?" Duncan burst out laughing.

"It is not a tale," Patrik all but snarled. "I saw her hiding in the shadows during the rebel meeting."

The laughter faded on Duncan's face. He glanced from Patrik to Alexander. "You are serious?"

Alexander nodded.

"Then why did neither of you say anything to Seathan?" Duncan demanded.

"She protested her innocence to Patrik," Alexander explained. "Claimed she was restless and out for a walk." Still, he couldn't believe she'd betray him.

"A lie," Patrik spat, "proven by her disappearance."

Disheartened, Alexander remained silent.

Duncan looked toward the portcullis. "When did she leave?"

"Her bed has not be slept in, so we estimate last

night," Alexander replied. "She only has a few hours start. Her trail should be fresh and easy to follow."

Duncan frowned. "If she slipped from her chamber last eve, the gate had been secured and the drawbridge raised."

"What of the men who left late to rescue Wallace?" Patrik countered. "The gates were kept open later than usual."

Dread washed over Alexander. A sword's wrath, he'd forgotten. It would have offered her the perfect opportunity to slip outside, and she would have traveled in the dark. Had she stolen a knife to use as protection? As if she could wield it with any skill. Blast it.

"We will gather a search party," Alexander said.

"We cannot tarry," Patrik said. "We still need the ransom she will bring."

The ransom. At the moment, money was the last thing Alexander gave a damn about.

"A rider approaches," the guard atop the gatehouse called.

Alexander made out the figure galloping toward them as if chased by the devil himself.

"It is the runner Seathan sent to fetch the ransom," Duncan said.

The rider flew across the drawbridge, the thunder of hooves hard and fast. He galloped into the courtyard and yanked his horse to a halt before the brothers.

"What is wrong?" Alexander demanded. Nichola. Had he found her en route home? Dead? Oh, God.

The rider dismounted. "It is the Lady Nichola," he said in between breaths.

Fear squeezed Alexander's chest. "She is—" He couldn't utter it.

The horse snorted. The man's eyes darkened with anger. "She is penniless."

"What!" his brothers exclaimed together.

At first, the runners words didn't register in Alexander's mind. Nichola was alive. They weren't too late. That's all that mattered.

Then, the messenger's news sunk in.

Alexander did not flinch. "It is a lie." If it were true, she would have told him. How could she have deceived him from the start?

The messenger shook his head. "When I delivered the ransom note as we discussed, I received a missive from the steward. The household ledgers are nothing but paper and ink. Nichola is penniless."

"How is that possible?" Duncan sputtered, asking Alexander's unvoiced question.

"Lord Monceaux's excessive drinking and gambling the past year," the runner explained.

"There is nothing," Patrik burst out. "Nothing to justify our acceptance of her during her stay."

The knight nodded. "The debtors have already begun to seize her property in return for outstanding debts owed."

"Christ!" Patrik snarled. His expression grew violent. "The cunning bitch. The entire time, she deceived us." He glared at Alexander. "Tell me that she did not hide her poverty from us from the start?"

Stunned, Alexander shook his head. She'd known. Her subtle comment as they'd traveled here that she had nothing to go back to had been the truth—a truth she'd never trusted him enough to tell. What did she think, that if he discovered her monetary state, he would kill her? Did she distrust him so much?

Yes. 'Twould seem so.

And when Nichola had said she loved him, 'twas said in desperation. She'd sought to buy time.

And what of her spying on their rebel meeting? Had she done so with intent to be paid for information she passed to the English? Aye, apparently she was desperate enough.

The softer emotions he'd sheltered yielded to anger. He turned to his brother. "Duncan, stay behind. When Seathan arrives inform him of Nichola's escape."

Duncan nodded.

"Patrik, tell the master-at-arms that I need several of his best men—immediately."

"I am riding with you as well," Patrik stated as he started toward the stables.

Alexander nodded, beyond denying his brother's help a second time. His heart ached at her distrust, that after they'd made love, after she'd told him she loved him, she could leave. They would find her, and God help her when they did.

Chapter Nineteen

Nichola shoved a limb up and ducked underneath. Sweat trickled down her face and clung to her gown. It'd taken most of the night, keeping covertly to the side of the road, to reach the loch shore. Precious time she could ill afford to waste. Now, the sun sat high in the sky, its golden rays coating the earth and the fresh smell of pine sifting through the air.

Her heart squeezed as she thought of the man she fled. By now Alexander would have noted her disappearance. How had he reacted to her missive? To the revelation of her lack of funds? Would he hate her? Understand her fears?

What of Patrik? He would be furious, anger that would skew his telling his brothers that she was spying on the rebels.

Alexander would come after her, she had no doubt. Not because he believed she was a spy, but because of his wounded pride that she had escaped.

A loud crack sounded in the distance.

She whirled, her heart pounding. Had Alexander found her already?

A raven's cry pierced the shush of wind. Then silence.

With trembling hands, Nichola relaxed her grip on the sack that held her precious food stores. Exhaustion from traveling was allowing her imagination free rein. No one was out there.

After taking her bearings, she started walking south. The forest floor once again curved up. Muscles screamed as she pushed herself on. At the top of the small hill, Nichola leaned against a tree, her breaths coming in gulps. She rubbed her aching neck. A moment's rest, then she would continue.

Through the break in the trees, the loch came into view. The angled banks, the swaths of shore that framed the blackened waters now rippling with waves. To the right, seeming to rise from the water, stood Lochshire Castle.

She thought of Alexander. His smile. His tenderness when they'd made love. No matter what the future held, right or wrong, she would always love him.

He, meanwhile, chose war over her. The past over the future.

Twigs cracked behind her.

Her nerves jumped. Nichola searched the nearby stand of trees. Again, she saw nothing.

Another crack of wood in the distance, this time accompanied by muted voices, sounded to her right.

Alexander!

Nichola stumbled forward, damning each snap of a stick beneath her slippers, every shuffle of leaves as she shoved a branch aside.

"Scour the hillside," a deep, terse, male voice ordered. "I want every possible hiding place searched. She could not have traveled far."

"Aye, Sir Patrik."

Patrik? Of course he would come. He wanted her dead. She needed to hide! The thinning trees to her south offered little cover. To the east and down the sharp slope, a denser swath of trees lay. She couldn't turn back. Nichola sprinted east.

The ground rushed into a steep decline. The grass and leaves of the forest floor shifted to loose rock peppered with an errant spray of flowers and vines.

Nichola stumbled and barely righted herself.

"Alexander?" another male voice called, a man she didn't recognize.

They were closing in on her! She half stumbled, half slid the rest of the way down the embankment. Rocks cut her hands, loose dirt around her clogged her throat, but she kept moving.

At the bottom, her legs aching, she crossed the small valley. Thankful, she slipped within the forest that grew denser on the other side.

Another voice called out, this time farther away. A reply echoed throughout the woods, even more distant.

Hope built. They'd turned their search elsewhere, leaving her free to find her way to England.

She moved deeper into the thick shield of leaves interspersed with pine. A fallen tree loomed before her, thick tangles of brush cluttering each end. She dismissed wasting time to go around the jumbled mess. The men were too close.

Gathering her strength, she ran and jumped over the moss covered trunk. A tearing rent the air as the hem of her dress caught on a limb. Her body was jerked back. Nichola slammed against the ground.

For a dizzying second, she lay there, gasping for breath, the forest spinning around her. On a groan, she rolled up into a sitting position to untangle her dress from the broken branch. The fabric held.

"Give way!" She gave a hard pull. The linen ripped

free, and she tumbled once again onto her back. She closed her eyes, frustrated. All things considered, it could be worse. At least the men were searching elsewhere. Ready to continue, she opened her eyes.

And stared straight into Patrik's triumphant face.

Hazel eyes pierced her with an enthralled fury. "You thought you would escape?"

Fear pounded in her heart. She dug her slipper into the soft earth to scoot back, but he reached down, clutched the front of her dress and hauled her to her feet.

"You will not escape me. I am not Alexander who is swayed by your comely face or your willingness to become his whore."

"Let me go!"

"You were a fool to believe the cover of night would give you any advantage."

Last night? The memory of the unidentified footfalls, then seeing Patrik cross the courtyard flashed through her mind.

"You saw me leave? Why did you not alert the guards?"

"And have them return you to your chamber?" he said with loathing. "What good would that have done?"

Then she understood. "You kept the guards occupied to ensure I could escape," she accused, her voice shaking with fear. "So when Alexander found me gone this morning, he would believe your claim when you told him I was a spy."

He sneered. "With you gone, who would doubt that with your brother's ties to King Edward, your intent was to warn the English king of the rebel plans?"

Tears burned in her throat. His twisted plans all made sense. "And my missive to Alexander?"

"Destroyed."

Mary's will!

Insanity cradled the violence in his eyes. "He hates you." The caustic joy of his words further battered her heart. Patrik wrapped his hands around her throat.

She fought, but his iron grip held her.

"When he finds you dead, he will be thanking me for destroying another English traitor."

Nichola screamed.

He tightened his grip, making it impossible for her to yell a second time.

She gasped for a breath that never came. The forest dimmed. Blackness flickered before her. The need for air burst through her lungs.

In the murky light, hooves thrummed across the forest floor.

As the world dimmed around her, she couldn't understand if she was being saved or delivered straight to the bowels of hell.

Nichola! Alexander urged his mount faster toward where her scream had cut through the forest. He burst through the shield of trees.

Patrik knelt several paces away, pinning Nichola to the ground, choking her.

Clods of dirt and twigs flew as Alexander jerked his mount to a halt and jumped to the ground. "Release her!"

Surprise whipped across Patrik's face as he turned.

His grip easing, Nichola slumped to the ground and fell into a fit of coughing.

In a lightning swift move, Patrik unsheathed his dagger. He caught her shoulders and pressed the blade against her neck. "Stay where you are."

The wild look in his brother's eyes made Alexander

take a step forward. "Patrik, a sword's wrath, what are you doing?"

"She cannot live," Patrik stated with a mundane calm as if asking for no more than a crust of bread. "She is a spy. When she feared she would be exposed, she ran." His voice jumped to a fevered pitch. "From the runner this day, we have learned that she is a pauper. She has lied to you over and again and proven she cannot be trusted. She must die."

Nichola's fearful gaze pleaded with Alexander.

Stunned, he stared at her. God in heaven, did she think he would let Patrik kill her? That he could harm her in any way? Hurt built inside as she waited for his response, her eyes like mirrors to her soul. He saw the doubts, the nerves, but also a fragile trust in him as well.

In that moment, matters of war and treachery paled in significance to Nichola. Without her his life would be empty. The freedom he sought an hollow victory.

He loved her.

It was that simple. And that complex.

"Sheath your blade," Alexander said. "I will take her to task for her deceptions."

Patrik shook his head. "She will wield her well-honed lies. In the end, you will forgive her."

Alexander took another step toward them, fear for Nichola's life driving his every step.

Patrik jerked her back against his chest; she screamed. "Another step and I will kill the English bitch!"

"No," Alexander replied, keeping his voice calm as he searched for a reason to convince Patrik to set her free. "You want Nichola dead because she is English." He stared at his brother straight in the eye. "She does not deserve this."

"We will send a missive to the English with regrets

that during her travel home she was killed by thieves," he rambled as if he hadn't heard Alexander. "They will believe that. If anyone even cares of a penniless woman's demise."

Nichola's eyes widened with pure terror.

Alexander hadn't felt this helpless since the day he'd held his dying father in his arms. Frustration built to fury. No, he would not lose her. He'd watched his father die. He would not lose her as well. Whatever it took, he would save her.

"If you kill her," Alexander said, drawing his brother's attention, "it will be murder."

Crimson stained Patrik's face. "Murder? As if the English hesitated to butcher my family while they slept in their beds. No, they claimed their actions just, of preserving peace between our lands. Enough of this foolery! You had an opportunity to leave. Now you will witness her death."

In that second, Nichola tore her hand free. A scream gurgled from her throat as she fought to shove the knife away. "The missive I left for you," she cried out.

"Quiet!" Patrik secured her hand with a rough grab.

"What missive?" But even as Alexander asked, he remembered Patrik's fisted hand as he had walked away from her bed and the sound of crumpled parchment after he'd found her gone.

"She would say anything to save her life," Patrik spat.

"I left a missive explaining everything on the bed," she whispered, her tone frantic.

Patrik pressed the knife harder. A trickle of blood slid down the blade. "I said quiet!"

"You had it in the chamber, put it in your pocket, didn't you?" Bedamned his brother's order. Alexander strode forward.

"Stay back!" Patrik panted, his eyes wild, that of a rabid wolf. "Do not force me to harm you as well."

As if Patrik had left him any other options. "Seathan, now!" Alexander yelled.

Patrik whipped his head to the side.

His brother's distraction gave Alexander the break he needed. He lunged forward and caught Patrik's hand. He ripped the knife away from Nichola's neck. Jamming his forearm against his brother's throat, Alexander pulled her free.

"Run!" Alexander yelled as Patrik struggled.

Nichola jumped up and staggered back.

Patrik yelled. He shoved his feet against Alexander's chest and pushed him away. He attacked, his fist plowing into Alexander's jaw.

Stars burst before Alexander's eyes, then his brother's furious expression swam into view.

"He still has the knife!" Nichola screamed.

"Nichola run!" Alexander's vision cleared. He feinted to the left, then dove straight toward Patrik. He caught Patrik's wrist and squeezed. "Stop. Do not do this."

He caught Nichola digging in her bag. She withdrew a dagger. Alexander shook his head in warning for her to stay away, then turned back to his brother.

Hazel eyes glittered with fury. "I warned you." Patrik drove his knee into Alexander's gut.

Air rushed from him in a painful exhale. With a yell of pure rage, Alexander lunged forward, toppling them both. Fists flew, grunts of pain spewed.

Alexander gained his feet. He withdrew his dagger. "I am taking her back."

Blood oozed from a cut in Patrik's brow as he shoved to his feet, his breaths coming hard, his eyes black with malice. "Touch her and you are dead."

Alexander's heart broke. "You are my brother."

"Am I? My brother would never choose a traitor over blood."

"Damn you, Patrik—"

With a cry of outrage, Patrik charged.

Alexander delivered a solid blow.

Patrik's head jerked back. His brother staggered, his lip already swelling. He charged again; his blade aimed toward Alexander's heart.

Alexander shifted.

This time Patrik anticipated his movement and boxed him into an alcove of trees.

He shot his foot out, catching Patrik's leg. Alexander jerked hard.

Flailing, Patrik went down hard. A thunk sounded as his head met stone. His brother lay there. Still. His face pale.

Alexander sagged, his dagger loosening in his grip. His body shook with emotion as he turned to where Nicola had pressed back against a tree. She watched him, her expression a mix of hope and fear. He started toward her.

Her hand shook as she stowed the blade. She gasped. "Behind you!"

He turned as Patrik charged. His brother's dagger flashed.

Pain shot through Alexander as the blade sliced into his arm. With his breaths coming fast, Alexander stared in shock at the blood seeping from his wound. He lifted his gaze to Patrik; met his wild stare.

And understood.

Patrik wouldn't stop.

In his frenzy, Patrik would kill him to reach Nichola.

His heart broke as any other option fell away, Alexander gave Patrik one last chance. "Do not do this."

Patrik lunged.

Screaming out his grief, Alexander sank his dagger deep into Patrik's chest.

And a part of Alexander died.

Eyes wide, Patrik stared at him. "Saint's breath." He slumped to the ground.

Patrik's blood stained Alexander's blade. Alexander dropped to his knees beside Patrik. "Damn you," he whispered, each word tearing him apart.

A trickle of blood oozed from the corner of Patrik's mouth. "She is English. She will never be good enough for you."

Alexander hugged him, damning the events, not wanting to lose him. "Nichola was never a threat."

His brother coughed, closing his eyes as his body rattled with a ferocious jerk. He blinked his eyes open, the urgency in them shaking Alexander to the core.

Patrik exhaled one last time, a soft, empty sound.

As the breeze flowed soft and warm, the birds chirped happily in the distance, the light faded from Patrik's eyes until they grew blank.

Alexander pressed Patrik's lids closed and bowed his head. "She is good enough," he whispered, but Patrik would never believe that. To him she was English. The enemy.

"I am sorry."

At Nichola's raw whisper, Alexander looked up. Hurt, aching, and wishing Patrik's life back. But it was gone, forever. He released Patrik.

On shaky knees, he stood. "I am sorry as well," he replied, wondering if he would ever overcome the pain of losing his brother, or his guilt.

"It was not your fault." Her face was stained with tears. "If I had not run—"

"Regardless of your actions, Patrik would have tried

to kill you." A fact he accepted. How would he explain Patrik's senseless death to his brothers?

Nichola's body trembled. He saw the fear, the questions on her face, but behind that, he saw her love. Her fragile expression had him opening his arms. She stepped into his embrace. He hugged her, needing her, loving her more. Never had he thought to find love. Yet, like a gift, he'd found Nichola.

Alexander stroked his hand down the length of her auburn hair, inhaling the goodness of her scent. "I never saw the missive you left."

Gray eyes raised to him with hope. "You believe me?"

He stared at Patrik's lifeless body. Tiredness and the weight of death swept through him. "He must have destroyed it."

Sorrow clung to her eyes like broken dreams. She glanced toward the south, toward England.

Toward her home.

Alexander's hope of her choosing to remain with him in Scotland dimmed. He caught her shoulders in a gentle hold. "Do you love me?"

She stared up at him. Doubt, uncertainty, and need waged a war within her eyes.

Fear at losing her battered his already battered nerves. "Answer me."

"Nichola," a deep male voice yelled, "get back!"

From the side, Alexander caught a blurred glimpse of a huge man a split second before he slammed him to the ground. His breath whooshed out.

Nichola screamed.

Chapter Twenty

Nichola stared at the large, well-muscled man attacking Alexander. Her breath caught. Her heart stuttered. Her legs threatened to give. Mary's will!

She stumbled forward. "Griffin!"

"Stay back," her brother commanded her as he raised his fist to strike Alexander.

"Do not hit him!" With a half laugh, half cry, she wiped the tears from her face. Griffin wasn't dead. The news of her brother's death had all been a lie. She stared at him, taking him in.

A leather thong secured his brown hair, enhancing the hard angles of his face. He wore a cloak she'd never seen, a rich brown color that made him blend in with the surroundings. His eyes, clear of drink, honed with fury on Alexander.

Alexander caught Griffin's fist, using her brother's momentum to flip him. Before she could stop him, Alexander slammed Griffin on his back.

He landed with a grunt. With a curse, he wedged his foot against Alexander's chest, shoved him back, then sprang to his feet. Her brother unsheathed his dagger.

The scar along Alexander's left cheek tightened. Alexander jumped up, his dagger readied.

Fear pounded in her heart. No one else would die this day! "Griffin listen!" Nichola yelled. "I love him!"

Both men ignored her.

Fear for both their lives spilled through her. Unsure how else to stop them, she ran between them.

Griffin reached out to grab her arm.

She dodged his hand.

"Saint's wrath, Nichola, move out of the way!" he ordered, never taking his eyes off Alexander.

Alexander's eyes narrowed on her. "Nichola, move!"

She gave a wilting glare to first one, then the other, her breath coming in unsteady rasps. "I will not." Both of the pigheaded men were intent on saving her life.

"Do you know him?" Alexander demanded as he stared at his opponent with cold distrust.

"Yes, it is my brother."

"Lord Monceaux is dead."

"I will show you dead," Griffin muttered, his body coiled, ready to attack Alexander. "Nichola, who is he?"

Alexander's lip curled with anger. "A man who will carve your heart out, you bloody Sassenach." He tried to skirt her and lunge forward, but she fended off the clash and ended up wedged between their well-honed bodies.

Both men's blades shot upwards in fear of hurting her.

She didn't know whether to laugh with joy or scream with frustration. She had to make them listen before one of them was injured or killed.

Nichola shoved her palms against their chests. The tremble of enraged muscles pressed against her hands. "Both of you stop so I can explain!"

Explain? Alexander didn't move or relax his guard. Neither this man, nor any other, would take Nichola from him.

The thrum of hooves increased. Men's voices grew louder.

His men. Appeased, Alexander waited. Oddly, her brother didn't appear worried by the approaching riders.

A horse neighed. Hoofbeats increased. Seathan, Duncan, and several men rode into the clearing.

Alexander and Griffin eased away from each other, their daggers held out in readiness.

Seathan's gaze swept past the trio and fell on Patrik. Grief ripped through his face until it drowned in devastation. "By the lance of God!" With shaky movement, he dismounted and knelt by Patrik.

His face pale, his eyes ravaged, Duncan dismounted as well and ran to Patrik.

Head bowed, Seathan drew several deep breaths and whispered a prayer. His eyes burning with loss, he looked up at Alexander. "What happened?"

Alexander swallowed hard. He flicked a wary glance toward the stranger Nichola named Griffin; he hadn't moved.

He turned to his brothers. "Patrik had a blade to Nichola's neck. He was going to kill her." His chest ached. "I—I tried to stop him. He was so angry. He wouldn't listen." A sword's wrath! There was no easy way to explain. To forgive himself. "When I freed Nichola, he turned on me—"

"And left you no choice but to kill him," Seathan finished. A tremor washed through his body. He laid his hand on Patrik's shoulder, then stood. "Since his parents' murder, hatred guided Patrik."

Duncan's sad gaze raised to Alexander. "It was your only choice, Alexander."

Alexander remained silent. However true that Patrik had given him no choice, his brother's death would always haunt him.

"She was English," Duncan comforted. "To Patrik it was enough."

Seathan gave a sad nod.

Alexander was a fool to believe Nichola would ever betray him. His shame grew. To salvage his pride, he'd not told them of Patrik's suspicions.

Seathan glanced toward the man by Nichola's side. A frown creased his brow. "Wulfe?"

"Wulfe?" Alexander stared at the large warrior opposite him who stood readied for battle, his face notorious in its English heritage.

Seathan was wrong. This couldn't be the English lord who aided the Scottish rebels. The same man who supplied them English troop movements—and other decisive information that could make the outcome of their uprising a success.

"Wulfe?" Nichola asked. She frowned at the striking man, who matched Alexander's own strength. "Griffin, what is he talking about?"

Alexander's hand fisted. Her familiarity with him helped not the man's cause. "Who is he?"

"I told you he was my brother," Nichola replied. "Had you both not been so incensed on maiming each other, you would have heard."

"Your brother is Wulfe?" Seathan and Duncan demanded in unison.

"Wulfe?" Alexander added stunned. Then he stared at Nichola, unsure if the fact he'd almost abducted Wulfe was more incredible than the fact that he'd ended up abducting Wulfe's sister.

Seathan met Griffin's gaze. "I never knew your real name. Only your face." He paused. "I see you have not told your sister as well?"

"No," Lord Monceaux said. He relaxed his stance. "Until now, I saw no need."

Seathan nodded. His gaze fell upon Patrik. On a heavy sigh, he gestured to one of his men. "Take him back to Lochshire Castle. Ensure his body is taken care of."

"Aye, my lord." With quiet, discreet moves, the knight lifted Patrik and laid him over his horse. The knight mounted, then rode north, disappearing through the trees.

A somber silence fell over the group.

Seathan glanced toward Lord Monceaux. "The timing is not as I would like, but Wulfe, I would introduce you to my brothers, Alexander and Duncan."

Alexander evaluated the man who matched his skill, his pride eased in that he was a legendary man, a knight the Scots viewed as a symbol of freedom. A man who though English, disagreed with his king's tyranny and dared to defy his liege lord for Scotland's cause.

The Baron of Monceaux nodded to Duncan, the warmth in his eyes fading to wariness as they turned upon Alexander.

"Why are you here?" Seathan asked Lord Monceaux. "Once we had parted after reclaiming Wallace's body, I thought you would have returned to England?"

"I had," Griffin replied, "only to learn my sister had been abducted for ransom."

"The decision to abduct you was mine," Seathan said. "No one was aware that Lord Monceaux and Wulfe were one and the same."

Lord Monceaux's brows lifted. "But you took my sister?"

"Who was treated with great respect during her stay," Seathan said. "When my brother, Alexander, arrived, you were absent."

"My concerns were to raise coin for our cause. My decision to abduct her came out of duty," Alexander stated.

Nichola turned from one man to the other. "Will someone tell me what this is all about?"

"Wulfe's identity," Alexander explained, the irritation simmering in her eyes all too familiar and endearing, "is only known by a few Scots." He gestured toward Seathan. "Though my brother knows him, he never was told his real name. Only a handful of people are aware that Wulfe is Lord Monceaux."

Her brother was Wulfe. As the men continued to speak, Nichola worked to accept the revelation. She turned toward her brother, her mind spinning with this newfound knowledge.

"What do you do?" Nichola asked.

"I aid the Scots," Griffin replied, his eyes softening on hers.

"You are a spy?"

His expression hardened, his conviction for his actions clear. "Aye."

"But you are King Edward's advisor to the Scots?"

Griffin nodded.

She hesitated, then it all made sense. A new thought crossed her mind. Panic raced through her. "And what of the times you were gone? The money? Our finances. Mary's will. We are—"

Her brother took her hand. "I need to explain," he said quietly. "When our parents died, they were en route to try and free me."

"I know. You had been imprisoned."

Hurt creased his face. "Over drink, an argument broke out. I was imprisoned on the charge of attacking a noble. Thankfully, no one ever made the connection of my true reason for being there. At the time, like our father, I was already working in secret for Scotland and passing sensitive information to King Balliol."

"Our father was a spy for Scotland as well?" she asked in shock.

Her brother shrugged. "A family tradition you might say." He sobered and gave her hand a gentle squeeze. "I am sorry. I never meant to put your life or that of our parents at risk."

A tear slid down her cheek, then another. A sob escaped her lips. The slight blur of Alexander moving toward her was stopped as she saw Seathan shake his head. Then it was only Griffin, his arms wrapped around her, his quiet whispers soothing her, asking for her forgiveness.

She clung to him. She'd not lost him after all. Stronger, she stepped away from her brother. Alexander laid his hand upon her shoulder, his strength and comfort filling her soul.

"Griffin, I was wrong to blame you for our parents' death. After, I thought you hated me."

"No. You are my sister. My blood. I love you. That will never change."

"The last year you would not even speak to me. You let me believe—"

"The worst," her brother finished with a grimace. "Women, gambling, and that we had naught left but a pittance."

Her breath caught. "And Lord James?"

"He died in a duel with another man. Our argument earlier that evening was what spawned the gossip that I had killed him. I was falsely accused and was being sought, which is why I left through the secret passageway. Until I could prove my innocence, I could not allow myself to be caught."

She was trying to absorb everything he was telling her. "I have checked the ledgers. What else have you not shared?"

"With my secret activities, I feared for your life. I thought to keep you safe. My being a drunkard and a scoundrel were a cover." Griffin gave her a tender smile.

"We are not impoverished?" she whispered.

"No," he said gently. "Far from it. There is a second ledger I have hidden that holds our true accounts."

Relief swept through her. Then Nichola remembered the heirlooms she'd sold in a misguided attempt to keep coin in their coffers. Possessions passed down through their family. Tapestries that'd reminded her of their parents. But he'd never explained it, had allowed her to sell them.

No, he'd never known. If he had told her the truth, they would still hold the items that reminded her of those they'd dearly loved and honored.

"You could have told me," she said, angry.

"The risk was too great," Griffin replied. "Had you known, you might have done something, unknowingly to endanger your life."

"And what if you died?"

"The seneschal knows and would have explained everything. Unfortunately," Griffin gave Alexander a hard look before turning back to her, "he was away when the runner arrived with the ransom."

Mary's will. Now she had her own confession. "Unaware our coffers were full, while you were away I sold several heirlooms."

A smile touched his mouth. "Each of which I have purchased through various channels."

Joy rushed through her. "They are not lost?"

"No." Then his mouth grew solemn. Griffin brushed a wisp of hair that'd slipped onto her cheek. "I regret what you have endured, more so, your abduction. And for whatever treatment you have suffered." He slanted an ominous look toward Alexander. "By God, if you have harmed my sister in any way, you will answer to me."

Alexander bristled.

Nichola shook her head, her heart aching. "No, he never harmed me."

"Then why did you leave?" Alexander asked.

She searched Alexander's face, plagued by doubts. "I thought you did not want me."

Alexander stepped closer, blocking out all of the others. "How could I not want you? I am in love with you."

Her heart stumbled. "You love me?"

"You are my life, Nichola."

"When I came to tell you our coffers were bare," she scowled at Griffin before turning back to Alexander, "you would not speak to me."

"I was torn between my feelings for you and my country." He searched her face. "Why did you not tell me you believed your coffers were bare?"

"I believed you would not harm me, but I was unsure of my fate if the other rebels learned of my impoverished state. I could not take the risk."

Alexander shook his head. "It was already too late."

"Too late?"

A tender smile skimmed Alexander's mouth. "I never would have harmed you. When I first saw you in the solar, I think I fell in love with you then."

Nichola's heart swelled. He loved her.

Alexander's brothers inhaled.

Lord Monceaux bristled. "I demand to know your intentions toward my sister."

Alexander drew himself to his full height and faced her brother. "If she will have me, I would ask her to hand fast with me."

Seathan and Duncan nodded toward Alexander. Their surprised expressions shifted to understanding, then pride.

Lord Monceaux caught his sister's hand, his dark eyes intense as he scoured hers. "And what do you wish, Nichola?"

Time stilled. Alexander's breath caught as he waited for her reply.

Warmth softened her gaze. "I love him as well."

Her brother sighed. He turned to Alexander. "It would seem you have won my sister's heart. I entrust you with her care, but hear me well, harm her not or it will be me who serves you punishment."

"I will guard her with my life."

With a satisfied grunt, Lord Monceaux stepped back.

"It is time to return home," Seathan said.

Alexander wrapped his hand around her waist and drew her to him. "Nichola will ride with me." He cupped her face in his hands. "After I have kissed the woman I love." Blood pounded in his veins as he drew her to him, wanting her, needing her with his every breath.

Their lips touched, melded. Alexander groaned. Aye, he'd found his heart.

* * *

A short distance away, Alexander broke away from his brothers, Nichola seated before him on his mount.

"Where are we going?" she asked.

"You will see."

He guided his bay to the familiar path, up to where he'd first shown Nichola Lochshire Castle so many days before. Then, he'd not known he'd loved her, that he would wish her to stay by his side forever.

Now he knew.

At the top of the incline, the trees fell away and as before, the loch spilled out before them in all its splendor. Except so much had changed. He'd lost his brother this day, a man he'd loved.

And he'd found love to last a lifetime.

Alexander dismounted. He lifted her to the ground. With his heart in his throat, he took her hand in his and led her a few feet away to where sunlight shimmered through the trees like dancing fairies. To where pine needles scattered the earth, their scent fresh against the turmoil in his soul.

"Nichola," he said as they stood bathed in the sunlight's embrace. "Will you be my wife, take me as I am, a knight who has naught to offer but his heart?" She stared at him, her eyes unreadable.

He stilled.

She'd said she loved him, but he'd never contemplated that she'd not said yes. He made to drop her hand, but Nichola held tight.

"When I first saw you, I thought you a rogue. As time passed, I saw a man who loves his family and a man who is loyal to his country." She reached in her gown and withdrew her hand. In her palm glistened the other half of his azurite. Her smile grew. "And the man I hopelessly fell in love with who made me believe in magic. Yes. I will marry you."

The azurite twinkled.

Warmth filled his soul. Aye, the chamber indeed held magic. By his grandmother's guiding hand, 'twould seem he would make her wish come true.

Alexander swept Nichola into his arms. He drew her into a heated kiss, overwhelmed by the blessing of her in his life. After his father's death, he'd believed himself incapable of ever loving again—until now.

Until Nichola.

Aye, her love was truly the most precious gift.

Epilogue

Pipes played and men filled with drink yelled in the great room. Alexander danced with Nichola in a heady whirl.

Caught up in the moment, she laughed in his arms.

He stared down at her, the bliss of this day's wedding swelling inside. The sennight since her brother's startling appearance had whisked by. Each bringing a riot of emotion from sadness of Patrik's death to anticipation of his marriage to Nichola.

Finally, the day of their vows was here. Now she was his wife. Never had he thought to dare love again. She'd destroyed his every reserve and won his heart.

The dance ended and Alexander drew her to him. He devastated her senses with a blazing kiss, oblivious to the calls and cheers of the onlookers surrounding them.

He stared at her. On a finely-crafted chain around her neck next to the pendant her mother had given her, a dark, greenish blue stone hung.

The other half of the azurite.

Though his brothers would laugh if they knew, he now believed his grandmother had cast a spell upon their stones. That each stone would draw their respective mate, a woman who would teach them to love and make them whole.

As with Nichola.

Sadness welled in his heart as he thought of Patrik. He and his brothers had agreed Patrik should be buried within the castle grounds. Though anger guided Patrik, he was still their brother.

Oddly, after Patrik's burial, Alexander had visited the tower chamber. The malachite his grandmother had gifted Patrik had vanished. Never would he believe that someone had stolen the stone known for its ability to promote inner peace. His grandmother had taken it back, to counteract the malice that Patrik could never overcome.

Now only two halved stones sat within the bowl, Seathan's and Duncan's. Except Alexander had decided he wouldn't worry about the magic or the women his grandmother had chosen for them. Before him stood the lass who held his heart. A woman he would love forever.

"I still cannot believe we are married," Alexander said. "The waiting for this day has crept by like an old man."

Nichola laughed. "It was not as if we have not shared my chamber for the past sennight."

Alexander winked, remembering his nocturnal trips up to her room. "Only after my brothers—and yours—were abed."

Her smile drove him insane with wanting.

"Leave the hall with me now, Nichola. I cannot wait any longer to be alone with my wife. To watch the flicker of candlelight dance across your breasts."

"Surely your patience can extend awhile yet?" But he saw the desire that lurked beneath her expression of reproof.

A commotion at the entry to the great hall had them turning. A knight who'd sworn allegiance to William Wallace pushed through the crowd.

Alexander tensed. What had happened now? At the somber looks of Griffin, Seathan and Duncan, he feared the news would be bad.

Nichola touched his arm. "Alexander?"

"Come."

The crowd parted as he escorted her toward his brothers. His unease grew. Hours ago he'd given his vow to Nichola. Now was he to head off to war?

They had both known the time would come. Except he hadn't expected the news so soon. Or had English soldiers been spotted in the distance and could Nichola's life be at risk?

A sword's wrath! He should have wed her earlier, should have taken her to the Highlands where she would be safe. As if she would have agreed to that. Whatever the decision, the option to whisk her away to safety was gone.

With Nichola at his side, Alexander halted beside his brothers and new brother-in-law. He was still amazed that Lord Monceaux had turned out to be the revered spy for Scotland, Wulfe, but at the moment, that was of no consequence.

Wallace's knight halted before them.

"Let us go to the solar," Seathan said, his tone somber.

The knight shook his head, his face breaking into an excited smile. "No need, my lord."

"Your news is not of the English troops?" Seathan glanced with surprise toward his brothers and Griffin, then back to the runner.

"No." The man held out a simple yet well-crafted dagger.

Confusion wrinkled on Seathan's brow. He clasped the weapon. "Wallace's dagger?"

"He sends it to you along with his promise that Scotland shall be free," the knight announced, his voice choked up.

Unsure he'd heard right, Alexander glanced at his brothers. They seemed as confused as he.

"Sir William died a sennight ago," Seathan stated.

The runner shook his head. "I believed the same, but he was not dead."

Seathan's face filled with anger. "By God, you dare draw out our county's mourning? I helped carry his body into his nurse's cart."

"And it was after the nurse was alone with Wallace in her home that she laid her head against his chest and heard the slight flutter of his heart."

Alexander stared at the knight, wanting to believe in the miracle he offered. "It is true?"

The runner simply nodded.

Seathan shook his head, his expression dazed, adding to the thick emotions clogging Alexander's throat.

"Wallace is alive." Seathan turned and faced his people. He held up his hands for silence. The rumble of expectant murmurs fell silent. "I have great news to add to our celebration. Sir William Wallace lives!"

The great room, crowded with gentry and peasants alike, broke out in pandemonium. Cheers roared through the room, men caught women in bawdy kisses, and tankards clanked as toasts were made.

"My thanks," Seathan said to the knight once the volume had dimmed marginally.

"Aye, my lord. It is news that for once I looked forward to delivering."

"Go pour yourself a tankard of ale," Alexander said

as he lifted his own tankard. "We are celebrating a wedding." He grinned. "Mine." He pressed a kiss on Nichola's hand.

The knight's eyes lifted. "Congratulations, my lady." He winked at Alexander. "And a lucky man you are." He nodded and made his way to where a group of men were refilling their own mugs.

Alexander turned to Nichola. His body ignited at the thought of this night, of touching her, loving her for the rest of his life. "Come."

He caught her within his arms and headed toward the turret, his action reminding him of not too long ago at a certain inn when he'd done the same. But this night, he wouldn't be holding back.

With mirth shining in her eyes, she wrapped her arms around his neck. "Where are we going my husband?"

"Where we will not be interrupted," he said in a seductive whisper.

Desire darkened her eyes. "I would wish that as well."

His body hardened as he wove through the crowd, sidestepped two knights who looked ready to hinder them with their congratulations. He made a dash for the stairs.

At the bottom step he set her down and took her hand. "Run for it."

With her face flushed with happiness, Nichola laughed and ran alongside him as he bolted up the stairs.

Near the top, with his heart pounding, and love for her in his every breath, Alexander caught her and pressed her back against the curved stone. He covered her mouth in a demanding kiss that promised a future of happiness for both.

He shuddered as he lifted his head to gaze upon his wife. The flicker of torchlight illuminated her eyes warm with love. "I love you so much, Nichola." How had he ever been so blessed to have been gifted with her in his life?

She shuddered at his touch. "Take me to bed, Alexander."

He scooped her up. Aye, he would love her forever. He'd stolen the lass from her home, but she'd stolen his rebel heart.

Discover the Romances of
Hannah Howell

My Valiant Knight	0-8217-5186-7	**$5.50**US/**$7.00**CAN
Only for You	0-8217-5943-4	**$5.99**US/**$7.50**CAN
A Taste of Fire	0-8217-7133-7	**$5.99**US/**$7.50**CAN
A Stockingful of Joy	0-8217-6754-2	**$5.99**US/**$7.50**CAN
Highland Destiny	0-8217-5921-3	**$5.99**US/**$7.50**CAN
Highland Honor	0-8217-6095-5	**$5.99**US/**$7.50**CAN
Highland Promise	0-8217-6254-0	**$5.99**US/**$7.50**CAN
Highland Vow	0-8217-6614-7	**$5.99**US/**$7.50**CAN
Highland Knight	0-8217-6817-4	**$5.99**US/**$7.50**CAN
Highland Hearts	0-8217-6925-1	**$5.99**US/**$7.50**CAN
Highland Bride	0-8217-7397-6	**$6.50**US/**$8.99**CAN
Highland Angel	0-8217-7426-3	**$6.50**US/**$8.99**CAN
Highland Groom	0-8217-7427-1	**$6.50**US/**$8.99**CAN
Highland Warrior	0-8217-7428-X	**$6.50**US/**$8.99**CAN
Reckless	0-8217-6917-0	**$6.50**US/**$8.99**CAN

Available Wherever Books Are Sold!

Visit our website at **www.kensingtonbooks.com**